spy school GOES SOUTH

STUART GIBBS

spy school GOES SOUTH

A **spy school** NOVEL

Simon & Schuster Books for Young Readers

New York London Toronto Sydney New Delhi

SIMON & SCHUSTER BOOKS FOR YOUNG READERS
An imprint of Simon & Schuster Children's Publishing Division
1230 Avenue of the Americas, New York, New York 10020

Text copyright © 2018 by Stuart Gibbs
Jacket design and principal illustration by Lucy Ruth Cummins,
copyright © 2018 by Simon & Schuster, Inc.
Supplemental jacket elements copyright © 2018 by Thinkstock.com

SIMON & SCHUSTER BOOKS FOR YOUNG READERS
is a trademark of Simon & Schuster, Inc.
For information about special discounts for bulk purchases, please contact
Simon & Schuster Special Sales at 1-866-506-1949 or business@simonandschuster.com.
The Simon & Schuster Speakers Bureau can bring authors to your live event.
For more information or to book an event, contact the Simon & Schuster Speakers
Bureau at 1-866-248-3049 or visit our website at www.simonspeakers.com.
Interior design by Lucy Ruth Cummins
Endpaper art by Ryan Thompson
The text for this book was set in Adobe Garamond Pro.
Manufactured in the United States of America
0818 FFG
First Edition
10 9 8 7 6 5 4 3 2 1
Library of Congress Cataloging-in-Publication Data
Names: Gibbs, Stuart, 1969– author.
Title: Spy school goes south / Stu Gibbs.
Description: First edition. | New York : Simon & Schuster Books for Young Readers,
[2018] | "A Spy School Novel." | Summary: Thirteen-year-old spy in training Ben Ripley
is sent to Mexico to try to thwart the evil organization SPYDER—the CIA's main enemy.
Identifiers: LCCN 2017038945|
ISBN 9781481477857 (hardcover) | ISBN 9781481477871 (eBook)
Subjects: | CYAC: Spies—Fiction. | Adventure and adventurers—Fiction. |
Friendship—Fiction. | Schools—Fiction. | Mexico—Fiction.
Classification: LCC PZ7.G339236 Sph 2018 | DDC [Fic]—dc23
LC record available at https://lccn.loc.gov/2017038945

In memory of Suzanne,
my incredible, wonderful, amazing wife

Contents

spy school
GOES SOUTH

March 27, 2017
To: ███████████, Agent Emeritus, Central Intelligence Agency
Re: Inmate 62615, aka ████████████

As you are certainly aware, our attempts over the past month to
get ███████████ to give up information on SPYDER have been
unsatisfactory. While I have no doubt that ███████████ knows more
than he is letting on, he has been surprisingly effective in his refusal
to reveal any of it. (The one time he *did* reveal information, it turned out
to be false, leading to last week's regrettable CIA raid on a Boy Scout
jamboree.) ███████████ has remained surprisingly immune to our
methods of persuasion, and while there are other things I would like
to try, they are all illegal under the Geneva Conventions. After the bad
press of raiding the jamboree, the last thing the CIA needs is another
lawsuit.

Therefore, I am optimistic about the sudden change of attitude shown by
███████████ this morning. While I share your skepticism about anything
concerning the prisoner, I'm not about to look a gift horse in the mouth.
Learning anything we can about SPYDER is the top priority for you and
your team. SPYDER is certainly plotting another diabolical scheme, and
they have infiltrated the Agency to the point where almost no one can
be trusted. At this point, sadly, ███████████ is the best lead we have to
bringing them down once and for all.

So cut a deal with the kid. Give him whatever he wants. (Or at least, let
him think you're doing that.)

And if he says he'll only talk to ███████████, then let him talk to ███████████.

Also, thanks for recommending Dr. Raker. She really took care of those
bunions!

Sincerely,
███████████
Director of Information Retrieval

Destroy this memo after reading.

GOOD CITIZENSHIP

Washington, DC

Streets in proximity to the Academy of Espionage

March 28

1500 hours

"Stop that man!"

Alerted by the cry, I glanced back over my shoulder. Five storefronts away, an extremely tall man with muscles the size of cantaloupes was charging down the sidewalk, clutching a leopard-print purse. Behind him, an elderly woman lay sprawled on the ground.

My first reaction was to think that it was a test.

That might not seem like the correct reaction for a normal thirteen-year-old boy, but then, I *wasn't* a normal thirteen-year-old boy. I was a spy-in-training at the CIA's top secret Academy of Espionage, and it was standard practice at the school to spring fake emergencies on the students to see how we handled ourselves. This happened surprisingly often. Three days earlier, I had to defuse a phony bomb *and* survive an attack by ninjas before I even got to breakfast.

These pop quizzes rarely took place off campus, though. And they usually concerned serious criminals like terrorists or assassins, rather than plain-old muggers. But I wasn't completely sure about this.

"Someone please help!" the elderly woman cried.

Even though the sidewalk was crowded with people, no one was trying to stop the thief. This was somewhat understandable, as the thief was built like a brick wall and looked as mean as a wounded bear. He was bowling over anyone who happened to be in his way; therefore, people were scrambling to clear a path for him. Trying to stop him would only be asking for trouble.

He was now three storefronts away.

I glanced at Erica Hale for guidance.

Erica was two years ahead of me at spy school and by far the most accomplished student. In fact, she was probably more accomplished than most of the teachers. She was a legacy, a descendant of Nathan Hale, whose entire family tree was chock-full of secret agents, and she'd been learning the ropes from her relatives since she was old enough to wield a billy club. In addition, she wasn't above springing a sudden sneak attack on me herself.

The whole reason we were off campus together was that Erica was giving me extra tutoring in advanced survival techniques. I was only in my second year at the academy, but due to an unusual set of circumstances, I had managed to thwart the plans of SPYDER, our main enemy, four times so far. SPYDER was a covert organization dedicated to plotting chaos and mayhem for a price, and its operatives were getting rather annoyed at me for thwarting them. Now they wanted me dead.

Unfortunately, the CIA wasn't great at adapting to unusual circumstances. School rules specifically stated that, as a second-year student, I wasn't allowed to take classes beyond Self-Preservation 202, even though I could really have used some more advanced training. So Erica had stepped in. She was tutoring me without permission, on her own time.

Now, out on the street, watching the incoming criminal, she shook her head. It was a very small shake, almost imperceptible, but I understood both meanings of it:

1) This wasn't a test. It was a real crime.

2) I shouldn't get involved.

The biggest problem with being a secret agent was the "secret" part. Once your cover was blown, there was no getting it back. My own parents didn't even know I was a student in spy school. In fact, the very existence of spy school itself was a secret. (There was quite obviously a campus, only a few blocks away, but it was hidden behind a great stone wall and claimed to be St. Smithen's Science Academy for Boys and Girls.)

Erica was insanely talented at martial arts. She could have flattened the thief in less time than it took most people to tie their shoes. But then she'd have to explain *how* a sixteen-year-old girl like her could do such a thing, which would open up a dozen cans of worms.

Erica Hale wasn't going to do anything that would jeopardize her potential career as a spy. Even if that meant letting some jerk get away with stealing a poor old lady's purse. And she wanted me to know that I ought to do the same.

There was only one problem with that:

It didn't seem right.

"All my money is in that purse!" the old lady wailed, a desperate last-ditch attempt to get some bystander to actually do something.

The thief was almost on top of me. Close enough to look me in the eye. It was a look that said he was considering shoving me into the street merely for being within arm's reach.

I couldn't beat this guy in a fight. I had the martial arts skills of a box turtle. (That was a direct quote from Professor

Simon after my latest self-preservation exam.) But I did have other talents that could come in handy.

For starters, I was extremely good at math. I could do advanced calculations in my head, I never forgot a phone number, and I could instantly work out complicated concepts like trajectories or gravitational forces with relative accuracy.

In addition, I was learning to be hyperaware of my surroundings. This was one of the things Erica had been teaching me. It was much easier to escape an attack by evil assailants when you knew they were coming, as opposed to being caught by surprise. As it was, I had clocked everyone on the sidewalk ahead of me, and thus had registered:

1) The heavyset man walking toward me with a bulldog on a six-foot leash.

2) The waiter wheeling a loaded dessert cart out of the sidewalk café just ahead and to my right.

3) The three young women dining at an outdoor table at the same café. The one closest to me had a triple-decker club sandwich.

Erica, who was even more aware of things than I was— hyper-hyperaware—registered that *I* had registered all of this and shook her head again, more firmly this time, meaning that she *really* didn't want me to get involved.

I did anyway.

As the thief bore down on me, I made a show of leaping out of the way, banging into the table with the three young women hard enough to upset their water glasses into their laps. While they were distracted by this, I deftly snatched two strips of bacon from the club sandwich and tossed them to the ground at my feet.

The bulldog, being a dog, lunged for the bacon, snapping its leash taut right in front of the thief. If I had done this with a smaller dog, such as a toy poodle or a bichon frise, my plan wouldn't have worked, but the bulldog was the size and weight of a sack of concrete. When the thief ran into the leash, the bulldog held fast like an anchor. The leash caught the thief at shin height, tripping him and sending him flying.

At this point, I gave the dessert cart a small "accidental" nudge, just enough to knock it from the waiter's grasp—and place it directly in the thief's path.

The thief landed on it so hard that a Boston cream pie exploded on impact, coating a few nearby diners with custard. The thief himself ended up face-first in a double-chocolate torte, which caught him by such surprise that he dropped the purse. However, the force with which he landed made the dessert cart roll faster than I'd expected. (In the few seconds I'd had to concoct a plan, I hadn't been able to calculate *everything*.) The cart now raced down the sidewalk, which sloped gently downhill, increasing the cart's speed even more. Startled pedestrians scrambled out of the way as it careened past them. The thief, though blinded by chocolate, was still aware that something bad was happening, and he screamed as he hurtled along. The cart gained more and more speed—until it slammed into a fire hydrant at the corner and stopped abruptly. Meanwhile, the thief *didn't* stop. He was large enough to have considerable inertia, and his body was now greased with various mousses and gelatins, so he shot right off the cart and flew through the air.

It was only now that I noticed something about my surroundings I had failed to register before:

The street beyond the corner was under construction.

Several utility workers in bright orange vests were overseeing a project that required three major pieces of construction equipment. A trench had been gouged into the road to allow access to a large sewer pipe, which had been cut open as well. The thief tumbled right through the gap and plunged headfirst into the sewage. He landed with a sickening squelch, which was followed by his cry of abject disgust.

Every person around had recorded the entire incident on their phones.

However, no one had noticed my involvement. I had

been cautious enough to make it look like a freak accident.

Erica grabbed my arm and dragged me away before anyone even realized we were there.

The waiter picked up the purse and returned it to the old lady, who had struggled back to her feet.

Everyone else began to either forward the videos they had recorded to friends or upload them to the Internet. It didn't seem to have occurred to anyone that they could use their phones to call the police.

Thankfully, the old lady didn't appear to be hurt. In fact, she was laughing so hard at the fate of the thief that her false teeth had come loose.

I tried to head toward her, just to make sure she was all right, but Erica kept her iron grip locked on my arm and hustled me across the street. "That was an unnecessary risk," she said angrily under her breath.

"The man was a criminal," I argued. "We're supposed to stop criminals."

"*Major* criminals," Erica corrected. "International arms dealers. Terrorists. Lunatics determined to cause chaos and mayhem. Not common thieves. That's a job for the police."

"I didn't see any police around. And besides, I was subtle about the way I did it."

"Subtle? You call sending a man cannonballing down the street on a dessert cart subtle? Why didn't you just trip him?"

"I was trying to look like I wasn't involved! You can't trip someone without them noticing."

"Of course you can."

"No you can't—" I began, though I didn't get to finish the thought, because Erica tripped me. At least, I *thought* she did. It happened so fast, I didn't actually notice her doing it. One moment I was arguing with her; the next I was sprawled in a flower bed.

"See?" Erica asked.

"Point well made." I got back to my feet, brushing mulch off my shirt. "Okay, maybe it wasn't subtle. But it was effective."

"Sending the man flying into the open sewer was a bit much."

"Er," I said uncomfortably. "Well . . ."

Erica sighed. "Let me guess. You didn't notice the open sewer until it was too late."

There didn't seem to be any point in denying it. "Yes."

"You didn't notice a giant, gaping hole in the street with a dozen men in bright orange vests surrounding it?"

"It was almost a block away. And there were other things going on. Like a robbery in progress."

"There are *always* going to be other things going on, Ben. But you need to be on the alert at all times. People are trying to kill you."

I probably should have been upset by Erica's exasperation with me. But I wasn't. Despite the fact that my life was in constant danger and Erica was berating me for my lack of skills, I couldn't help but feel pleased.

Because Erica Hale was worried for my safety. Which meant she cared about me.

In addition to being the most competent spy at school, Erica was also the most beautiful girl I had ever met. She had hypnotic eyes, lustrous hair, and the intoxicating scent of lilacs and gunpowder. Plus, she could beat a man twice her size senseless.

However, Erica generally didn't like other people. Until recently, she had considered having any friends at all a liability. This had earned her the nickname "Ice Queen" at school. But over the past year, I had earned her respect—and, even more importantly, her affection. Or the closest to affection that Erica could allow herself. She wasn't willing to go on a date, or even consider the idea of being my girlfriend, but she had once kissed me when we thought we were going to be vaporized by a nuclear bomb. And now she was teaching me to survive, rather than leaving me to the wolves.

However, she still had some work to do where basic social skills were concerned.

"Why are you smiling?" she asked me.

"Am I smiling?" I asked, then realized that I was, given how thrilled I was that Erica cared about my safety. "Sorry, I'll stop."

"Good. This is serious stuff." Erica still hadn't released her vise grip on my arm. She hooked me around a corner, aiming me back toward campus. "You already have enough problems with SPYDER being after you. If you pull another stunt like that and get outed as a spy, the CIA will cut you loose, and then no one will be able to protect you anymore."

"*You* will," I said.

"No I won't. It'll be against the rules."

"You'll still do it. Because any attempt SPYDER makes on me will be a lead to SPYDER."

"You're smiling again," Erica said.

Which was true. However, Erica was also dodging the subject.

Even though we had thwarted SPYDER four times, we still didn't know much about them—and neither did anyone else at the CIA. In fact, until a year before, no one at the CIA had known that SPYDER even existed. We didn't know who ran the organization or where they were holed up. We didn't know how many moles they had in the government or who they might be. And we didn't have the slightest idea what they were plotting next. The few slim leads we'd found had come up dry.

Until that very moment.

Erica's phone buzzed in her pocket.

This struck me as odd, because only three people on earth knew Erica's phone number: her grandfather, who was a very good spy for the CIA; her mother, who was a very good spy for MI6 (so good that even Erica's grandfather didn't know about her); and me. Even then, Erica had only given me her number grudgingly, insisting that it was exclusively for life-and-death emergencies. Her own father, who was also a spy, didn't even have it. This was because Alexander Hale was a lousy spy—although he had been clever enough to hide this from most of the CIA until recently.

Erica seemed moderately concerned that anyone was calling her. She pulled out the phone, checked the caller ID, then answered curtly. "What's the situation?"

She listened for a few seconds, then said, "I'm with him now. I'll bring him right in." Then she hung up and said, "Granddad wants to see you. Immediately."

"Why?"

"Murray Hill says he's finally ready to talk."

That caught me by surprise. Murray Hill was only a year older than me, but he was one of SPYDER's most devious operatives. He had been a mole at spy school for months and nearly succeeded in blowing the place up. Since then, he'd been caught and had escaped several times. For the past month, he'd been incarcerated at spy school, during which he had steadfastly refused to say anything he knew about SPYDER, no matter how much he was offered in return.

"Why's he ready to talk now?" I asked.

"Granddad didn't know. He said Murray just decided to do it."

"And what's this got to do with me?"

Erica rolled her eyes, the way she always did when I wasn't putting things together fast enough. "Isn't it obvious? You're the only one he'll talk to."

NEGOTIATION

Sessions Center for Juvenile Incarceration

CIA Academy of Espionage

Subterranean Level 2

March 28

1600 hours

Murray Hill was locked up in the academy's rela-
tively new jail for students, which had been built inside the
Cheney Center for the Acquisition of Information. The reason
the jail was relatively new was that, until recently, no one had
believed there was any need for it. Everyone had felt that, even
if a kid under eighteen *had* been devious enough to commit
a serious crime against the country, then a standard juvenile
detention center would have been good enough to hold them.

That hadn't been the case with Murray Hill.

SPYDER had sprung him from state custody twice. Therefore, the academy jail had been built, although Murray wasn't one of the original prisoners. (He had still been at large at the time.) The originals had been two students from SPYDER's training center for future evil agents: Nefarious Jones, who was still imprisoned, and Ashley Sparks, who had escaped.

The new jail also served as a school, providing Nefarious and Murray with classes specifically tailored for them, such as "Why You Should Defect from SPYDER and Help Us Defeat Them" and "Informing on the Enemy 101." I hadn't seen Murray since he had been incarcerated, but I'd heard through the grapevine that the classes weren't working. This was quickly confirmed by Cyrus Hale, Erica's grandfather, as he led Erica and me through the center.

"The little dirtbag hasn't said one useful thing the whole time he's been here," Cyrus groused. "No matter what we've tried."

"Even torture?" Erica asked.

"The CIA isn't allowed to use torture anymore," Cyrus replied testily, like this was a bad thing. Cyrus was a talented spy, but, like Erica, he wasn't much of a people person. He was gruff and curt on a good day—and this obviously wasn't a good day. "But then, there are plenty of other approved techniques. We're not exactly making the kid comfortable down here."

"So what are you doing?" I asked.

"Standard procedure for prisoners who refuse to cooperate. Reduced sleeping hours. No TV or any other perks. Only vitamin-enhanced gruel and water to eat."

"No junk food?" I asked. "Murray's the least-healthy person I've ever met. I'm pretty sure he's never eaten a vegetable unless it was garnishing a hamburger. Without junk food, I'm surprised he lasted a day without saying anything, let alone a month."

"Oh, he said plenty," Cyrus muttered. "The kid never shuts up for a second. Problem is, none of it's useful. It's all just hot air and banana oil."

We arrived at a door flanked by two guards. Both snapped to attention when they saw Cyrus, but glanced at Erica and me warily.

"They're with me," Cyrus said.

The guards obediently stepped aside. One entered a code into a keypad, and the door clicked open. Cyrus led us through it into the incarceration area. The two cells sat side by side, with a narrow corridor for us to stand in.

Nefarious Jones was in the first cell, just as he'd been the last time I'd visited. In fact, Nefarious was in the exact same spot where I'd last seen him. He was seated on his cot, facing the large-screen TV that had been a reward for his turning in evidence against SPYDER. He was playing video games, as usual, surrounded by a dozen empty bags of Cheetos. Now that I thought about it, Nefarious ate even worse than Murray. Cheetos were his primary food source—and possibly his only one. The area around his mouth was bright orange from Cheeto dust. He looked like he had a radioactive goatee.

"Hey, Nefarious," I said. "How's it going?"

"Mneh," Nefarious replied, which was actually rather communicative for Nefarious. He simply ignored most people.

"Is that Ben Ripley?" Murray Hill called from the next cell over. "Don't waste your time talking to that that gamer freak. You might as well talk to a turnip. C'mon over and say hello."

I continued down the corridor . . . and stopped in shock before Murray's cell.

Erica did too. And Erica wasn't easily shocked.

Murray looked like an entirely different person. The whole time I'd known him, he'd been an out-of-shape slob: He had a potbelly, a permanent slouch, and the stamina of a koala bear; his hair was oily, his skin was greasy, and his clothes were usually so covered with food stains that they looked like Jackson Pollock paintings. But now, Murray was trim, fit, and a good twenty pounds lighter. His hair was cut short and even appeared to have been washed in the past day, revealing eyes that were much brighter than I remembered. His belly was now flat as a tabletop—and he had muscles. They weren't huge, but still, they were on display, as Murray was doing push-ups. Murray Hill, who had always acted as though the simple act of sitting up straight was exhausting, was *exercising*.

"Erica!" he exclaimed upon seeing her. "Glad to see you're here too. Not that I would have expected you to let Ben visit solo. I mean, big things are about to happen, and I know you want to be a part of them." He sprang to his feet in a smooth and distinctly un-Murray-like movement, then began doing jumping jacks.

"Hello, Murray," Erica said. She was trying to speak with her usual reserved cool, but she was obviously still caught off guard.

Murray picked up on this too. "Checking out my new bod? Well, not *new*, I guess. Technically, it's the same body I've always had, but now it's been tuned up, courtesy of the CIA." He grinned at Cyrus. "I've been meaning to thank you, Agent Hale. I'll admit, for the first day or two, after you locked me down here with nothing to eat but pig slop and absolute zero in terms of mental stimulation, I was not a happy camper. Which I suppose was the point. But after a while, I realized that moping around feeling sorry for myself wasn't going to get me anywhere. So I decided to make the best of my situation. I asked the guards for some exercise tips and started working out, and I have to tell you, this has been an incredible month. As your granddaughter noticed, I'm in the peak physical condition of my life, my skin has cleared up, I feel fantastic—and mentally, I'm even better." He returned his attention to Erica and me. "I've taken up yoga, mindfulness, and tantric meditation. It's amazing. I feel like I've really gotten in touch with the real me."

"The real you is a backstabbing sleazeball," I said.

"The *old* me was a backstabbing sleazeball," Murray corrected. "Also a money-grubbing jerk and an all-around schmuck. But I've changed. I know you won't believe this, but I am truly sorry for my behavior."

"I don't believe it," Erica and I said simultaneously.

"I deserve that," Murray said, sounding genuinely upset. "But it doesn't change the fact that I *am* sorry. The way I behaved to you both was very bad."

"You tried to *kill* us," I pointed out. "On multiple occasions."

"Okay, the way I behaved was *worse* than very bad. It was terrible. Horrible."

"Reprehensible," Erica suggested. "Repugnant. Odious. Loathsome. Abhorrent. Subhuman."

"Those too," Murray agreed. "My experience here has allowed me to realize that. I put my own well-being ahead of yours, and while that seemed like a good idea at the time, it wasn't very smart from a karmic perspective. So . . . I want to atone. I want to do something good for both of you to make up for all the awful things I've done." He stopped his jumping jacks and gave us a big grin, revealing the gold tooth that had replaced one of his front incisors. "What if I gave you SPYDER? For real this time."

I took a step back, stunned. Then I looked at Erica, unsure what to believe. She looked at her grandfather in turn.

If Cyrus was caught by surprise, he didn't show it. Instead, he gave Erica a slight nod, indicating he thought this might be on the level.

"How?" Erica asked Murray.

"I'll put the whole organization in a box, stick a bow on it, and then leave it under your Christmas tree," Murray said sarcastically. "How do you *think* I'll give it to you? I'll take you to where everyone who runs SPYDER is hiding out."

My astonishment grew even greater. I had been expecting Murray to give us a few names, at most. And here he was, offering to hand over the entire organization.

Cyrus immediately became skeptical. "For the past month, you've told the inquisitors you didn't have the slightest idea where SPYDER was holed up. And now, just like that, you've changed your mind?"

"First of all, the inquisitors never asked nicely," Murray

said. "Secondly, I have seen the error of my ways. And I can prove it with two words: Adam Zarembok."

Cyrus blinked at him, confused. "Who's Adam Zarembok?"

"He's a sixth-year student here," Erica replied. "Weak on self-defense, but otherwise scores top marks all around. Well-respected. President of his class. Has a work-study job with the school administration."

"He's also a mole for SPYDER," Murray said. "And has been for the past two years. If you toss his room, you'll find a trove of top secret documents he's stolen from the school."

Cyrus looked to Erica. "Is he on your radar?"

"No," Erica admitted. "But you might as well check it out."

Cyrus strode to the door and told the guards stationed there, "Get a team to Zarembok's room right now and search it thoroughly. If you find anything suspicious, call me."

One guard saluted and hustled off, leaving the second on duty.

Meanwhile, Murray grabbed a pipe that hung from the ceiling and began doing chin-ups. "It's not a question of *if* he finds anything. It's *when*. Zarembok's dirty. Just like I used to be. And he's only a little fish. I'm offering you the whole organization."

Cyrus returned from the door. His skepticism had faded significantly. "You're really willing to take us to your leaders?"

"Not *you*." Since his hands were occupied, Murray pointed to Erica and me with his feet. "*Them*. And only them. No one else from the CIA comes along. That's the deal. Take it or leave it."

"I can't send two kids to face SPYDER, and you know it," Cyrus said.

"Well I can't bring a whole brigade of CIA agents," Murray returned. "And *you* know that. This needs to be a stealth operation, not the D-day invasion. Plus, the CIA is crawling with double agents. If you alert too many people, one of those scumbags will tip SPYDER off before we even get out the door. Now, if the dynamic duo here wants to call in the cavalry *after* I've shown them where SPYDER is, that's up to them." He looked toward Erica and me. "However you crazy kids want to handle this is your business."

"Why us?" I asked.

Murray paused in the midst of a chin-up to look at me curiously. "What do you mean?"

"If you really want to bring SPYDER down, why not take two pros?" I clarified. "Like Agent Hale here and whoever he wants to bring along?"

"Because I don't *like* Agent Hale here, and I'm sure I'd like whoever he wants to bring along even less." Murray dropped to the floor and approached the bars of his cell. After his chin-ups, his newfound muscles were bulging. "But

I like you, Ben. Before you knew I was working for the bad guys, we were friends." He shifted his attention to Erica. "As for you, I have to admit, I always respected you. You might have treated me like pond scum, but I deserved it. I did you guys wrong, so you're the ones I'm looking out for now."

"Both of us?" Erica asked skeptically. "I heard you only wanted to speak to Ben."

"I wanted to speak to *both* of you," Murray insisted. "But I knew Ben wouldn't be allowed to see me unless I demanded it. Furthermore, I know Ben won't agree to go on any mission without you. You're a team. A good one. Possibly the best at the CIA—even if the CIA won't admit it. That's about to change, though. I'll help bring SPYDER down—but I want both of *you* to get the credit for it, not anyone else."

I glanced at Erica, expecting her to say something like *It doesn't matter who gets the credit for bringing down SPYDER. All that matters is bringing SPYDER down.*

But she *didn't* say anything like that. She didn't say anything, period. She just gave Murray a hard stare. Only, there was a tiny glint of excitement in it.

Murray had struck a nerve with her, and he knew it. He leaned against the bars now, selling his plan. "Both of you have helped thwart SPYDER four times now, and how much credit has the CIA given you? Zip. Nada. The big old goose egg. The first time, your own daddy stole the credit, Erica.

The next three, they kept everything a secret and swept your contributions under the carpet." He shifted his attention to me. "Yeah, you got a medal from the president last time, but that was only public relations. The CIA had to cover its butt after letting you take the fall for blowing up the White House. And even then, you only got credit for saving the president, not thwarting SPYDER." His eyes flicked back to Erica. "Which is still more credit than *you* got, Hot Stuff. As smart as Ben is, he would have been dead ten times over without your mad skills. You've bailed him out of trouble time and time again, and for what? You know more than most *teachers* here, and they still only consider you a spy-in-training. Well, once you give them SPYDER on a silver platter, that won't be the case anymore. So what do you say? Are we a team?"

Erica said, "I'm not committing to anything until I know how this plan of yours works."

"It's simple. The CIA has lots of aircraft at its disposal, right? All we need is a small private jet, one capable of traveling a few thousand miles—and with an in-flight entertainment system of some sort. 'Cause I've had nothing to watch except mold growing on cinder blocks for the past month, and that story line has gotten very boring. You guys covertly spring me from this lockup, the three of us fly to where SPY-DER is hiding out, I point them out to you, and you take it from there. Easy peasy, lemon squeezy."

"Not exactly," Cyrus grumbled. "I'm guessing this plan of yours doesn't entail your making a round trip back here."

Murray acted surprised, as if this hadn't even occurred to him. "Now that you mention it, Agent Hale, it does seem like my freedom might be a nice reward for helping engineer the capture of the most ruthless and cunning group of enemies this country has ever had."

"No dice," Cyrus said. "You've committed too many crimes to walk."

Murray shrugged. "Fine. Be that way. Good luck finding SPYDER on your own." He dropped to the floor and started doing push-ups again.

"We're done here," Cyrus told Erica and me, then walked out of the incarceration area.

Erica and I hurried after him. Nefarious didn't even glance at us as we passed his cell. He was still riveted to his video game.

"Nice seeing you guys!" Murray called out cheerfully. "Feel free to drop by again next time you're in the neighborhood!"

We caught up to Cyrus in the hall outside the cell block. "What do you think you're doing?" Erica asked him.

"Putting the kibosh on this." Cyrus kept walking at a fast clip through the Cheney Center. For a man in his seventies, he was in excellent shape. "That kid has committed serious crimes against this country. I'm not about to let him go free."

"He's offering us *SPYDER*," Erica said heatedly. "Not just the low-level schmoes we've caught before. The people who run the organization. If we get them, then SPYDER dies once and for all—and all the chaos and mayhem they cause ends too."

"*If* they're not ten steps ahead of us, as usual," Cyrus muttered. "I'm not sending you into the lion's den with only Ben as backup. The kid might be smart, but he has the survival skills of a potato bug."

"Um . . . ," I said. "I'm right here."

"We won't do anything on our own," Erica said. "We'll simply confirm SPYDER's location, radio it back to you, and keep a close eye on them while you bring in the big guns."

"It won't be that simple," Cyrus warned. "Things never are with SPYDER."

"It's a babysitting operation. I can handle it, Grandpa, and you know it."

Cyrus scratched the stubble on his chin, mulling this over. I knew that, despite his concern for Erica, he valued her skills more highly than most other spies at the agency. After all, he was the one who'd taught them to her. "I still don't like the idea of that weasel in there getting a Get Out of Jail Free card."

"So we don't free him," Erica said with a smile. "We tell

him we will, but then we sack him with the rest of SPYDER."

"You want to go back on your word with him?" I asked.

"It's exactly what he'd do to us," Erica replied. "In fact, he *has* done it to us. Too many times to count."

"What's to say he isn't double-crossing us *now*?" I asked. "What if this whole thing is a setup?"

"It's possible," Cyrus conceded. "Let's see how this Adam Zarembok thing shakes out. If Murray is really willing to expose a mole SPYDER has spent years developing, then I'd say he's definitely turned against them. In fact, he'll *need us* to take SPYDER down, because once they find out he's fingered someone, they'll want him dead."

We passed out of the Cheney Center and into the maze of subterranean tunnels beneath the academy. The entire network was designed to be as confusing as possible. There was no signage, and all the exits were cleverly concealed. However, Cyrus moved through it without hesitation. He and Erica were probably the only people who knew their way around it without a map. Our own principal had once been lost down there for two days.

"So if Murray has really turned, this mission is a go?" Erica asked.

Cyrus fixed Erica with a stony gaze as we walked. "Tell me you're not only doing this for the credit," he said. "I saw the look on your face when that snake-oil salesman gave you his spiel. I know the CIA hasn't given you what you deserve, but you can't get into this game looking for glory. Once you start putting yourself ahead of the mission, things go south fast. If you need any evidence, look at your father."

"It's not about the credit," Erica assured him. "It's about getting SPYDER. *That's it.*"

Cyrus considered Erica a little longer, then nodded. "All right. If Zarembok is really a mole, you're on. We'll let Murray sweat it out in there another couple hours, though. Make him think we really have nixed this thing. Then we cut a deal on our terms and send you guys in."

"Great!" Erica said. "We won't let you down, Grandpa."

"Er . . . ," I said.

Cyrus and Erica both turned to me, looking as though they had forgotten I was with them.

"You have a problem with this?" Cyrus asked.

"No," I said. "I have *many* problems with it."

Cyrus glared at me. Erica didn't look much happier.

I soldiered on anyhow. "For starters, neither of you asked *me* if I wanted to do this. . . ."

"That's not how spying works," Cyrus informed me. "You get your mission and you see it through. End of story."

"I understand that in theory," I said. "But I've gone up against SPYDER several times before, and things have never worked out the way we hoped."

"And yet we've always thwarted them," Erica said impatiently.

"Yes," I conceded. "But before that happens, there's always been an awful lot of me almost dying. Which I have never enjoyed. And now you and I will be confronting SPYDER alone, with Murray Hill, who's as slippery as they come. It sounds awfully dangerous."

"This is the Academy of Espionage," Cyrus said gruffly. "If you didn't want danger, you should have enrolled at the Academy of Scrapbooking. Any other problems?"

"Yes," I said. "I'm worried that people might recognize me. Six weeks ago I was the most wanted kid in America for trying to assassinate the president."

"You just came here from walking around in public, didn't you?" Cyrus asked. "Did anyone recognize you?"

"No," I admitted.

"How many people have recognized you in the last month?"

I thought about that then gave my answer. "None."

"Exactly as suspected," Cyrus said. "People have terrible memories. Most can barely recognize someone they've met a dozen times, let alone someone who was famous for fifteen minutes a month and a half ago. The chances of you being noticed are minuscule at best—especially because you're going to be trying your best to not even be seen in the first place. The whole point of this mission is to lie low. Now, if there are no other issues . . ."

"Actually, there's one more," I said weakly. "It's spring break next week. I'm supposed to go home to see my parents."

"Not anymore," Cyrus informed me. "If we want to get the jump on SPYDER, we can't waste any time. So call your parents and let them know that plans have changed. You have a big science project, and you're gonna need the whole week to finish it."

"They won't be happy about that," I said.

"I'm sure they won't," Cyrus agreed. "But the fate of the free world is at stake here. We can't put it on hold so you can spend the week with your mommy. Your spring break is now officially Operation Tiger Shark."

"Tiger Shark?" Erica asked, impressed. "I thought the CIA had run out of cool names like that."

This was true. The CIA had been naming operations for several decades, and the good options were running low. Our last mission had been dubbed Pungent Muskrat.

"I made an executive decision," Cyrus replied. "I'm not initiating ops with names like Mangy Weasel or Scrawny Chicken anymore. It's bad for morale. So I recycled an old mission name. Now go get packing. I want you moving out at oh-two-hundred."

"That's two in the morning!" I exclaimed.

"I know when oh-two-hundred is," Cyrus snapped. "The best way to catch your enemy by surprise is to get to them before they've even had their morning coffee. I'll put everything in motion immediately." With that, he spun on his heel and marched down the hall.

"But we don't even know where our enemy *is* yet," I said to Erica.

"We will soon enough." Erica's eyes were wide with excitement. "C'mon. Let's get to the armory." She started down the hall in the opposite direction her grandfather had gone.

I stayed rooted to my spot.

Erica turned back to me. At first she seemed to be annoyed, the way she would have been back when we'd first met, but then she seemed to think better of it. She shifted to a tone of concern. "Ben, I know we've ended up in danger every time we've gone up against SPYDER, but this mission is different. It's easy. We're only keeping an eye on SPYDER, not confronting them. They won't even know we're there."

"And what if something goes wrong? Something *always* goes wrong."

"Not this time. I promise. This is as simple as missions get."

I wasn't sure if Erica was saying this because she truly meant it—or because she knew it would make me feel better to hear it. I *hoped* it was the former, though. After all, Erica liked me, which hopefully meant she wouldn't lie to me. However, I knew she wanted to bring SPYDER down more than anything. It wasn't merely about the credit. It was also personal; Joshua Hallal, the last spy school student Erica had liked, had betrayed her and defected to the dark side. He was certainly one of the higher-ups Murray was promising to hand over to us. And yet, while Murray might have respected Erica, he certainly didn't consider her a friend. If I didn't agree to go on the mission, Murray would probably kill it.

So it was definitely possible that Erica was only sweet-talking me.

Still, I fell in behind her and followed her through the tunnels. Partly because I really wanted to trust her intentions. And partly because, without her help, I probably wouldn't be able to find my way out again. It was a real labyrinth down there.

"I know you're worried," Erica said, "but this won't turn out as badly as you fear. In fact, it might even be fun."

I realized that might be true. If the mission *really* did turn out to be easy, then going away with Erica for a few days could be enjoyable. Maybe even romantic. I found myself smiling at the thought of it. "Yeah, I suppose it could."

"Then let's start packing." Erica led the way through the tunnels toward the armory.

I fell in beside her, growing more and more excited about the mission. Which was a mistake.

As it happened, Erica was right about one thing: The mission didn't turn out as badly as I had feared.

It turned out far worse than I could have ever imagined.

DILEMMA

CIA Academy of Espionage

Armistead Dormitory

March 28

2015 hours

"I have a problem," Mike Brezinski said. "A *big* one."

"Join the club," I told him.

"You don't understand," Mike said. "This problem is huge. Bigger than anything you could possibly be dealing with right now." He was standing in the doorway to my cramped dormitory room, wearing his customary shorts-and-T-shirt combo.

"Wasn't that door locked?" I asked.

"Yes. But I picked it."

"Why?"

"I didn't think you would answer if I knocked." Mike pointed to the DO NOT DISTURB sign I'd taped to the door as evidence. "See? You apparently don't want to be disturbed."

"I don't," I agreed. "I'm in the middle of something very urgent here." I was packing for my mission. Adam Zarembok had turned out to be a mole. Campus security had found thirty-six highly classified documents hidden in his room. They hadn't busted him, though, as that would have tipped off SPYDER that something was wrong. But this had convinced Cyrus that Murray had truly turned. Only two minutes before, I had received a coded text from him: **Tiger Shark approved and initiated. Be ready at 0200. Murray Hill says dress for warm weather.**

My knapsack was laid out on my spindly bed. (It didn't seem right to take a suitcase on a mission. I had to be prepared for any eventuality, and the knapsack was far more versatile.) Luckily, I had only placed a few shorts and T-shirts in it so far, and not the cache of survival gear that Erica and I had procured from the school armory. I had quickly covered it all with my bed sheets when I'd heard Mike picking the lock.

Mike closed the door and plopped himself into my desk chair. Either he was ignoring me, or he was too wrapped up in his own problem to have heard what I'd said. "It's Jemma," he groaned.

"Your girlfriend?" I asked.

"She's not my girlfriend," Mike said quickly. "She's just a girl who's a friend."

"The national news seems to think you're her boyfriend," I told him, then added, "And so does Jemma, I think."

"That's the big problem." Mike was my best friend from growing up. I had been recruited to spy school first and done my best to keep it a secret from him, but Mike had eventually caught on—and then proved he was potential spy material as well. So he'd been recruited too, although he'd had to start a year behind me.

Mike was the kind of guy who breezed through life. Back in regular school, he had never really challenged himself, only taking classes he knew he could pass. Spy school had been tougher, but he was still doing fine, mostly because Mike tended to think rules were only for other people, which was an attitude that served him very well at the academy. At spy school, you could sometimes ace a test simply by coming up with a clever enough way to avoid taking it in the first place.

Jemma was Jemma Stern, the daughter of the president of the United States of America. She had noticed Mike at my medal ceremony, and I'd made an introduction. The two of them had been hanging out ever since. Up until that point, though, I had thought Mike was enjoying his time with Jemma. Two nights before, he'd been her date to a huge gala at the White House and ended up meeting his favorite comedian *and* the quarterback for the Washington Redskins.

"Jemma wants me to go to Hawaii with her family for spring break," Mike groaned.

"That sounds terrible," I said sarcastically. "No wonder you're so upset. And you'll probably have to fly on *Air Force One* instead of a regular plane."

"It *is* terrible," Mike insisted. "A girl doesn't invite a guy to Hawaii unless she's *serious*. And I don't want to be serious with Jemma."

"So tell her you're not that into her."

"It's not that easy! She's the First Daughter. You can't just break up with the First Daughter!"

"Why not?"

"Because she's famous! She's America's Sweetheart. She has a hundred million Twitter followers! I just found out we might be in *People* magazine next week. If I break her heart, I'll become the most hated person in the country."

I hadn't thought of that. "Oh. That *is* a problem."

"Plus, her father controls the Secret Service. He already isn't a fan of mine. If I really upset Jemma, he might have them whack me."

"I don't think the Secret Service does that for the president."

"Oh yeah? How many ex-boyfriends of First Daughters have you ever heard about?" Mike put his head in his hands. "This is a real dilemma, Ben."

"Yes. A Jemma dilemma." I glanced at my watch. Although I felt bad for Mike, I really needed to get him out of my room and finish packing.

"I don't want to go to Hawaii," he said. "I mean, I *do*. Especially on *Air Force One*. But once that happens, everyone's going to think we're a thing—especially Jemma—and then I'll never be able to get out of this alive."

"So come up with an excuse," I said. "One that doesn't sound like you're breaking up with her. Like you have to go to a family reunion or something."

"That'll never work. I already told her everyone in my family hates each other."

"I'm sure you can come up with something else."

Mike lifted his head from his hands, looking at me suspiciously. "Why are you trying to get rid of me?"

"I'm not trying to get rid of you," I said. Though I'd probably hesitated a moment too long before saying it. Mike had caught me off guard.

His eyes flicked to my knapsack. "What are you packing for?"

"My week at home."

Mike sprang to his feet and snatched a pair of shorts out of the knapsack. "These are shorts! It's only supposed to be forty degrees in Virginia this week."

"I'm hoping it warms up," I said quickly. "And I still have pants at home."

Mike snatched a tube of sunblock out of the knapsack as well. "Aha! Sunblock! No one takes sunblock to Virginia in March. You're going on a secret mission, aren't you?"

"No."

"That's exactly what I'd expect someone who was going on a secret mission to say!"

"As well as someone who *wasn't* going on a secret mission. Which I'm not doing. Because I'm going home to see my parents." I defiantly removed a pair of jeans from my dresser and threw them into the knapsack. "See? Pants."

"Where are you going?" Mike asked. "Does it have something to do with SPYDER?"

"It couldn't have less to do with SPYDER. I'm going to be helping my parents at the grocery store."

Mike dramatically yanked back the covers on my bed, revealing the cache of supplies. Then he grinned knowingly at me. "Exactly what do you need a grappling hook for at a grocery store?"

"Some of the stuff on the top shelves is very hard to

reach," I said. But I couldn't sell it. Mike had me figured out, and I had always hated lying to my friends. It was my least favorite thing about being a spy. After the nearly being killed by my enemies, of course.

"What's the mission?" Mike asked. "Can I come?"

"No."

"Aw, c'mon! I'm your best friend! Take me with you!"

"That's not how these things work. I don't get to invite whoever I want. It's a top secret mission, not a birthday party."

The door to my room suddenly flew open, revealing Zoe Zibbell. "You're going on a secret mission?" she asked excitedly.

Zoe had been my best friend at spy school until Mike had been recruited. From the moment I met her, she had been my biggest supporter, believing that I had what it took to be a great spy even when I hadn't believed it myself. Unfortunately, our relationship had grown awkward since I had discovered that she'd had a secret crush on me. Even worse, our fellow student Warren Reeves had had a secret crush on Zoe. Warren had been so upset with my stealing her attention from him that he'd defected to SPYDER and nearly gotten me killed.

Zoe and I really hadn't dealt with this since it had happened. Both of us had been too embarrassed. But avoiding the subject had only made things worse. Things had been weird between us for the last few weeks.

"Doesn't anyone knock anymore?" I asked. "Or pay attention to 'Do Not Disturb' signs?"

"I wasn't eavesdropping," Zoe said. "I swear. I merely happened to be passing by when I overheard you. The walls in this dorm are paper-thin."

"So you decided to pick the lock?" I asked accusingly.

"Actually, that's my bad," Mike owned. "I didn't lock the door after *I* picked it."

"Are you going after SPYDER?" Zoe asked me excitedly. "Can I come?"

"No!" I went to the doorway, peered into the hall to see if any other fellow students were eavesdropping, then locked the door and lowered my voice to a whisper. "You're not even supposed to *know* about this mission, let alone be invited to tag along."

Zoe frowned angrily. "I thought we were friends."

"We are."

"Friends don't go on missions without telling each other about it."

"They do if they're *secret* missions," I said. "If you got sent on a secret mission, you wouldn't be allowed to tell *me*. And I wouldn't take it personally."

"Yeah right." Mike dug into the box of survival gear.

"Wow. Night-vision goggles, telephoto scope, camo face paint. Looks like someone's doing some surveillance!"

Zoe peered into the box as well and grabbed a pack of gum. "Cool! Is this putty explosive that's designed to look like gum?"

"No," I said. "That's actual gum."

"*Mint* gum," Mike said suspiciously. "So you're thinking about keeping your breath fresh. Erica must be going!"

Zoe glowered jealously, then tried to hide it.

"She's not," I lied.

"Of course she is," Zoe said flatly. "Any time you go on a mission, Erica goes too. You two are the Wonder Twins. You get to go off and have all these amazing adventures while the rest of us are stuck back here doing homework."

"Adventures where people try to kill me on a regular basis," I reminded her. "And you've been able to come on some of them."

"Only as backup," Zoe muttered. "You and Erica always get to be the principals. No one ever frames *me* for the assassination of the president. Or forces *me* to defuse a nuclear bomb while hanging from a helicopter. . . ."

"Most people would consider that a good thing," I said.

"Well I don't!" Zoe huffed. "I'm a straight-A student here! I've proved myself on missions. And I have *way* better fighting skills than you do."

"There are slime molds with better fighting skills than Ben," Mike put in.

"But you're the one who always gets the missions," Zoe told me petulantly. "I *never* get to have any fun!"

I signaled her to lower her voice before the entire dormitory heard about the mission. "I wish I could take you," I whispered. "But it's not my call."

"Then put in a good word for us," Mike suggested. "Who's running this op? Cyrus?"

"No," I said too quickly.

"It's definitely Cyrus," Zoe said. "Yes, ask him. He likes you."

"Cyrus doesn't like anybody," I said.

"He likes Erica," Mike offered. "So ask her to ask him about us. Zoe and I have been with him before. We did good work. We kept all of Colorado from getting nuked. That has to be worth something."

"I can try," I told them. "But I don't think it's going to get us anywhere. This mission is supposed to be pretty bare bones."

"Please," Zoe pleaded. "You know we'd be helpful, right?"

"I do." I truly meant that. Despite my previous success on missions, I still felt as though Zoe and Mike had far better talents than I did in many areas. They might not have been as incredibly adept as Erica, but they would still have been a welcome addition as far as I was concerned. Four spies seemed far better than two. And yet . . . "It's still going to be a long shot."

"Thanks," Mike said. "I mean, if I had a mission, that'd be the perfect excuse for getting out of going to Hawaii with Jemma. She couldn't get upset at me if the fate of the free world was at stake."

"Hold on," Zoe said. "Are you asking to go on a top secret mission solely to get out of breaking up with Jemma?"

"Kind of," Mike admitted.

"He's having a Jemma dilemma," I explained.

"Why don't you just be a man and break up with her?" Zoe asked Mike. Which gave me the impression that Mike might have told Zoe a lot more about Jemma than he'd told me. The idea that my two best friends were bonding behind my back made me a little jealous, but then, I'd had a lot going on lately.

"It's not that easy!" Mike protested. "But I'm working on ways to do it. Ones that will still let me look like a pretty good person. Like maybe faking my own death."

"Mike!" Zoe gasped. "You can't do that!"

"Sure I could. It wouldn't even be that hard. If I go on the mission, then we could say that something went wrong and I was killed in action."

"There are three problems with that," Zoe pointed out.

"First of all, it's idiotic. Second, it's a horrible thing to do. And third, Jemma isn't even supposed to know that you're a spy. She thinks this is a science academy."

"Crud," Mike grumbled. "You're right." Then he brightened suddenly. "Maybe I could die in a tragic science experiment!"

"No!" Zoe said so forcefully that Mike shrank away from her.

"Guys," I said, "I'm sorry, but I really need some time to pack. And if you want me to see about getting you on the mission, then I'd better do it right away—so that *you* have time to pack. We're leaving at oh-two-hundred."

Mike and Zoe were so excited by this prospect, they practically sprang for the door.

"Sure thing!" Mike told me.

"Thanks for doing this," Zoe said. "I really appreciate it. Sorry I got upset at you earlier."

"No worries," I told her, following them out the door. "I'll go talk to Erica and let you know what Cyrus says."

They thanked me again and hurried off to their own rooms, whispering excitedly to each other. I quickly set off in the other direction, heading for Erica's room. I was quite sure I was on a fool's errand, but I figured it couldn't hurt to try. I took the stairs down a floor, cut through a small common area where a few fellow students were doing homework, and approached Erica's room.

Instead of my simple DO NOT DISTURB sign, Erica had dozens of threats posted on her door. Most promised bodily harm to anyone who bothered her.

I was considering whether or not to risk knocking when the door opened anyhow.

Erica had apparently known I was standing there.

She yanked me into her room, cased the hall to see if anyone was watching, then shut the door and locked it.

It hadn't occurred to me until that moment that I had never been in Erica's room. I doubted anyone else had either. Erica wasn't much for socializing.

What I saw astonished me.

It looked completely normal. I had been expecting walls lined with weaponry. Or cold, bare walls that concealed secret rooms with walls lined with weaponry.

I had *not* expected posters with kittens on them. Or a baby-blue comforter on the bed. Or a plethora of throw pillows.

Erica noticed the stunned look on my face. "What's wrong with you?"

"Nothing!" I said quickly. "I just didn't think that, uh . . ."

"I was human?"

"Er, that's not quite what I . . ."

"I like kittens, okay? And throw pillows."

"Is that a *teapot*?" I asked, stunned. The one I was staring at was porcelain, and it had delicate paintings of flowers on it.

"I'm half British," Erica said curtly. "Liking tea is genetic. Also, the pot is very good for brewing antidotes for poison. In case I've ingested too much."

"Too much? Don't you mean 'any'?"

"No," Erica said, like I was an idiot. "You have to ingest *some* poison if you want to build up an immunity to it."

"Oh. Of course."

"You do that, right? In case SPYDER ever tries to poison you, you need to be prepared."

"I'm working on it," I lied. "Listen, before we go, I have a question for you."

"The answer is no."

"You don't even know what the question is!"

"Is it 'Can Mike and Zoe come with us on the mission?'"

"Okay," I said. "You *do* know what the question is. How'd you do that?"

"I'm studying to be a spy, Ben. It's my job to know things."

"Do you have my room bugged?"

"We don't have time for this," Erica said. Which was a dodge, rather than an answer. "Murray set the parameters for this mission. Only you and I are going. That's it. That's what Grandpa sold to the CIA, and it's too late to make changes now. Plus, Mike and Zoe aren't strong enough agents yet.

They'll make this mission *more* dangerous, rather than less."

"So will I."

"True, but Murray requested you personally, so you're going. And your friends aren't. End of story. Now go get packed."

I sighed in defeat and turned back to the door, knowing any further arguments would be completely ineffectual. "All right."

"Oh, and Ben?"

"Yes?"

"If you tell *anyone* about the kitten posters or the throw pillows or the teapot, I'll kill you."

"I figured as much." I exited into the hallway and heard Erica triple-bolt the door behind me.

In only a few hours, I was going to begin a dangerous mission to confront people who wanted me dead in a place I didn't yet know with a double agent I didn't trust. And now I had to give my best friends the bad news that they couldn't come along.

In other words, it was shaping up to be a typical mission at spy school.

AVIATION

CIA Jet A415

Somewhere over the Gulf of Mexico

March 29

0600 hours

I was jolted awake when the jet hit an air pocket at thirty-five thousand feet. The sudden turbulence shook me so hard in my seat that my head cracked against the window.

I came to, disoriented, momentarily having forgotten where I was.

"Good morning!" Murray Hill said cheerfully. "Ready for breakfast?"

I blinked at him a few times, trying to clear my mind. Even though I had seen the new, improved Murray before, the sight of him was so disorienting that I figured I might still be dreaming. He was buckled into the seat across the aisle from me, squeezing a hand strengthener in his left hand while eating a bowl of Greek yogurt and granola with his right.

This seemed wrong on many levels:

1) Murray was awake before noon—and was alert and chipper, to boot.

2) Murray was doing exercise without anyone forcing him to at gunpoint.

3) Murray was eating granola.

Back at school, Murray had slept more than your average house cat, had the muscular conditioning of a sloth, and rarely consumed any meal, let alone breakfast, that did not have bacon in it. He had also, on many occasions, disparagingly referred to granola as "hamster food."

Murray noticed me staring at his meal. "I know I gave this stuff a bad rap," he said. "But I'd never actually tried it. Turns out, it's good! And obviously, it's way better for the bod than my old diet used to be." He flexed his arms, making his biceps bulge. "This is my own special blend: milled oats, compressed kale bits, and Mongolian whey, with just a hint of agave syrup for some flavor. It's got tons of antioxidants, fiber, *and* riboflavin. I brought some extra if you want to try it."

"Maybe in a bit," I told him. What I *really* wanted to do

was go back to sleep. We had left spy school at two a.m. on the dot, exactly as planned, then been driven to a covert CIA airstrip somewhere in the Virginia countryside. Murray was already there, locked and handcuffed in the back of a CIA sedan, as were two CIA pilots, a man and a woman, who Cyrus said we could trust. While the pilots had prepped the jet for our flight, Cyrus had frisked Murray for any weapons (he didn't have any) and reviewed our mission with us.

The plan was simple. Murray would have the pilots fly us to wherever SPYDER was hiding out. (He still hadn't revealed where this was, wanting to keep it a secret until we were in the air.) Once there, Erica and I would make visual confirmation of SPYDER's presence and send the exact coordinates to Cyrus, who would mobilize a select team of agents tasked with the ambush and capture of our enemies. Erica and I were not to engage SPYDER in any way until the team arrived; instead, we were only to keep a close eye on the organization. Even so, we would still be given full credit for engineering SPYDER's downfall.

Our only other task was to keep a close eye on Murray to make sure he didn't escape. Although Murray had been told he'd be able to go free, he was going to be apprehended along with everyone else from SPYDER. He would go right back to jail, though he might have a few years shaved off his sentence for turning over evidence.

At 0300 hours, we had boarded the jet and taken off.

I had been exhausted, but even then I couldn't go right to sleep, because Murray was too fired up to allow it. He was thrilled to be out of his cell and on his way to an adventure and was annoyed that I didn't want to catch up on old times or play cards. (I *did* want him to tell me where we were going, but he'd refused to do that, only giving the coordinates to the pilots.) I finally had to curl into a ball and pull a blanket over my head before he got the message, and I had eventually fallen asleep.

Now that I was awake again, I checked my watch. Normally, I had an extremely accurate sense of time—it went hand in hand with my math skills—although sometimes it was off when I had just woken up.

Six a.m. I had been asleep only two and a half hours.

The jet vibrated as it hit another air pocket.

I had always dreamed of flying on a private jet. It sounded so glamorous and exciting.

It wasn't.

This jet was owned and operated by the CIA, who appeared to have bought it secondhand, if not third- or fourthhand, possibly from someone who had used it to transport farm animals. It was quite old as private jets went, and it smelled funny. It was also much smaller than I'd expected, with only six seats in the cabin, a tiny cockpit in the front, and an even tinier bathroom at the back that reeked of septic fumes. (The cockpit was concealed behind a door that had been closed since shortly before takeoff.) The furnishings were several decades out of date. To Murray's great disappointment, the only entertainment system was an eight-track-tape player, and there did not appear to be any tapes for it, as none had been manufactured since the 1980s. The plane rattled constantly as it flew, even when there was no turbulence, giving the unsettling impression that the wings might fall off at any moment.

The seats were the nicest thing about the plane. They were big and plush, like the recliner my father had in our TV room. They tilted back a decent amount, which had helped me sleep, and they could also swivel around so you could face the seat behind you. There were three on each side of the plane.

Erica Hale was asleep in the first row, in the chair on the right. Though I suspected she might only be *pretending* to be asleep. It wasn't like Erica to drop her guard around an enemy.

Murray and I were in the second row, with Murray directly behind Erica. The third row was empty, as we were the only passengers on the plane.

I looked out the window that I had whacked my head on. The sun was peeking over the rim of the earth, turning the clouds around it an iridescent pink. Below me was a great expanse of water, although I could make out a distant fringe of land ahead of us.

I was sitting on the left side of the plane. If the sun was coming up outside my window, that meant . . .

"We're heading south?" I asked.

"Of course," Murray said cheerfully. "Where else are we supposed to go for spring break?"

I did some quick calculations, given what I knew about the speed of the plane, how far we would have traveled since taking off, and the direction we were heading, which—now that I thought about it—appeared to be more south-southwest than due south. "We're way past the United States. Is that Mexico up ahead?"

"That's my buddy Ben! Always thinking!" Murray downed a heaping spoonful of granola and yogurt and then spoke with his mouth full. He might have improved the nutritional value of his food, but his manners were still atrocious. "I can never get anything past that big old brain of yours."

"Is SPYDER's hideout in Mexico?"

Murray grinned, granola flecking his teeth. "I can't just tell you. That's no fun at all."

I sighed and looked back out the window. The land ahead was so flat it appeared to have been planed with an enormous power sander. There wasn't a single hill. "That's the Yucatán peninsula."

Murray's eyebrows raised slightly, giving away that I was right.

I tried to see if I could provoke another reaction. "Is SPYDER in Quintana Roo?"

No response this time. Murray managed to stay completely stone-faced.

"Belize?"

Nothing.

"Guatemala? Honduras? Nicaragua?"

Nothing. Nothing. And more nothing.

"C'mon," I groaned. "I thought you wanted to talk."

"Yes. But not about this. You'll see where we're going when we get there. Thirsty?" Murray fished a bottle of acai-berry-infused water from his duffel bag and offered it to me.

"No thanks," I said. Even though the CIA had searched everything Murray had brought on the plane, I still didn't trust him.

"Suit yourself." Murray cracked the bottle open and took a big gulp. "You're missing out, though. It's delicious—and full of priambic electrolytes."

Something was really bugging me about Murray's behavior. Even more than I was normally bugged by Murray's behavior. His habitual cockiness was cranked to greater levels than usual, like he was playing a joke on me and couldn't wait for the payoff.

"What's going on with you?" I asked.

"I'm just excited to be going on this mission," he said. "It's fun to be working *with* you, rather than *against* you."

I gave him a skeptical look. "Really?"

"Really."

"You don't have any tricks up your sleeve?"

"Tricks?" Murray asked innocently. "Like saying that you'll let me go free once I lead you to SPYDER, but secretly plotting to capture me with them anyhow?"

The way he asked this caught me off guard. But I did my best to act like betraying him had never crossed my mind. "I wouldn't do that to you."

Murray narrowed his eyes, like he saw right through this. "Of course you wouldn't," he said coldly.

The plane hit another pocket of turbulence and jolted wildly. If I hadn't been wearing my seat belt, I would have flown out of my chair. Murray lost his grip on his yogurt and granola, which shot straight up out of his hands and splatted on the ceiling.

Erica appeared to sleep soundly right through it.

There was a thump from the rear of the plane, which sounded like some luggage bouncing around, followed by a yelp, which didn't sound anything like luggage at all.

It sounded human.

I turned toward the back of the plane, concerned.

"Don't get so freaked out," Murray told me. "It's only Zoe."

"Zoe?" I asked, surprised.

There was another thump. And another yelp. A more masculine one.

"And that other pal of yours," Murray added. "The one you grew up with."

"Mike?" I exclaimed.

"They snuck aboard while Grandpa Hale was giving you guys your final orders to betray me," Murray said, then called out, "You might as well show yourselves! We know you're here!"

A flimsy door in the rear of the plane popped open. Mike and Zoe tumbled through it onto the floor, looking embarrassed and banged up.

Thankfully, the turbulence ended before they could get thrown around the cabin.

Erica remained sound asleep.

"Hey, guys!" Murray said cheerfully. "Grab some seats. It's way more comfortable than hiding in the luggage compartment."

"I'll say," Mike muttered, getting to his feet. "We've been

getting bounced around in there like pinballs." He flopped into one of the rear seats and buckled himself in.

Zoe moved slower. She couldn't take her eyes off Murray, astonished by his transformation. "Murray? Is that really you?"

I swiveled my seat around to face them. Murray did the same thing.

"Sure it's really me," he said. "The *new* me." He flexed for Zoe. "What do you think?"

"It looks like someone Photoshopped your head onto someone else's body." Zoe sank into the chair across the aisle from Mike's and buckled her seat belt. It took her a few tries, because she couldn't remove her gaze from Murray.

"What are you doing here?" I asked them.

"We came to help you," Zoe said weakly.

"But you were denied permission to join this mission," I reminded her.

"We thought that, if we ended up helping capture SPY-DER, the academy might overlook the fact that we'd disobeyed orders," Mike said.

In his defense, this was probably true. But if they failed—or screwed up the mission—they could get expelled from the academy. However, I decided not to bring this up; they were certainly well aware of it.

"How did you even get to the plane?" I asked.

"We tailed you," Zoe replied. "You'd told us you were leaving at oh-two-hundred, so we called a cab for then and had it waiting off campus. When the car left with you, we followed it to the airstrip."

"And you did a darn good job too," Murray said. "Those covert surveillance classes are really working out for you."

I looked to him. "You knew they were on board the whole time?"

"I'm a seasoned criminal," Murray informed me. "You don't get as far as I have without learning to keep a very close eye on your surroundings."

Zoe glared at him. "If you knew we were in the luggage compartment all along, why didn't you let on earlier? We could have been in real seats rather than crammed back there with the bags."

"I was waiting to see if either Ben or Erica figured it out," Murray replied. "But they didn't. Obviously Ben here is pretty surprised by the whole thing, whereas Sleeping Beauty over there has been out cold since we took off. Anyhow, I'm glad you guys could join us. I'd offer you some food, but mine's all stuck to the ceiling." He pointed up to the splotch of yogurt and granola.

I swiveled my chair toward Erica, stunned that she really was still sleeping. But then, I decided this might be for the best. I swiveled back to Zoe and Mike. "Erica is going to *kill* you both when she finds out you've stowed away on her mission."

"After all our help in Colorado?" Mike asked. "Or at the Pentagon?"

"This is different," I told him. "We're going right to SPY-DER headquarters this time. It's going to be dangerous, and we have to be extremely careful, or things could go wrong in a big way."

The cockpit door burst open, and both pilots stormed out, aiming guns at us. "Put your hands up," the first ordered.

"Wrong like that?" Mike asked me.

"Yes," I agreed sadly. "Wrong like that."

AERIAL MANEUVERS

CIA Jet A415

Mexican airspace

March 29

0630 hours

Both pilots were wearing parachutes. Along with the guns they had pointed our way, I took this as a bad sign.

The plane continued flying normally, indicating they had activated the autopilot.

I raised my hands, trying to stay calm. Zoe and Mike did the same thing.

Murray didn't. The smug grin he'd worn all morning grew even wider. "It's about time," he said to the pilots. "I was wondering when you were going to show."

"Murray!" Zoe screamed. "You scumbag! You set us up!"

Murray shrugged. "I *am* evil." He unbuckled his seat belt and returned his attention to the pilots. "Where's my parachute?"

"Oops," the male pilot said. "We must have forgotten it." He and his partner laughed, enjoying watching us squirm. Cyrus Hale might have vetted them himself, but it appeared he had made a very serious mistake.

Murray's grin faded. "That's not funny. C'mon. Where's my parachute?"

"Parachutes are for SPYDER agents who don't get caught," the female pilot said. She grabbed the emergency release for the external door, despite the fact that we were several miles above the earth.

At that height, the air pressure outside the jet cabin would be far lower than the pressure inside it. Once the door was opened, we could get sucked right out. However, since both pilots had guns trained on us, there didn't appear to be much we could do to stop them.

"I knew we shouldn't have trusted you, Murray!" Zoe shrieked. "You are the worst person ever!"

"Me?" Murray asked, now on the edge of panic. "These guys are about to kill all of us!" He spun back to them. "SPYDER won't be happy when I don't show up alive!"

The pilots broke into laughter again. "SPYDER?" the

man asked. "That's who gave us the order to kill all of you."

His finger tensed on the trigger of his gun.

Erica suddenly lashed out a foot, kicking the man's hand so hard we heard the bones crack. He howled as the gun flew from his grasp.

Erica really *had* been faking being asleep. Now she sprang from her seat and slammed into the man. Both of them crashed into the female pilot, driving her into the door so hard that her head clonked off the metal frame.

Zoe was on her feet in a second, catching the gun before it hit the floor. She spun it around and aimed it at both pilots—just as the woman yanked the emergency release on the door. It popped open, instantly depressurizing the cabin. Both pilots were sucked out in the vortex.

In the split second before the door opened, Erica had dived for the cockpit. If her reflexes had been the tiniest bit slower, she would have been plummeting toward Mexico, but she made it to the relative safety of the tiny room.

Those of us in the main cabin were in trouble, though. Mike and I still had our seat belts on, but I was yanked against mine so hard that it felt as though my body might rip in half.

Zoe threw herself against the back of my seat so that it blocked her from being pulled out. The gun was ripped from her grasp and tumbled out the door.

Murray was so stunned by SPYDER's betrayal, he didn't act to save himself. He would have been sucked right out of the plane if his foot hadn't got caught in the strap of his own pack. The pack jammed underneath his seat, holding him on board while his body was tugged toward the open door.

I felt my mind clouding almost immediately from the sudden lack of oxygen. My vision began to tunnel, shadows creeping in around the edges.

Then oxygen masks dropped from the overhead compartments. I quickly strapped mine on. Zoe, pinioned to the back of my chair, was able to get one too, as was Mike.

Despite the incredible suction trying to drag her out the door, Erica hauled herself into the pilot's seat and strapped on a mask as well.

"Do you know how to fly this plane?" I yelled to her.

"Not this one in particular," she called back, seizing the controls. "But I've taken flying lessons, and I read the pilot's manual for this jet yesterday afternoon, just in case of trouble."

It was preparation like this that made Erica the best partner on earth.

Meanwhile, Murray was still being pulled toward the door, held back only by the strap wrapped around his ankle. His survival instincts had finally kicked in, and he was desperately trying to find something else to grab on to, while still freaking out about SPYDER's double cross. "They set me up!" he whined. "They *used* me! After all I've done for them, they tried to kill me just like I'm one of you losers!"

"How is this a surprise to you?" Zoe asked. "They've left you for dead before!"

"But this time they *promised* they wouldn't!" Murray wailed. "I had them put it in my contract—and they welched on the deal, those jerks!"

Out my window, I could see the pilots in the distance. They had deployed their parachutes and were gently drifting to the ground.

We had crossed over the Yucatán peninsula from the ocean. Directly below us was a huge green swath of tropical jungle, fringed by white-sand beaches and vacation resorts. Unfortunately, it was still *very* far below us, given that we were in a crippled airplane.

In the cockpit, Erica was pushing the stick forward, slowly lowering us toward the ground. The pressure outside the plane was gradually equaling the pressure inside the cabin—but Murray was still in serious danger of being sucked out the door. The strap circling his ankle was starting to tear. He was now straining to fold himself in two so that he could grab the seat, but despite his new physique, this was incredibly difficult given the forces working on him. It was like trying to do a sit-up with a gorilla sitting on his chest.

I leaned toward him, extending my hand toward his.

"Let him go," Zoe said bitterly. "He set you up! He was never going to show you where SPYDER was hiding! This was only a ruse by SPYDER to get rid of you and Erica."

"And *me*," Murray sniveled. "Obviously I'm just as expendable as they are!"

"How did SPYDER engineer this?" I asked him. "Did they get word to you in the jail?"

Murray pointedly didn't answer. But he kept straining for my outstretched hand.

So I pulled away from him. "Fine. You can help yourself."

"Okay!" Murray screamed. "You're right! Somehow, SPYDER slipped a coded message into my food a few days ago. I don't know how they did it. Maybe they have someone in the school cafeteria."

"That would explain the food," Mike observed. "It certainly *tastes* like SPYDER has someone working in the cafeteria."

"Anyhow," Murray went on, "the message told me to cut a deal to bring you to them."

"What about Adam Zarembok?" Erica yelled from the cockpit. "Was he even a real mole—or was he just a patsy?"

Murray hesitated, like he didn't want to admit the truth.

I crossed my arms over my chest, making a show of refusing to help him.

The strap of Murray's pack tore some more. Only a few stitches were now keeping him inside the plane.

"All right!" Murray cried. "Yes! Zarembok's clean! SPY-DER knew I had to give you someone to sell the story, but they didn't want to cough up a real mole. So someone planted the documents in Zarembok's room."

"Who?" Zoe demanded.

"I don't know!" Murray dug his fingers into the plane's grimy carpet, desperately looking for something to hold on to, but found no purchase. "They barely told me anything about what was going to happen."

"But you knew Erica and I were supposed to die, right?" I asked. "You thought the plan was for you and the pilots to bail out and leave Erica and me to crash?"

Once more, Murray hesitated before answering.

Erica tilted the plane to the left, so that gravity was now tugging Murray toward the door as well. Some of the few remaining stitches in the strap popped.

"Okay! Okay!" Murray yelled. "Yes, I knew the pilots and I were going to bail out. But I swear, the plan was never for you to die in a plane crash!"

I got the sense that he was telling the truth. Which concerned me even more than his lying.

"Heads up back there!" Erica called from the cockpit. "We have a slight problem!"

This was also concerning. When most people said they had a slight problem, it meant they'd done something like burn the toast. For Erica, it was most likely something far worse.

For example, a missile attack.

A kid my age really shouldn't have known what an incoming missile looked like. But sadly, I had seen one more times than I'd seen *Star Wars*. And so I instantly recognized the shiny silver object racing toward us outside my window.

I instinctively traced its smoke trail to see where it had launched from. It led down to a tract of jungle near the coast.

Zoe wheeled on Murray. "Erica and Ben weren't supposed to die in a plane crash because they were supposed to die in a missile attack?"

"Yes," Murray conceded softly.

"You are the worst!" Zoe screamed at him. "Let him die, Ben! He deserves it!"

To be honest, I was tempted. It was infuriating to know that almost everything Murray had said over the past day was a lie designed to lure me to my death. My first impulse was to grab the fraying strap and tear it loose, sending Murray tumbling out of the plane.

But then I would be just as bad as he was.

So I reached for him again.

"Ugh," Zoe groaned. "Ben, you are way too decent for your own good."

"Erica?" Mike called up to the cockpit. "Any chance you can ditch this missile?"

"I'll do my best," Erica replied. "Make sure you're all buckled in tight. This is going to be rough."

Zoe shoved off the back of my seat with all her strength and landed in her own seat, then quickly fastened her belt.

Murray was still hanging by what remained of the strap.

Outside the window, the missile grew bigger and bigger, glinting in the morning sun. It was now close enough for me to make out Cyrillic letters on the side. I was pretty sure that made it a Russian DX380: heat seeking.

"Everyone ready?" Erica asked.

"No!" I said, but it was drowned out by Zoe yelling "Do it!"

Murray made a last-second lunge. He clamped his hand around my wrist, and I did the same to him.

Erica pushed hard on the stick. The plane suddenly banked to the right and dove.

We were all thrown toward the left-hand wall.

The strap ripped. Murray flew toward the open door. I held on to his arm as tightly as I could, and since he had been working out a lot, he held me even tighter. His body was whipped around so that his feet were almost at the door. My muscles screamed in pain, but I didn't let go.

The missile screamed through the air above us, missing us by fifty feet, then arced around to give us chase.

The ground was coming up fast. We were suddenly close enough to make out individual trees.

And then close enough to make out individual branches.

"Erica!" Mike called out. "Anytime you want to pull up would be good with me!"

"I'm trying!" Erica yelled back. "The pilots dismantled some of the controls before they bailed!"

And just when my day was going so well, I thought.

Mere seconds before we smashed into the forest, Erica managed to right the plane. We swooped out of the dive and rocketed along above the treetops.

We were now low enough that the pressure inside the plane was the same as that outside, so there was no longer much danger of getting sucked out the door. Instead, we only had the dangers of crashing or getting blown up to worry about.

Murray thudded to the floor and let go of my arm. He'd grabbed me so tightly, I had red craters in my flesh from his fingertips.

I couldn't see the missile out the window anymore, but I could hear the flare of its booster rocket, meaning it was still homing in on us.

"Get to the luggage!" Erica ordered. "There's a grenade launcher in my duffel bag!"

There was a time, back before I had come to spy school, when a statement like that would have struck me as unusual. Now it was music to my ears. We no longer needed the oxygen masks, so I tore mine off, unbuckled my seat belt, and scrambled for the storage room at the rear of the plane.

Mike and Zoe were doing the same thing.

Murray merely lay on the floor, gasping for breath after his near-death experience.

An unending expanse of green jungle stretched below us in every direction. There was nowhere to land the plane.

Mike reached the storage room first. He yanked the door open, unzipped the duffel bag, and yelped in concern. "Erica! There's no grenade launcher in here! Only a bunch of T-shirts, bras, and makeup!"

"That's because you're looking in *my* duffel bag," Zoe informed him. She then unzipped the bag next to it.

Sure enough, it held the stubby, silver tube of a grenade launcher.

Mike and I let her have it. We both knew Zoe could use it better than we could. Mike was still new to spy school and, thus, hadn't used much heavy artillery, while I simply didn't have much aptitude with it. I had received an F on my last exam in weaponry, along with a comment from my professor that read *This kid is so incompetent, he shouldn't be allowed to use a fork, let alone a gun.*

"Come steady me," Zoe ordered, then slung the launcher's strap over her shoulder and raced back through the plane to the open doorway.

Mike and I followed her. We had to leap over Murray, who was now curled up on the floor in the fetal position and bargaining with God. "Please don't let me die," he whined. "If you save me, I'll be good. I swear!"

Zoe sneered at him. "If you don't want to die, why don't you try helping us fend off the missile instead of crying about it?"

"Because it's a *missile!*" Murray exclaimed. "A giant heat-seeking weapon of doom! You might as well be firing a peashooter at it!"

"That attitude is *not* helping," I told him.

"Steady me, guys," Zoe instructed. "Ben, I need you to make some calculations really fast." She edged toward the open door.

Mike grabbed the wall by the cockpit with one hand and the back of my waistband with the other. I then wrapped my arms around Zoe, who braced herself against the frame of the open door and shouldered the grenade launcher.

From this position, I could see the treetops hurtling past right below us. The leaves shuddered in the wake of the jet.

"Hey!" Mike exclaimed. "I think I saw a monkey!"

"Mike!" Zoe snapped. "Focus!"

"Sorry," Mike said. "I've never seen one in the wild before."

Behind the jet, through the shimmer of its exhaust, I could see the missile closing in on us. It was narrowing the gap with disturbing speed. And to make things worse, the tail of our own plane was blocking a direct shot at it.

Murray was still on the floor, praying to any god he could come up with, covering all his bases. In short order, I heard him run through the religions of Christianity, Judaism, Islam, Buddhism, Shintoism, Zoroastrianism, and a few I'd never even heard of before.

Somehow, in the midst of all this, it occurred to me that Zoe smelled amazing. Despite having been friends with her for so long, I had never held her this tightly before. I was pretty sure that, with death approaching, I reeked of sweat, but Zoe smelled like she had just been traipsing through a rose garden.

I shook my head, wondering why that had even occurred to me, and focused on the missile. My mind filled with numbers as I calculated and recalculated the possible trajectories of a launched grenade, taking into consideration the speed of the jet, the speed of the missile, the ambient heat, and a dozen other factors. "Erica!" I yelled over the rush of air.

"In exactly five seconds, I need you to cut hard to the left! Starting now!"

"Roger," Erica replied coolly.

"Fire on my command," I told Zoe.

"Okay," she agreed.

The missile was now only a few feet from the tail of the plane.

"Fire!" I yelled.

Erica jagged to the left a split second before Zoe pulled the trigger.

The grenade launcher boomed. The recoil was so hard that it threw Zoe and me backward into Mike. We sailed across the cabin and slammed into the far bulkhead.

The sudden turn of the plane had given us a slightly wider angle on the missile. Zoe's shot was perfect. It nailed the warhead full on. The missile erupted into a fireball right behind us, so close that we were buffeted by the shockwave. Our tail tipped upward, and the jet slewed wildly as Erica fought to get it under control.

Several trees below us were charbroiled in the blast, but we escaped it.

Except for the shrapnel.

Large chunks of missile scattered in all directions. Several hit our plane, punching holes through the walls like they were made of tissue paper. One whistled right past my head, then left a gaping exit wound on the far side of the cabin. Within seconds, the jet looked like a flying piece of swiss cheese.

Our tail caught the worst of it. Red-hot debris nearly sheared it right off.

The jet shuddered worryingly. The controls trembled in Erica's hands. "Crash positions everyone!" she announced. "I need to land this thing now!"

"Land it *where?*" Murray howled. "There's nothing around us but jungle!"

"Not quite," Erica said.

Through the cockpit window, I saw what she was looking at. In the midst of all the greenery, a slash of dark blue was quickly approaching.

"Um, Erica," Mike said warily. "I hate to break it to you, but I don't think this plane is designed for water landings."

"Maybe not," Erica agreed. "But I don't see any other options. Hang on!"

We scrambled back through the perforated plane, threw ourselves into our seats, buckled up, and folded ourselves into crash positions. Even Murray stopped praying to do this.

Erica pushed the stick forward, bringing the jet down in as flat an angle as she could. Through a brand-new hole in the floor, I watched the terrain change from green to blue as the jungle ended and the lake began.

Zoe reached across the aisle. I took her hand in mine and held it as we quickly lowered toward the water.

Murray was reciting the Lord's Prayer.

We skimmed across the surface of the water, then dropped down onto it. The plane jolted abruptly, as though Erica had slammed on the brakes. We were thrown forward against our seat belts once again. Anything that wasn't bolted down flew toward the front of the jet and clanged off the bulkhead.

A wave exploded over the front window, and the jet shuddered to a stop.

We were alive.

We had a good three seconds to be thankful about that. Then the plane started sinking.

Water gushed through the numerous holes in the floor and sloshed through the open doorway. Within seconds we were ankle deep in the lake.

We hastily unbuckled our belts and scrambled from our seats. "Get my gear!" Erica ordered. "We'll need it to survive!"

Mike hustled to the rear of the plane, opened the door to the luggage compartment—and found nothing there at all. The entire tail of the plane had snapped off during landing and was now twenty feet away, quickly disappearing beneath the surface. "The gear is gone!" Mike reported, then came running back up the aisle.

There was now more than a foot of water in the jet. It was going down fast.

"Abandon plane!" Murray announced. "Abandon plane!" When he got to the cabin door, however, Erica was standing in his path, blocking the exit. "Why aren't you abandoning the plane?" Murray demanded.

"I'm a little concerned about the crocodiles," Erica replied. She said it very calmly, as though she was talking about a pack of stray dogs, rather than a bunch of enormous, prehistoric man-eating reptiles.

I glanced out my window. We had skimmed all the way across the lake and almost made it to the far bank, which was lined with dozens of very large crocodiles. Until a few seconds before, they had been basking in the sun, but the plane crash had jolted them out of their stupor. Sensing easy prey, they were slithering into the lake and coming for us. It turned out, hungry crocodiles could move much faster than I'd realized. They raced toward us through the water, their beady little eyes poking just above the surface.

"Crocodiles?" Murray gasped, then turned his eyes to the heavens. "What did I ever do to deserve this?"

"Attempted murder, for one," Zoe answered, then ticked more things off on her fingers. "Plus terrorism, assassination, destruction of public property, and being an all-around jerk. The question is really, what *haven't* you done to deserve this?"

We were now up to our knees in water. The plane was tilting down and toward the left, where the lake was surging through the open door.

Erica scrambled to the opposite side of the plane and opened the emergency exit. Because of the tilt of the plane, this side was drier, with the right wing jutting up above the lake's surface. Erica swung through the doorway onto the wing.

The rest of us followed her without hesitation. After all, Erica seemed to have a plan while we didn't. (Well, I *did* have a plan, but it was simply swimming away from the crocodiles as quickly as I could and hoping they'd eat Murray first. Plus, I wasn't sure it would work.)

More crocs were closing in on the right wing, but there was also a large tree with vine-draped branches extending out over the lake. The vines dangled seven feet above the tip of the wing, tantalizingly out of reach.

However, since the left side of the plane was sinking faster than the right, the right wing was slowly tilting upward. Erica edged out to the tip as it rose a few more inches, then leapt up and grabbed a low-hanging vine. She quickly shimmied up it into the branches of the tree, well out of crocodile range.

As she jumped, though, the wing trembled ominously. It had suffered serious damage in the crash and seemed ready to pop off. If we didn't want that to happen, we'd all have to be very calm and careful.

Which was exactly the opposite of how Murray behaved. "I'm next!" he yelled, shoving the rest of us aside and racing up the wing. "Me me me me me!" Then he bounced on the wing like it was a diving board and grabbed a vine himself.

The wing shook wildly from his actions. Part of it tore from the hull of the plane with a sickening screech of rending metal.

Erica glared at Murray as he scrambled up into the branches, looking like she had half a mind to send him back down and tell him to wait his turn. Only, that wouldn't have done the rest of us any good, and we were running out of time.

The broken wing dipped back down toward the surface of the lake. A crocodile the length of a car bobbed up only a few feet away from me, its mouth gaping open like a bear trap.

I heard some guttural reptile noises from behind me as well. Several crocs had swum through the open door of the plane and were now inside the cabin. One was gnawing on the grenade launcher.

Zoe and Mike went next. Since Zoe was short, Mike gave her a boost to get to the vines. Then he leapt up himself. He tried to do it carefully, without putting too much force on the wing, but it still quivered dangerously. More metal tore along the joint where the wing met the plane.

There was a sudden roar and a roiling of water inside the jet. Two big crocs were fighting each other for dibs on me.

I scurried out to the end of the wing, hoping it would hold long enough for me to jump off it.

It didn't.

I had almost reached the tip when the wing tore from the jet hull and dropped back down to the lake's surface with a resounding slap. The enormous crocodile who had been lurking close by wasted no time. It lunged from the water, dug its claws into the metal, and began hauling itself up. The two crocs who had been fighting inside the jet immediately put aside their differences, squeezed through the door of the plane, and flopped onto the wing as well.

Their added weight pulled it even farther down into the water.

A dozen more crocs surfaced around me.

When you chose to become a spy, in the back of your mind, you always knew there was a chance you could get killed by various things: guns, knives, bombs, missiles. Up until that morning, I had never considered crocodiles to be a possibility. But now it looked like Death by Crocodile was increasingly likely.

"Ben!" Erica yelled.

I tore my attention from the advancing reptiles to find Erica dangling upside down above me. She had hooked her knees over a branch, braced her feet below another one, and was reaching down to me like an acrobat hanging from a trapeze.

The closest croc was now only a few feet away and moving fast.

I leapt up and grabbed Erica's hands. In the branches around her, Mike and Zoe struggled to pull her and me up into the tree.

As they lifted, the big croc lunged for me. I did the only thing I could think of.

I kicked it in the nose.

I gave the kick everything I had. It barely fazed the croc at all, but it prevented the beast from biting my legs off. It dropped back to the wing, sneezed, then sprang at me again.

Thankfully, my friends hauled me out of range just in time. The croc's jaws snapped shut right beneath my toes. It plopped back into the water, then angrily turned on the other crocs nearby, roaring so loud it shook the tree. The smaller crocs quickly swam away in fear.

I found myself clustered with Zoe, Mike, and Erica in the branches, clinging to them with all my might, my heart thudding in my chest.

Below us, there was a final *blorp* of air as the jet sank beneath the surface of the lake. It quickly vanished into the murky depths.

Murray was picking his way through the branches ahead of us, working on saving his own skin without any thought for anyone else. Sensing our angry stares, he turned back to us with a sheepish smile. "Well, that sure was exciting, wasn't it? Glad to see you all survived."

"No thanks to you!" Zoe snarled. "You are the lowest, most despicable, slimiest weasel who ever walked the earth!" She swung through the branches as nimbly as a gibbon, quickly catching up to Murray. Even though he was bigger than her, she was amped up on anger and adrenaline. She slammed into him, grabbed him by the neck, and prepared to fling him into the lake, where several hungry crocodiles waited below.

"Stop!" Erica yelled.

Zoe reluctantly paused her attack. "Why?"

"We need him."

"For what?" Zoe asked bitterly. "This whole thing was only a trick to get us on a plane and blast us out of the sky."

"Not quite," Erica insisted. "It wasn't a lie that SPYDER is holed up somewhere down here."

"How do you know?" Mike asked. "Murray's lied about everything else."

"But not this," I said, realizing what Erica meant. "SPY-DER fired that missile at us. And those pilots are certainly heading to rendezvous with them as well."

"Exactly." Erica turned to Murray. "You really thought you were going to SPYDER's headquarters, didn't you?"

"Yes," Murray mewled. "I thought I'd meet up with them after bailing out of the plane. I had no idea they wanted to kill me. Man, you can't trust anyone these days." Even though it made sense that he might only be saying this to save his skin, I believed him. Murray's reaction to his betrayal had been too real.

"Good." Erica picked her way through the branches, heading toward Murray, oblivious to the man-eating reptiles below us. "Okay, team, here's the deal: We are in serious trouble. We might have survived for now, but we are still stranded in the middle of the jungle, and all our supplies just sank into the middle of Crocodile Central. I estimate our chances of survival at around fifty percent. And if we actually succeed in getting back to civilization, we still have to confront an adversary who obviously wants to eliminate us."

"Excellent," Mike said sarcastically. "Good pep talk, Erica."

Erica ignored him. "There is one bright spot, though. SPYDER thinks we're dead, which gives us an advantage against them." She reached Murray, grabbed his wrist, and deftly wrenched his arm behind his back.

Murray yelped in pain.

"You know where they are," Erica told him calmly. "So take us to them."

ORIENTEERING

Somewhere in Quintana Roo, Mexico

March 29

1200 hours

"We're in the wrong Mexico," Mike said.

I turned to him, concerned. We had been hiking for hours, and even though there were trees to give us shade, the temperature was still broiling. I figured there was a good chance that Mike might have gone delirious from the heat. "What do you mean?"

"Whenever you see a commercial for Mexico, they never show *this* part," Mike groused. "They always show these beautiful white-sand beaches, and quaint little towns, and fiestas full of happy people. They never show jungles and crocodiles and"—he paused to smack an insect on his arm—"clouds of mosquitoes. I want to be in the Mexico in the commercials. Not this one."

"There are much worse parts of Mexico than this," Erica pointed out. "If we'd gone down in one of the southern deserts, we probably would have fried to death by now. At least here, there's shade and water."

"I suppose," Mike said, then added under his breath, "though this still stinks."

I didn't argue with him, as I was in complete agreement. It was a testament to how lousy our situation was that Mike was in such a grumpy mood. Normally, Mike was an unflappable optimist; I'd once heard him refer to a glass with a tiny bit of water in it as "almost one percent full." But now, given our dire circumstances, all of us were miserable. In addition to nearly having died several times that morning alone, we were now lost in a jungle filled with poisonous snakes and malarial insects. The plant life was impenetrable and full of thorns; we constantly had to work our way around large thickets, which made our progress maddeningly slow. Meanwhile, all our phones, sunblock, and food had gone down with the plane. I was hot, sweaty, hungry, and exhausted. And yet there wasn't any choice but to keep pushing onward.

There was only one positive to our circumstances: We

were with Erica. If it hadn't been for her, our situation would have been even worse.

We all knew how to survive in the wilderness, at least in theory. We had taken rudimentary courses in it at spy camp. But that didn't mean we were *prepared* to survive. We weren't. Erica, meanwhile, was prepared for almost anything.

As usual, she was wearing her utility belt. From it, she had produced a compass, a collapsible flask, and water-purification tablets, all of which had proven exceptionally useful. (Erica's mother had recently bought me my own utility belt, though I had never taken the time to load it with survival supplies—not that it would have mattered, as I had also forgotten to bring it.) After we had climbed down from the tree, we had found a relatively crocodile-free section of the lake, filled the flask with water, and purified it. Once everyone had drunk their fill, Erica had determined that the best course toward the coast was north-northeast and led us that way. Most of the development in the Yucatán was along the water, and the missile had come from that direction as well, so Erica figured it was the best way to go.

Short of the compass, there was no other way to get our bearings. Once we had left the lake, the trees had become too spindly to climb, and the land was ridiculously flat; there wasn't so much as a hill in any direction. Thankfully, we had found occasional pools of water along our route, so we had managed to allay the danger of dehydration for most of the morning.

Now, however, it had been well over an hour since we had last seen water. In the searing heat, whatever fluid I had in my body was quickly leaching out of my skin. I felt as though I could fry an egg on my forehead, while my tongue was like a dry lump of sawdust in my mouth.

There had been one moment, only fifteen minutes after starting our trek, when we had thought we might not have to walk at all. A helicopter had come skimming along above the trees, heading for the lake where we'd crashed. Mike, Zoe, Murray, and I had assumed it was a rescue operation and wanted to flag it down, but Erica had refused. "It's SPY-DER," she insisted. "Coming to confirm we're dead. If you let them know we're here, they'll finish the job." So we hid in the thick underbrush and watched the chopper through the leaves. When it reached the lake, it hovered over the point where the plane had sunk for a few minutes, as if the people on board were searching for signs of life, and then raced back toward where it had come from. That direction was north-northeast as well, the way we were already going, confirming that Erica had made the right call. We weren't only heading toward civilization; we were heading toward SPYDER as well.

If we ever got there.

Mike and Zoe appeared to be suffering as much as I was,

but Murray looked far worse. His upbeat, cocksure persona had vanished. He was a shell of his former self, and he made no secret of how miserable he was. He shuffled his feet through the dirt, pausing every now and then to moan despondently. He didn't even bother to swat the mosquitoes away.

Finally, somewhere around moan number 362, Zoe snapped. "All right!" she screamed at him. "We get it! You're unhappy! Will you shut up?"

"No," Murray replied morosely. "I *deserve* to be unhappy. I just found out SPYDER wants me dead."

"Big deal," Mike said. "SPYDER wants all of us dead."

"Yes," Murray conceded. "But you already knew that. I thought these people liked me. I thought they were my friends! And now it turns out, they felt I was expendable."

"Really sucks to get betrayed by people you trusted, doesn't it?" I asked pointedly.

"I'm well aware of the irony here." Murray stepped over a log, acting like this small act was as exhausting as climbing Mount Everest. "But that doesn't make it any less upsetting. I know why they wanted *you* dead. You're the good guys! You're the enemy! But why would they want *me* dead? I'm Murray! I'm fun! I'm charming! And clever! A lot of their evil plots would have gone nowhere without me."

"They didn't go anywhere anyhow," Zoe said. "Ben and Erica always thwarted them."

Murray ignored this and kept rambling on. "Apparently, I don't mean anything to them at all. As far as they're concerned, I might as well be one of these mosquitoes." He pointed to his arm, where a dozen of the bloodsuckers were feeding. A few had been gorging themselves so long, they had swollen to the size of raisins. "I always did everything they asked me to. I was always a team player. So why did they turn on me all of a sudden?"

"Maybe this *wasn't* all of a sudden," Erica said. Unlike the rest of us, she didn't seem the slightest bit worn out by our slog through the jungle. Instead, she looked as refreshed as if she had spent the last several hours napping. She hadn't even broken a sweat; the armpits of her shirt were miraculously perspiration free. "Maybe SPYDER *always* thought you were expendable."

Murray's jaw dropped open like a trapdoor. "You mean, they lied to me from the very beginning? They were *never* going to give me my own island? Why would they do that?"

"Because they're greedy and they have no morals." Zoe sidestepped a large web with a particularly ominous-looking spider in the center. "If they get rid of you, then they have one less person to share with. Assuming Ben and Erica don't thwart their plans again."

I paused to take a better look at the spider. It was the size of my fist and had tiny fangs covered with what looked disturbingly like blood. I shivered and hurried past it, wondering how much farther it was to the nearest hotel.

Murray was hanging his head in shame now, looking even more morose than before. I had expected he'd try to argue that Zoe was wrong, but Murray wasn't an idiot. He could now see the truth as well as any of us. "I can't believe this. How could I have been so blind?"

"It doesn't matter," Erica said. "The real question you should be asking yourself is, how can I get even with them?"

Murray looked at her curiously. "What do you mean?"

Erica sidled between two plants bristling with thorns the size of human fingers. "SPYDER has led you on for years. They manipulated you into helping them perpetrate heinous crimes without any intention of letting you share in the wealth. Basically, they treated you like garbage. They should pay for that. And you know how to make them pay." She fixed Murray with a penetrating stare. "What are they plotting next?"

Murray frowned, looking extremely disappointed in himself. "I don't know."

"Don't lie to me," Erica said coldly. "These people have turned their backs on you. There's no point in showing any loyalty to them."

"I know that!" Murray exclaimed. "Believe me, I'd be happy to bring them down. But I have no idea what they're up to."

"None?" Zoe asked skeptically. "I thought you were high up in their organization."

"I *was*," Murray said defensively. "But SPYDER is always very secretive about what's coming next. And I couldn't very well go to the last few development meetings because I've been in jail. I didn't hear a peep from them until I got that message about flying down here. And even then, they obviously didn't tell me everything. They left out the whole part about killing me in a fiery plane crash."

"You must know *something*," Erica pressed. "*We* know SPYDER has been amassing illegal weapons of mass destruction from multiple buyers. You really don't know what all those are for?"

"No," Murray admitted sadly.

"Then tell us where SPYDER is hiding out now," Erica challenged. "The exact location. Where did you think you were going today?"

"I don't know," Murray said again. "My orders were simply to do what it took to get you guys onto the plane, head to this part of Mexico, and be ready to bail out with the pilots. I figured, after that, I'd get an update on where everyone is hiding."

"And you were perfectly okay with that?" Zoe asked angrily. "Knowing the rest of us were going to die?"

"First of all, it was only Ben and Erica who were supposed

to die." Murray gingerly stepped around a nest of fire ants. "I didn't ask you to stow away on the plane. And second, I don't make the rules here. SPYDER comes to me with a plan to escape jail and join everyone at headquarters. What am I supposed to do, question it?"

Zoe screamed. I thought it might have been her expressing exasperation at Murray's warped sense of morality, but it turned out she had nearly stepped on an iguana. The lizard scampered up a tree and disdainfully attempted to urinate on her.

Erica's frustration with Murray finally boiled over. She grabbed Murray by the scruff of the neck, forced him to his knees, and bent him over the fire ant nest. "That can't be all you know," she growled, losing her usual, cool aplomb. "You're no idiot. So you'd better start coughing up info, or you're getting a fire ant facial."

"I *am* an idiot!" Murray exploded back at her, although he seemed to be more upset at himself than at Erica. "I swear, I've told you everything I know! Apparently, I wasn't nearly as important to SPYDER as I thought! I wasn't told what they're plotting. I wasn't given the coordinates of their new secret headquarters. And what I thought was a clever plan to spring me from jail was really only a setup to get rid of me as well as you and Brainiac Ben over there. I'm sorry I don't know any more than that. Believe me, if I could, I would do whatever it takes to burn SPYDER to the ground right now. But I can't give you any more info because I don't have it. I guess I'm no good to anyone at all."

I almost felt sorry for him.

Almost. Then I remembered that he had been perfectly happy with the prospect of letting me die that morning.

Still, Murray's frustration did seem genuine. And yet, because I didn't trust him, I looked to Erica for confirmation.

"What do you think?" I asked her.

"I think he's right," she said. "He's useless."

I turned my attention to Mike and Zoe.

At least, I turned my attention to where Mike and Zoe had been three seconds earlier.

Mike was still standing in the jungle, watching Erica and Murray.

But Zoe had vanished.

SPELUNKING

Somewhere in Quintana Roo, Mexico

March 29

1230 hours

"Mike!" I exclaimed. "Where's Zoe?"

Mike looked around and gaped in surprise when he discovered Zoe was nowhere to be seen. "I don't know! She was right here a second ago."

I ran through the jungle toward the last place I had seen Zoe. For once, we were actually in an area relatively free of thick underbrush, surrounded only by the trunks of spindly palm trees. I could see several yards in every direction, which meant Zoe should have been visible. "What happened to her?"

"How should I know?" Mike asked. "One moment she

was here, and then she wasn't! Maybe a leopard got her."

"There are no leopards in Mexico," Erica said, casually tossing Murray aside to hurry over herself. "If anything got her, it was a jaguar."

"Or maybe a rogue crocodile," Murray suggested.

"What would a crocodile be doing this far from water?" Erica asked.

"Migrating?" Murray suggested.

"None of this is helping!" I informed them. I looked back to Mike to ask him another question.

Only, Mike had now vanished from sight as well.

"Where's Mike?" I asked.

"He's gone too!" Murray yelped. "Maybe aliens beamed them up!"

"That's not possible," I said.

"Do you have a better explanation?" Murray asked.

I didn't answer him for two reasons. First, I *didn't* have a better explanation.

Second, I had just fallen through the earth's crust.

The ground beneath my feet suddenly gave way, and the next thing I knew, I was tumbling downward. There was a period of time that seemed like an eternity—but which was probably only a fraction of a second—during which I was completely disoriented and terrified. Somehow, even in that brief instant, I deduced that I'd dropped through the roof of a cave, and then wondered how deep it was and whether I'd end up splattered all over the floor.

Instead of slamming into hard stone, however, I splashed into water.

It was bracingly cold. I sank down several feet until my feet touched a sandy bottom, then kicked off it and swam upward hard. It was pitch dark all around me except for three shafts of light, which I realized must be above me. I broke through the surface, gasping for breath, and wondered what on earth—or *under* earth—I'd fallen into.

"Ben!" Zoe shouted from close by.

I turned, treading water, and found her swimming toward me, sopping wet but otherwise okay. Mike was close behind her.

As my eyes adjusted to the darkness, I began to make out my surroundings. I was definitely in a cave. The roof was about thirty feet above me and covered with stalactites—except for the three holes where Mike, Zoe, and I had punched through the ceiling. Here and there, gnarled strands of tree roots dangled, many long enough to reach all the way to the water below.

As for the water, it was fresh and amazingly clear. At the spots where the shafts of light hit it, I could see all the way to the bottom. Tiny fish darted about in it; the species must have evolved in the caves, because they didn't have eyes, only white patches where the eyes had been generations before.

I had swallowed a good amount of water by accident—but it wasn't enough. I was still desperately thirsty, and fresh, clean water was a godsend. I dipped my head back into it and guzzled it down.

Above me, a fourth hole suddenly appeared in the ceiling. Murray plunged through it, flailing his arms wildly, and cannonballed into the water a few feet away.

A few seconds later, he resurfaced, spluttering and startled, the same way I had probably done. Only, he remained agitated, floundering in the water. "What's going on? Where are we?"

"You're in a cenote!" Erica yelled to us. She was peering through one of the new holes in the ceiling of the cave, her head silhouetted against the daylight outside.

"What the heck's a cenote?" Murray asked.

"They're sinkholes in the limestone bedrock that exposes the natural groundwater," Erica explained. "You're perfectly safe. There are thousands of them in the Yucatán. Looks like you've just discovered a brand-new one."

"There are thousands of caves like this?" Mike asked, amazed. "With this much water in them?"

"Well, the size of the cave and the amount of water obviously varies," Erica said, "but yes, there are thousands. This entire ecosystem is supported by groundwater. Surely, when we were in the plane, you must have noticed there aren't any rivers on this entire peninsula?"

"Not really," I confessed. "We were pretty distracted with the incoming missiles and the whole imminent-death thing." But now that I thought about it, it *was* unusual that there hadn't been a single river visible from the air. Especially when a thick jungle like this certainly needed plenty of water to grow.

"Well, all the rivers are underground," Erica went on. "In fact, you're in one right now."

"How do you even *know* all this?" Zoe yelled back.

"It's important to know the major geological features of every country," Erica replied matter-of-factly. "It's also worth familiarizing yourself with as much historical and cultural information as possible, in case you get stranded someplace. Like we are now."

"Hold on," Zoe said. "Are you saying that you've memorized the geology, history, and culture of every country on earth, just in case something like this happened?"

"Not *every* country," Erica replied. "I'm doing it alphabetically, and I've only worked my way up to Swaziland so far."

In the dim light of the cave, Zoe gave me an *Is she for real?* look.

It occurred to me that, since I had spent far more time on missions with Erica than anyone else at spy school, I knew her much better than anyone else. Therefore, I was already well aware of her photographic memory and ency-clopedic education, whereas my friends were only begin-ning to scratch the surface of Erica's many talents and compulsive preparation for any eventuality. "She's telling the truth," I said.

Zoe sighed. "That girl really needs some other hobbies."

Mike called up, "Erica! Given your extensive knowledge of cenotes, do you have any idea how we're supposed to get out of this one?"

"There ought to be some tree roots hanging down into it," Erica said. "Do you see any that are thick enough to shimmy up?"

There was a strand dangling quite close to me, although the roots looked much too thin to support my weight. I gave them an experimental yank. Sure enough, several of the roots snapped right off in my hand. None of the other strands looked any thicker. "I don't see any!" I reported.

"Use this to take a better look around!" Erica dropped something through the hole in the ceiling.

Although the object had been wadded into a ball in her hand, it quickly expanded to its full size and shape the moment she released it. It was a circle of silvery, reflective material, affixed to a thin, collapsible frame, kind of like a fabric Frisbee. It wafted down to us slowly, and Mike snagged it out of the air.

Up on the surface, we would have used it to reflect the sun's light and get the attention of passing planes. (Passing planes that weren't piloted by SPYDER, that is.) In the cenote, Mike quickly grasped how it would come in handy. He found a place shallow enough to stand on the bottom, then held the reflector underneath one of the shafts of sunlight and used it as a mirror, lighting up distant parts of the cenote.

The first thing I noticed was that the cenote was much bigger than I had realized. The walls of the cave were so distant, the reflected light barely illuminated them.

Mike slowly swept the makeshift spotlight around, searching for anything that would be of help. He came upon dozens of strands of roots, but none was thick enough for us to climb. He kept sweeping anyhow.

Thin strand of roots.

Another thin strand of roots.

Yet another thin strand of roots.

Pile of human skeletons.

Someone screamed in abject terror. Turned out, it was me.

I had hoped that I would have been more composed in such a situation, but then again, there aren't many things scarier than coming across a pile of human skeletons in an underground cave. My voice echoed off the walls of the cenote over and over, startling a small flock of bats into taking flight. They

swarmed around us—which did little to calm my distress—
and then found a new place on the ceiling to roost.

"What happened?" Erica asked, concerned. "Did someone get attacked by something?"

"No," Zoe said disdainfully. "Ben just freaked out
because there's some skeletons down here."

"There are *human skeletons* down here," I stressed. "In the
dark with us. That is completely worth freaking out over."

Mike had kept the light trained on the skeletons, studying them carefully. "I think those have been down here a
long time," he observed.

I focused more closely on them. What I had at first thought
was a pile of skeletons tall enough to rise out of the water now
turned out to be a significantly smaller pile of skeletons on a
small island in the center of the cenote. There were perhaps
only three or four—it was hard to tell for sure, as they were all
jumbled together—and they were brown from age.

Zoe swam to the island and waded ashore.

"Don't touch them!" Murray warned. Even though he
hadn't screamed in fear the way I had, he still sounded very
much on edge.

"Why would I touch a skeleton?" Zoe asked. "I'm only
getting a better look at them."

Mike had to stay in the water to keep the light on the
skeletons, but I swam over to the island as well. Murray

stayed in the water too, grumbling to himself. "First we fall into a cave. Then we find a pile of ancient dead guys. It's like we stumbled into a *Scooby-Doo* episode."

"These skeletons are *really* old," Zoe reported as I clambered out of the water. "Like prehistoric, maybe."

I didn't know my archaeology that well, but there definitely seemed to be something ancient about the bones. Most of the skulls seemed rather small and only had a few teeth left, like the skulls you might see in museums.

Something crunched under my feet.

I reached down and found shards of white, smooth material in the dirt.

"What's that?" Zoe asked.

"Seashells," I replied.

"That can't be right," Zoe said. "We must be twenty miles from the ocean."

"They're probably cherished possessions of the dead people," Mike said.

Zoe and I turned to him. It was hard to see his face, as the beam of light he was reflecting was shining right in our eyes, but he seemed to be quite proud of himself. "Erica's not the only one who knows things," he said. "There was a huge Mayan civilization here like a thousand years ago. The people inland probably traded with people from the coasts. Seashells would have been pretty rare and cool for them. I'm betting we're in some sort of ceremonial burial area. These people were laid to rest with their most prized belongings."

"How do you know all that?" Murray asked.

"I've been doing what Erica has," Mike told him. "Learning about the cultures of every country on earth just in case I ended up stranded in one of them."

"Really?" Zoe asked, impressed.

"No," Mike admitted. "I'm jerking your chain. I randomly saw the end of a National Geographic special on the Mayans while I was doing my homework last week."

"I'll bet you're right about the burial." Erica was still looking down through the hole in the ceiling, though she was too far away to see the skeletons clearly.

I looked at the ground around the bodies. There were hundreds more seashells, along with some potsherds and what might have been primitive jewelry: tiny flakes of metal that had probably been attached to a necklace string that had rotted away centuries before.

"So how did these bodies even get here?" I asked. "If someone laid them to rest, they didn't drop them in through a hole in the ceiling."

"There must be another way in!" Zoe deduced. She pointed down the length of the island we stood on. "Mike! Aim the light over there!"

Mike did as ordered. Sure enough, in the depths of the cave, there was an even darker passage.

"Erica!" I yelled. "There's a tunnel down here!"

"Great!" Erica said. "I'm going to throw down my flashlight. You guys take it and follow the tunnel."

"You're not coming with us?" Zoe asked.

"No," Erica replied.

"Why not?" Mike asked.

"Because there's always a chance that the tunnel has collapsed or is impassable for some other reason, and if that's the case, then we'll all be trapped down there together, I won't be able to mount a rescue, and we'll ultimately die a horrible death by starvation."

"Good point," Mike said. "You should definitely stay up there."

Zoe looked at Murray suspiciously. "I'll bet if that *did* happen, you'd try to kill us and eat us to make your own pathetic life last a little longer."

"Hey!" Murray cried, offended. "I might be a terrorist, a thief, and a traitor, but I'm not a cannibal!"

"Anyhow, heads up," Erica said. "Light's coming down. Be careful with it. This is my only one." She dropped a small headlamp through the hole to Mike.

Mike caught it, then flung the reflective circle to me, Frisbee-style, and slipped the elastic straps for the light around his head.

The beam from the headlamp was quite powerful, given its small size, and yet it barely made a dent in the darkness around us. Mike swam to the island and joined Zoe and me there, as did Murray.

"Head on down that tunnel!" Erica called to us. "Hopefully, it will lead to some sort of exit. I'll find you when you emerge."

"How?" I yelled back, but Erica didn't reply. She was already gone.

"This is great," Murray griped sarcastically. "First we're in a plane crash. Then crocodiles try to eat us. And now we get to go down a spooky underground tunnel full of bats and skeletons. We'll probably end up in a school of piranhas next."

"Stop whining, you pinhead," Zoe told him. "We're only in this mess because of you."

"Here goes nothing," Mike said. He started along the island toward the tunnel. Zoe and Murray fell in line behind him.

I took one last glance at the ancient skeletons piled on the island behind us, worried this cave might end up being my last resting place as well. I shivered at the thought, then hurried after the others, following them into the dark.

ARCHAEOLOGY

Unexplored Cenote

Somewhere in Quintana Roo

March 29

1400 hours

I had imagined that working our way through a
half-flooded subterranean burial ground with only one tiny
headlamp would be awful.

It was worse.

Most of the time, we were up to our armpits in water, if
not swimming. The heat quickly drained from our bodies,
leaving us shivering. The tunnel often constricted around us:
The walls would close in, or the ceiling would dip down,
leaving us only narrow, claustrophobic passages to squeeze

through. In the dim light, I repeatedly whacked my head on stalactites. And yet, even that far from sunlight, there was plenty of life in the cave. If I had been a biologist, I might have been thrilled. But I wasn't a biologist, and it turns out, nothing that lives in a cave is cute or cuddly. Instead, everything is nightmare inducing. In addition to the weird blind fish, there were gobs of freakish insects, some of them disturbingly large, scuttling along the roof of the tunnel.

I began to feel nostalgic for our slog through the jungle. Yes, we had nearly died from dehydration, but at least it had been sunny and warm.

At some point, shortly after we started, Zoe and I ended up holding hands. There was nothing romantic about the gesture: We were in a dark, potentially deadly tunnel, and it made sense to stay in physical contact. And yet, Zoe and I had never held hands before. In fact, despite how good friends we were, I couldn't remember if we had really touched each other at all, except for that morning with the grenade launcher and the occasional sparring in self-defense class, none of which was very romantic.

I didn't say anything to Zoe about it. She didn't say anything to me, either. None of us said much at all as we worked our way through the cave, save for the occasional "Watch your heads!" to warn the others about dangling stalactites and the inevitable "Ow!" as someone whacked their head on one anyhow. We just kept moving silently, our hands clasped together until long after our fingers had become waterlogged and pruney.

Finally, after what seemed like an eternity, we saw daylight in the distance.

Mike, being in the lead, was the first to spot it. He gave a whoop of joy that startled all of us and shouted, "Look up ahead! There's sunlight! We must be near the exit."

"And the water's getting warmer too," Zoe put in.

"Um . . . actually, that's because of me," Murray said sheepishly. "Mike really frightened me with that whooping."

"Ick!" Zoe shrieked. "Murray! You're disgusting!"

We would have all been in a hurry to get to the exit anyhow, but now, thanks to Murray, we evacuated the water even faster. Ahead of us, a flight of crude stone steps was hewn into the rock, leading up to a good-size hole. The steps had obviously been there a long time; thick, ancient tree roots snaked down them to the water. We clambered up them, emerging into the jungle once again.

Only, this jungle was different. The land we had trekked across that morning was flat and featureless. Now there were small hills and mounds all around us, thick with trees and brush. I got the strange sense that something was odd about the landforms, though I couldn't quite figure out what it was.

There were also iguanas everywhere. Tons of them. It was as though we'd arrived in downtown Iguanaville. They were lounging on rocks, clinging to trees, lurking under ferns. As far as I knew, they weren't dangerous, but they still looked mean, with sharp claws and bad attitudes. All of them stared at us disparagingly with their beady little eyes.

"Erica!" Mike yelled at the top of his lungs. "We're out! Can you hear us?"

His words echoed off all the hills and mounds, but no response came.

Mike yelled for her again, but the result was the same.

"Where do you think she is?" Murray asked, sounding genuinely concerned.

"I don't know," Zoe replied. "There's no way she could tell where that tunnel was heading from up on the surface. She could be miles away from here."

While that was disconcerting, it was still nicer to be out in the sun without Erica than it was to be in a spooky, damp cave without Erica. It was blazingly hot now, but that was a blessing after being in the chilly tunnel.

I looked back toward the entrance to the cenote. Even though we had emerged from it less than a minute before, I had trouble spotting it. The jungle was so thick, the entrance was almost invisible. It was only a shadow amid a tumult of trees and ferns.

Right above it, however, was a strangely squared-off block of stone.

I might have missed it if I hadn't known the cenote was there. It was covered with tree roots. But now that I was looking at it, I realized it wasn't a naturally formed rock. Its edges were too even. I ran over to it and pulled some of the roots aside, revealing a pattern of ancient markings and a faint trace of red on the white stone.

"That's a shrine!" Mike exclaimed. "A Mayan shrine! They probably built it there to mark the entrance to the cenote!"

I returned my attention to the hills and mounds around us, seeing them in a new light. I now realized what was unusual about them:

They didn't rise gradually from the ground, the way real hills did. Instead, they tilted upward too abruptly.

I ran to the closest one, pulling away the underbrush. Beneath it were more square-cut stones with crumbling ancient mortar between them.

"Those aren't hills," Zoe gasped. "They're buildings. We're in an ancient city!"

All of us took in our surroundings with new eyes. Every feature around us was man-made, but had been swallowed by the jungle over the centuries. Even the strip of flat ground we stood on turned out to be made of crushed stone, rather than a solid slab of bedrock. "This is a road," I said.

"Of course!" Mike exclaimed. "According to the special I saw, scientists think there could be hundreds of Mayan cities in the jungles around here. No one's had the time or money to excavate them all."

"This is so cool!" Zoe announced, her eyes glittering with excitement. "We've found a piece of an ancient civilization!"

"Big whoop," Murray said sourly. "Unless there's an ancient hotel with room service somewhere around here, none of this helps us at all."

"Maybe it does." Mike started following the road, taking care to avoid the many iguanas splayed out on it. "The Mayans didn't construct all their buildings out of stone. Only the most important ones. Which means we must be in the center of town, and at any town center, there's probably going to be . . ." He trailed off, pointing dramatically through a gap in the trees. "A temple."

Sure enough, another mound rose in the distance. This one was significantly taller than the others around us. It was bedecked with trees and plants, but was obviously a stepped pyramid.

"So what's the plan, exactly?" Murray asked blankly. "We go to the temple and pray that someone rescues us?"

Zoe swatted Murray on the back of the head. "No, you idiot. We *climb* the temple and see how close we are to civilization. Plus, maybe we can spot Erica from up there."

"Oh!" Murray said. "Good thinking."

The ancient road led directly to the pyramid. Lots of trees and brush had grown on the road over the past few centuries, but it was still easy to follow. Now that we'd had plenty of water to drink and were warm again, we were in good shape. Except for my wet shoes squelching on my feet and my wet underwear riding up my butt, I felt better than I had in hours.

We reached the base of the pyramid and worked our way up the stepped exterior. Like the other buildings, it was constructed of rough-hewn limestone held together with mortar and covered with centuries of dirt and plant life. There were also dozens of iguanas basking in the sun on it. Everywhere I looked, there was an iguana, many of them the size of lapdogs. It was like a display case for an iguana store. They watched us warily as we climbed past them, but didn't seem too threatened by us, as they rarely bothered to move out of our way.

The pyramid angled up sharply. Murray, being in the best shape, made his way up it the fastest, though the rest of us weren't far behind.

The heat and the humidity, originally so refreshing after our time underground, quickly grew oppressive. I had to stop halfway up the pyramid to catch my breath, taking care not to sit on any iguanas. Zoe stopped as well, her eyes fixed on Murray above us.

Mike came up alongside us. "Are you checking out Murray's butt?" he asked Zoe.

"No!" Zoe exclaimed, horrified. And yet her face turned so red, it seemed she might have really been caught in the act.

"There's no shame in it," Mike assured her. "The guy's pretty hot."

"He's Murray!" Zoe hissed. "I don't care what he looks like now. The guy's disgusting. He once found a piece of leftover cookie between two rolls of fat on his stomach and then ate it!"

"He's hot *now*," Mike said.

Zoe shivered at the thought of this and then continued climbing the temple.

Mike gave me a devilish grin, pleased with himself for getting under Zoe's skin, then followed her.

I resumed the climb, wondering if Zoe really had been checking Murray out. Even before we knew Murray was evil, Zoe had regarded him with borderline disdain, but maybe that had been a front. Maybe she had always thought he was cute, and now that he had transformed into Hot Murray, she was really attracted to him.

I realized I was jealous. I had always been so distracted by Erica that I had never thought of Zoe as anything other than a friend, but the truth was, she was impressive in lots of ways: She was smart, she was fun, she was always supportive—and she was cute. An adorable, girl-next-door sort of cute. And she had a crush on me. Or, at least, she'd *had* a crush on me. For all I knew, she had shifted her attention to Murray.

I now found myself feeling ashamed for having romantic thoughts about Zoe, rather than Erica, like I was betraying Erica somehow. But Erica had told me that we could never have a relationship, because relationships complicated spying, and Erica didn't want any complications. That had upset me, but I understood her argument. Which meant that I really should have been free to think about other people and shouldn't have felt bad about it. Only, I did. And I also felt weird for thinking about Zoe as anything more than a friend. And annoyed at Murray for being potentially attractive to Zoe.

And then I found myself amazed that I was thinking about this at all, rather than focusing on survival. Here I was, climbing an undiscovered Mayan temple in the middle of the jungle in Mexico, and I was getting all hung up on girls. I needed to be thinking about how to get to civilization and thwart SPYDER, rather than how cute Zoe looked. I needed to be thinking about where Erica was, and how to contact her, rather than whether she'd be upset with me for thinking that Zoe looked cute. And if anything, I should have been annoyed at Murray for double-crossing me and getting me stranded in the wilderness, rather than being a potential rival for Zoe's affection. After all, Murray was the enemy. Zoe couldn't possibly like him.

Unless she had a secret thing for bad boys. Yes, she had been telling me to let Murray die a lot lately, but maybe that had been a front for more conflicted feelings about him.

I shook my head, trying to clear all the thoughts of Zoe and Erica out of it and focus on the task at hand. As it was, I had reached the top of the pyramid.

There was a surprisingly large platform at the top, with a small stone hut in the center. The pyramid had been abandoned for so long that a copse of trees was growing around the hut. It was like a tiny forest in the sky.

We were at the highest point for miles in every direction. It was only about the height of a ten-story building, but the rest of the Yucatán was as flat as land got. The small forest prevented us from being able to take in a sweeping 360-degree view, but if we peered through the trees, we could get glimpses of the surrounding countryside.

For the most part, everything was an endless carpet of greenery, marked by the occasional spot of blue. There was a large lake not too far away that I *thought* might have been the one where we had crashed the plane, although I wasn't completely sure which direction we had come from, or how far we had managed to get through the jungle.

"Hey!" Zoe yelled. "Check it out!"

She was beside the stone hut, looking through the trees in the opposite direction from the lake. I hurried over and joined Mike by her side. Zoe pointed into the distance.

About fifteen miles away, the carpet of green ended abruptly, and an expanse of blue began. The coast. And when I looked the way Zoe was pointing, I could see three buildings along the beach. The tallest was about the same height as the temple we stood on, ten stories or so, and it looked vaguely like a Mayan temple as well. It was a stepped pyramid shape, but it was obviously much more modern. Sunlight glinted off windows in it.

"It must be a resort," Zoe said.

"I think it's Aquarius," Mike announced.

We both looked at him curiously.

"You guys haven't heard of Aquarius?" he asked. "It's supposed to be amazing. Like, the best resort ever. It even has its own water park. Jemma wanted her parents to take us there, but they didn't think it would look good for the president of the United States to go on vacation in Mexico when there are so many resorts in America."

At the mention of the president, something occurred to me. "Speaking of Jemma, how did you get out of going to Hawaii with her?"

Mike's eyes went wide. "Oh nuts. With everything that was going on last night, I kind of forgot about Jemma."

"You forgot to tell your girlfriend you weren't going to Hawaii with her?" Zoe asked, upset.

"I couldn't tell her we were going on a secret mission!" Mike said defensively. "And she's not my girlfriend."

"You should have told her *something*," Zoe insisted. "She's probably worried sick about you!"

I suddenly realized that we had an even more pressing concern than Mike's girlfriend issues: I had no idea where Murray was. It seemed strange that he wasn't with us at the moment. If anyone would have been excited about civilization—in the form of a luxury resort, no less—it was Murray. I spun around, searching through the tiny forest at the top of the temple, wondering where he had gone off to. He was nowhere to be seen.

That wasn't good.

I ran back through the trees, rounding the small stone hut to the rear of the temple.

Murray was there. My fears that he'd been trying to escape immediately faded. He was merely scanning the jungle below, perched at the edge of the platform. "Hey, Ben!" he said. "I was just about to call you. I think I see Erica!"

"Where?" I asked.

"Over there." Murray pointed to a thick clump of trees a quarter mile away. "You might need to stand over here to see her."

I came to the edge of the platform. This side of the temple was much steeper. There were no stairs, like the ones we had come up. Instead, there was only a precipitous drop down into the jungle below. Murray was clinging to a tree to steady himself at the edge. He stepped aside so that I could take his place.

I stood where he had been and gazed into the jungle, where he'd seen Erica.

However, even from where I stood now, the mass of trees seemed completely impenetrable.

Something disturbing now occurred to me.

When I had first come upon Murray, he hadn't been looking quite in the direction of the trees he had pointed to. Instead, he'd been looking slightly to the right.

I glanced that way myself. To my surprise, there was a tiny clearing in the forest with a dirt road leading to it. A pickup truck was parked in the clearing. It was an old, weather-beaten, dust-caked truck, but it was still a vehicle. A vehicle that could get us back to civilization. It was partially obscured by the trees, but it wasn't hard to spot, either.

Which meant Murray had certainly seen it.

Yet he hadn't mentioned it to me. Instead, he had tried to distract me from it, pointing into a stand of trees where he couldn't possibly have seen Erica. . . .

If I'd had another fraction of a second, it might have also

occurred to me that Murray had led me right to the edge of a man-made cliff.

However, I didn't have another fraction of a second. Because Murray suddenly rushed me, slammed his shoulder into my side, and sent me flying over the edge of the pyramid.

PURSUIT

Chxtxclub Settlement

Somewhere in Quintana Roo

March 29

1430 hours

The world spun around me as I went over the edge.

I saw jungle, stone, sky, then jungle again. Somewhere in there, I caught a glimpse of Murray racing back toward the steps of the pyramid. I also saw the ground far below me. The ground I was about to plummet into.

Thankfully, I also saw one other thing.

A vine. It was thick and green and close enough for me to grab on to. I lashed out with both hands and seized it, hanging on tightly as though my life depended on it.

Which, in retrospect, was actually the case.

The vine snapped taut in my grasp, and my arms were wrenched upward as my body jerked to a stop. I felt as though I had nearly dislocated both arms, but despite the searing pain, I didn't let go. Instead of falling, I swung back into the pyramid, slamming face-first into the rock wall.

It hurt. But not nearly as badly as doing a swan dive into the ground below would have.

"Mike! Zoe!" I yelled. "Murray tricked us! He's getting away!"

From the far side of the small stone hut, I heard them gasp with surprise.

"Ben!" Zoe yelled back. "Where are you?"

"Don't worry about me! I'm fine!" I called out, hoping that was true. "Get Murray!"

I heard footsteps on the opposite side of the pyramid, my friends and enemy racing downward, along with Zoe yelling, "Murray! Get back here, you jerkwad!"

I took stock of my situation. I was about ten feet below the edge of the top of the pyramid, dangling from a vine, my face smashed up against the rock.

A few feet to my left, a large iguana clung to the steep stone face, regarding me curiously.

In theory, I should have been able to climb back up to

the platform at the top. Only, my arms were already killing me—it wouldn't be easy.

Meanwhile, Murray had a jump on my friends and was in better shape than them. He was probably going to beat them down the pyramid. I also had an idea where he was going, whereas they didn't.

I looked down. The vine I was clinging to dangled most of the way down the pyramid.

It was always easier to go down than up.

I kicked off the wall, bracing my feet against the stone, and began to walk backward down the pyramid, lowering myself along the vine hand over hand as quickly as I could go. With each step, the vine strained, and the branches it dangled from juddered ominously, but now that I was committed to going down, I couldn't change my mind. I simply had to hope the vine and trees were sufficiently strong to hold me long enough to safely reach the ground.

In the distance, I heard the distinct sound of someone losing their step and tumbling painfully down the pyramid. I really hoped it was Murray.

My shoulders were aching. My palms were getting rubbed raw on the vine. I was relatively sure I had a bloody nose. But I ignored all the pain and continued downward as fast as I could go.

I reached the canopy of jungle below. Leaves brushed

against me, and branches scraped my back. I forced my way through it all, heading down, down, down. . . .

Now the shouts of my friends had grown faint. The pyramid was much wider at the base than it was at the top, and they were on the far side. I heard what might have been the sound of people running through the trees, but I couldn't tell for sure.

My vine ended abruptly twenty feet above the ground. I hung there for a second, trying to work out a safe way down from that point, then decided there wasn't time. I looked for a soft spot below, swung out from the rock face, and let go.

I crashed through the brush, hit the ground, tucked into a ball, rolled over, and came up on my feet. It would have looked pretty cool if there had been anyone around to see it.

There *was* one iguana who watched the whole thing happen, but it didn't seem very impressed.

I raced off into the jungle, in the direction of the small clearing I'd seen. There was no trail. I had to plow right through the underbrush. Thorns raked my skin. Branches whacked my arms and legs. I ran face-first into no less than three separate spiderwebs.

But I made it. I stumbled into the clearing before Murray got there.

The truck sat right before me. The words MUSEO ARQUE-OLÓGICO DE TULUM were stenciled in green on the doors.

Some of the mud spattered on the sides was still somewhat fresh; the truck had been driven that day. Junk food wrappers and empty coffee cups littered the dashboard.

At the far end of the clearing was the worst excuse for a road I had ever seen. It wasn't just off the beaten path. It *was* the beaten path. It looked like someone had beat it with a stick.

But still, it was a road.

Someone was coming through the jungle my way. I heard the thrashing of them fighting their way through the underbrush, then a scream of fear, followed by "Freaking spiders!"

Murray. Ironically for someone employed by SPYDER, he had a horrendous phobia of the real things.

I looked around for something to use as a weapon. A spare tire was mounted on the back of the truck with the tire iron screwed on beside it. I knocked loose the bolt that held it—a movement that sent a shock of pain through my shoulder—then whipped the tire iron free and held it like a samurai sword.

Murray burst into the clearing, then froze in surprise upon seeing me.

He appeared to have lost Zoe and Mike in the jungle behind him, although there was also ample evidence that he was the one who had fallen down the pyramid. His body was mottled with bruises, some the size of my fist. He also had a big cut over his right eye and what looked like a lump of iguana poop smushed into his hair above his left ear. Still, he was upright and mobile. The fall, while painful, had probably sped his flight down the pyramid.

Murray seemed to be considering several different tactics of how to address me. Finally, he opted for the most insulting: acting like he hadn't done anything wrong.

"Ben!" he exclaimed with a grin. "Great to see you're still alive! I was worried about you! You just slipped on that iguana and went right over the edge. . . ."

"Please tell me you don't really think I'm stupid enough to fall for this crap," I said.

Murray's grin faded, but only a little bit. "Well, I was *hoping* you'd be stupid enough. But I can't get anything past you and that big brain of yours, can I?"

"Stop flattering me. It's not going to endear you to me."

"Why would I want to do that?"

"So I'll think twice about beating your face in with this tire iron."

"That wasn't my plan, Ben." Murray strode toward me confidently. "I *know* you won't hurt me for no good reason. You have all those stupid morals that keep you from doing things like that."

"I'm considering giving them up. Just this once." I brandished the tire iron over my shoulder in what I hoped was a menacing fashion. "Don't take another step!"

"Like this?" Murray tauntingly took another step toward me.

He was right. I did have a stupid set of morals that kept me from hurting people unless they were directly threatening me. And even then, I wasn't particularly good at hurting people. Murray was unarmed and merely walking toward me. It was wrong to club him with a tire iron.

Then again, he had repeatedly double-crossed me and tried to kill me. And now I stood between him and his only means of escape. If I didn't stop him, he'd no doubt steal the truck and leave the rest of us stranded in the jungle while he raced on to alert SPYDER that we were alive and well, which would probably prevent us from being able to figure out what they were up to and allow them to launch their newest plot, whatever that might be, causing chaos and mayhem on a mass scale.

Plus, Murray was a real jerk.

So I swung the tire iron at him.

I wasn't looking to cave his skull in or anything. I was only hoping to incapacitate him. Nailing him hard enough in the abdomen to knock the wind out of him for the next half hour would do the trick.

Only, I didn't hit Murray at all. To my surprise, he deftly sidestepped the tire iron.

My momentum spun me around, like a batter whiffing at a baseball.

Murray then lunged at me, pile-driving me into the door of the truck. The sudden hit knocked the wind out of *me*, and the jolt of pain in my already aching shoulders made me drop the tire iron. It clanked uselessly into the dust.

Murray had gotten much better at fighting over the past few weeks.

The last time I had faced off against him, Murray had been weak, lazy, and out of shape, and I had still barely beaten him. Now he hadn't merely bulked up; he'd also sharpened his reflexes and somehow honed his fighting skills.

For one thing, he had never been able to throw a punch before. Professor Simon had once remarked that Murray "hit like a dead wallaby." But now I got a firsthand lesson in how he'd improved.

He punched me right in the stomach. I folded like a hinge, and Murray drove his knee into my chest.

My head clanged off the door of the truck, and I went down, seeing stars.

"Sorry about that, Ben." Murray's grin had returned to its full strength. "I hate doing things like this, but the fact is, I *really* need this truck."

He then casually stepped over my prone body and opened the door.

Before he could climb inside the truck, though, something slammed into him hard enough to send him flying.

Erica.

The two of them tumbled through the dirt, then sprang to their feet, ready to fight. Unfortunately for Erica, Murray had landed right next to the tire iron. He snatched it off the ground and swung it around threateningly.

Unfortunately for Murray, Erica was the best fighter at spy school. It didn't matter how much Murray had trained over the past month; he still couldn't hold a candle to her. Even if he had a tire iron and she didn't.

Erica simply reached down and grabbed the closest thing off the ground that could possibly be used as a weapon.

Not surprisingly, the closest thing to her happened to be an iguana.

It was a good-size male, and it had been lolling in the sunny clearing, lazily watching us fight. Erica snatched it up in a second and whipped it at Murray.

This caught both the iguana and Murray by surprise. The iguana reacted by going into a defensive posture, even though it was sailing through the air: back arched, teeth bared, claws extended.

It landed right on Murray's face and promptly dug its claws into his scalp.

Murray screamed in agony. He dropped the tire iron and tried to pry the lizard off his face, but that only angered it. It dug its claws in farther, and then, for good measure, bit down hard on Murray's ear. It then rode around on his face as he flailed about, like a rodeo cowboy clinging to a bucking bronco.

As Murray staggered past me, I did the only thing I could manage from my prone position. I tripped him.

Murray went down hard in the dirt. The iguana quickly released him and scuttled into the underbrush. Before Murray could recover and get his bearings, Erica was on him. She pounced onto his back and wrenched both his arms behind him.

Murray wailed in pain.

"Hey," I said to Erica, struggling to a sitting position. "How long have you known we were here?"

"Only a few minutes," Erica said calmly. "I heard you all yelling from the top of the pyramid."

"Why didn't you yell back?"

"I had my suspicions Murray wasn't with the program. I wondered what he'd do if he thought I wasn't around."

"He tried to kill me!" I exclaimed.

"Doesn't look like he succeeded," Erica observed. She then turned her attention to Murray, smashing his clawed-up face into the dirt. "You've been a bad boy. And I'm guessing that, since you made a beeline for this truck, you've known exactly where SPYDER is hiding out all along and were going to head directly to them. Am I right?"

Murray didn't say anything.

"I asked you a question," Erica said, anger creeping into her voice. "So let's try this again. Am I right?" She twisted Murray's arms, making him writhe in pain.

"No!" he cried. "I was only trying to escape! I have no idea where SPYDER is!"

Erica calmly flipped him over, then sat on his chest, pinioning his arms to his sides with her legs. "Murray, remember when I knocked your tooth out last summer?"

Murray's eyes widened in fear. "Yes."

"I'm going to knock the rest of them down your throat unless you tell me where SPYDER's hiding."

Murray gulped. It was evident that his loyalty to SPY-DER didn't go as far as losing his teeth. "Deal," he said.

OBSERVATION

Aquarius Resort

Tulum Region, Quintana Roo

March 29

1600 hours

"You have got to be kidding me," Mike said.

We were standing at a balcony off the lobby of the Aquarius Luxury Family Resort and Spa. From this vantage point, we had a sweeping view of the opulent grounds. The entire property was lushly landscaped with tropical plants and fake waterfalls to give the impression that we were in the jungle. There was plenty of *real* jungle right outside the resort, but the phony jungle was nicer for the guests, as it had far fewer mosquitoes and much better catering. Directly in front of us was an enormous swimming pool surrounded by hundreds of tourists basking in the sun. Beyond the pool was a fringe of gorgeous white-sand beach, and beyond that was a bay of brilliant turquoise water. The bay was packed with guests trying out various water sports: snorkeling, scuba diving, Jet Skiing, paddleboarding, sea kayaking, and parasailing.

"*This* is where SPYDER's new headquarters are?" Mike asked.

"They're renting the penthouse suite," Murray reported, nodding his head in the direction of the building. "And they have been for the past eight months."

"Ever since we blew up their headquarters?" Zoe questioned.

"Since right *before* that," Murray corrected. "Remember, all the higher-ups had evacuated HQ a day earlier so they wouldn't be around if anything went wrong."

"Which is why the CIA didn't catch any of them," I recalled. "They were living it up down here while leaving you, Ashley, and Nefarious to do their dirty work and take the fall for them."

Murray glowered at the memory of this, then shot a baleful stare at the penthouse.

The main building was to the left of the pool. It was the fake Mayan pyramid structure I had seen from the top of the actual Mayan pyramid. Each level was bedecked with wide balconies that looked out upon the beach. However, it was hard to get a good view of the penthouse, as the residence itself was set back from the edge of the roof and surrounded by private gardens. A big, muscular man stood at the railing, wearing sunglasses and a Hawaiian shirt. He looked like an average, everyday tourist simply taking in the view. But since I knew SPYDER was holed up there, I presumed the man was in fact a trained killer, keeping an eye out for trouble.

"Staying here fits SPYDER's modus operandi perfectly," Erica observed. "You'd assume an evil organization would *build* a secret hideout down in the tropics, but that takes time and money, and, frankly, they're probably not going to use it long-term anyhow. It's a waste of resources. Renting a penthouse suite makes much more sense. Plus, there's room service. In addition, hotels always provide additional security for high-paying guests. I can guarantee you the elevator to the top floor requires a special key and that there's already alarm systems built in, though SPYDER has certainly added their own."

There had also been guards at the front gate of the resort, though they hadn't caused any trouble for us. They only seemed concerned with people arriving by car, the idea being that no one would actually ever walk onto the property from the road. But the five of us weren't normal tourists.

We had stolen the truck from the Mayan temple site. I had felt bad about that, but Erica had pointed out that tracking down the archaeologists and asking them for a ride would only cause problems. They would probably call the police to report that they'd found some kids lost in the middle of the jungle, and SPYDER was certainly monitoring the phones of the police. Of course, we could beg them *not* to call the police, but that would be suspicious in itself, as would any story we made up to explain why we were off in the jungle without our parents. Since I was fluent in Spanish, I had left a nice note for the police on the dashboard of the truck after we abandoned it on the side of the road, explaining who the truck belonged to and where they could be found. It didn't really make up for what we'd done, but when the fate of the world was at stake, you occasionally had to do something uncool.

Erica had driven the truck. The route back from the archaeological site was more pothole than road, but it was still much faster than trekking through the jungle had been. Even though we had only been able to jounce along at ten miles an hour, we had still made it to civilization well before dark. The dirt road had emerged onto a four-lane highway that served as the major route up and down the Caribbean coast of the Yucatán peninsula. It was lined with resorts on the beach side and eco-adventure tourist spots on the jungle side. Judging from the billboards, the main eco adventures were snorkeling in cenotes, riding all-terrain vehicles, and zip-lining.

The entrance to Aquarius was extremely ostentatious, with elaborate fountains, an electronic gate, and a guard booth. However, it was all for show; the rest of the resort's perimeter was only protected by a spindly wire fence. We abandoned the truck on the side of the highway two hundred yards past the main entrance, easily jumped the fence, and then worked our way to the lobby.

At most resorts, anyone seeing five kids in our filthy, banged-up condition probably would have immediately called a hospital. But at that hour, tourists were returning by the vanload from eco adventures, and most of them looked to be in even worse shape than us. The ones who'd gone ATVing looked particularly bad: Most were so caked in dust and dried mud that they'd changed color, save for clean patches around their eyes where their safety goggles had been. Everyone sported welts and scratches and bug bites, which they bore as badges of pride, pleased with themselves for having done something as rugged as hiking through the jungle for a few minutes to go down a zip-line.

Given what we'd done that day, we weren't that impressed.

Still, they were easy to blend in with. We walked right

into the hotel lobby behind a vanload of mud-encrusted ATVers. Since Aquarius was located in a climate where it never got cold, the lobby was open air, without any doors or windows. Hostesses in fake Mayan outfits had offered us complimentary glasses of lemonade, which we gratefully accepted before proceeding on to scope out the surroundings. The balcony where we now stood was on the opposite side of the lobby from the front entrance, designed for new guests to pause and gawk at the beauty of the resort.

"So what was your plan?" Erica asked Murray. "Steal the truck, drive here, and offer to tell SPYDER where we were as a bargaining chip for them taking you back?"

"Pretty much," Murray admitted. He didn't *want* to admit it, but he was well aware that Erica's threat to forcibly remove all his teeth if he tried anything sneaky wasn't idle. For extra security, Erica had lashed his hands behind his back with a vine for the entirety of our drive to civilization, and she'd shoved a dirty sock in his mouth to keep him quiet. (There hadn't been any real security reason for the sock, but Erica didn't want to listen to him whining and felt he deserved the punishment anyhow.) Unfortunately, we couldn't have him bound and gagged in the hotel, so we were all keeping a very close eye on him instead.

"It wouldn't have worked," Erica informed him. "They would have still killed you."

"I don't think so," Murray said, though it sounded like he was trying to convince himself this was true. "You're the ones they *really* wanted dead. The information that they'd failed, along with directions to where I'd stranded you, would have been worth a lot."

Erica shook her head. "Get it through your thick skull, Murray. They're done with you. Nothing you do is going to change that. The moment they know you're alive, they'll toss you right in the shark tank."

That wasn't a euphemism. There really *was* a shark tank at the resort. It was in the water park. One of the water slides went through a glass tube that ran straight through it. The slide also had two corkscrews and finished with a twenty-foot plummet into a pool of water. It was called, quite insensitively, Montezuma's Revenge.

I hadn't seen the slide myself yet, but there were TV monitors throughout the lobby displaying all the fun things to do at the resort. There were many other slides in addition to Montezuma's. Several of them coursed down yet another fake Mayan pyramid, though this one was significantly smaller than the one with the hotel rooms. There was also a lazy river for tubing, a wave pool, a kiddie park, and some zip-lines that dropped you into a large basin. Apparently, Quintana Roo was the zip-line capital of Mexico.

The voice-over on the videos was entirely in English,

despite the fact that we were in a country where the official language was Spanish. Almost all the guests appeared to be from the United States, although, based on the accents, there was a smattering of Europeans as well.

The entire hotel staff was from Mexico, though. My first instinct, upon arriving at Aquarius, had been to ask the staff whether anyone unusual was renting the penthouse suite. After all, I spoke Spanish. However, Erica had cautioned me not to.

"There's a good chance SPYDER has warned them to report anyone asking too many questions," she said. "And besides, sometimes you can learn a lot more if they think you *can't* understand them."

Now, as we stood on the balcony, I found that, once again, Erica knew exactly what she was talking about. Two maids passed us, chatting in Spanish. They made no attempt to whisper or conceal their conversation in front of us, assuming we only spoke English, like everyone else at the resort.

"The one-eyed man in the penthouse wants fresh towels again," the first one said. "And he wants them fluffed like they were new."

"Again?" the other asked. "That guy is more picky about his towels than any guest we've ever had."

"Maybe," said the first. "But he's a good tipper."

"For a cyclops," the other said, and they both laughed.

I must have stiffened in response to this, because Erica sensed it. "What'd they say?" she asked. It might have seemed surprising that someone as smart as Erica didn't speak a language as common as Spanish, but then, she already spoke French, Russian, Mandarin Chinese, and Arabic.

"There's a one-eyed man staying in the penthouse," I reported.

Now everyone else stiffened slightly. Even Erica.

"Joshua Hallal," Zoe said.

Joshua only had one eye. And one leg. And one hand. He had suffered a terrible accident while fleeing the scene of a crime right around the time Erica had been forcibly removing Murray's tooth from his mouth.

I returned my attention to the penthouse, just in time to witness a shift change on the terrace. The big, muscular man with the sunglasses melted back into the patio garden and was replaced by a bigger, even more muscular man. He wore only a Speedo bathing suit and had a blond mullet.

Even though it was sweltering outside, I felt my entire body go cold.

I knew the new guard all too well. He had tried to kill me. Several times.

"Don't look up," I said quietly—as though the man could hear me from all the way across the resort. "But

Dane Brammage is at the SPYDER penthouse."

Everyone did exactly what I'd just asked them not to do and looked up. Except Erica.

Thankfully, Dane was gazing in the other direction. Otherwise, he would have noticed such an obvious display of staring.

Erica grabbed Murray and Zoe and dragged them with her behind some potted plants. "Nice work," she hissed sarcastically. "Why don't you guys just call him and let him know we're here? It'd be faster."

I yanked Mike into the shade of the potted plants as well.

My friends were all too shaken by the appearance of Dane to be upset by Erica's insult. "That's the guy from Vail!" Mike exclaimed. "I thought you killed him, Ben!"

"So did I," I agreed.

When we'd last seen Dane, he was plunging through the ice into a frozen lake. However, that hadn't been the first time we had thought he'd died that day. He had proven exceptionally hard to kill. He had already fallen from a helicopter and been buried by an avalanche. (For the record, what I had done was in self-defense.)

Zoe peeked out at Dane from behind a palm frond. "What's he even doing working for SPYDER? I thought he worked for Leo Shang!"

"Shang is in jail, thanks to us," Erica reminded her. "And

thugs need to pay the rent like everyone else. Shang's arms dealer, Paul Lee, is connected to SPYDER. He probably made an introduction."

"Or maybe Paul Lee is *here*," I suggested.

Erica cocked an eyebrow, considering that. "Anything's possible."

I pulled aside a frond and chanced another look at Dane. The only times I had seen him before had been in the mountains in winter, so he had always been bundled up in ski clothes. Now his bathing suit allowed me to see his whole, insanely muscular body. He looked like a Greek statue that had come to life and then spent three months in the gym while hopped up on steroids. He was also no longer pale, indicating he had probably been in Mexico for a while. His delicate Scandinavian skin hadn't tanned very well, though. He was as red as a boiled lobster.

Thankfully, he still hadn't looked in our direction. Instead, his attention was focused out on the water, beyond the beach.

I followed his gaze. There was a yacht anchored in the bay.

It was the biggest yacht I had ever seen. Not that I'd seen a whole lot of yachts, but still . . . It was like a floating mansion. It was four decks tall, sleek, and gleaming white. Two speedboats hung from davits on the stern, while a black helicopter perched on the roof.

"Is that the helicopter that came looking for us earlier?" I asked.

"Yes," Erica said in a tone that indicated she had noticed the helicopter well before I had. "The serial number on the tail is the same."

I couldn't make out the serial number. The helicopter was too far away. The writing on the tail was only distant hazy images.

"You can read that?" Zoe asked.

"You can't?" Erica asked.

"How good is your vision?" Mike asked.

"It's off the charts," Erica replied. "I eat a lot of carrots."

"So SPYDER has the penthouse *and* a yacht," I deduced.

"Or they have rich friends who brought their own yacht," Erica posited. She looked to Murray for an answer.

He shrugged helplessly. "I never heard anything about a yacht. All I heard was that they were staying at this resort. If you want to know more than that, you'll have to figure it out yourselves. I'm finished here." He started for the exit.

Before he could go two steps, Erica lashed out a hand and grabbed him by the throat.

Despite his newfound muscles, Murray was powerless against Erica's grasp. He made a strangled *urk* and quickly sank to his knees in the lobby.

"You're not finished until I say you are," Erica warned.

"Dane Brammage knows all of us!" Murray gasped. "If he spots me—or you—or any of us, then we really will all be finished."

"Um, Erica," Zoe said quietly. "If we want to keep a low profile, strangling Murray in the lobby probably isn't the best idea." She pointed toward the main entrance, where a new vanload of American tourists was funneling inside.

This group had obviously just returned from ATVing, which I could determine from the dust plastered all over their faces. And they were all in the same family, which I could determine from their matching T-shirts. The shirts were a garish neon yellow (at least, in the spots they weren't coated with mud) and proudly proclaimed FARKLES RULE! on the front and FABULOUS FIFTH FARKLE FAMILY FIESTA on the back. There were seventeen Farkles, greatly varying in age, size, and body type, but every last one of them was brash and boisterous. Luckily, they were all too busy high-fiving one another and loudly recalling the best wipeouts of the day to have noticed Murray being throttled.

Erica reluctantly let go of Murray's neck. Murray collapsed against a potted palm, sucking in air.

The Farkles all clustered around the ladies handing out free lemonade and began to discuss their plans for the rest of the day at the top of their lungs.

Once Erica determined they weren't paying attention to

us, she said, "Surviving was only the first step of this mission. Our primary objective is finding out what SPYDER is plotting and thwarting it. . . ."

"Actually," I corrected, "our primary objective is to let the CIA know where SPYDER is and simply keep an eye on them while waiting for backup."

Erica gave me a harsh stare that made me think she was now considering clenching a hand around *my* neck. "That was a stupid plan," she said.

"It was your grandfather's," I argued.

"That doesn't mean it's good," Erica countered. "Case in point, the whole thing was a setup by SPYDER to leave us all dead in a plane crash. And the very men Grandpa handpicked to fly us down here turned out to be double agents, which means the entire CIA is compromised. Meanwhile, SPYDER is obviously planning something big—and we're the only ones in position to find out what it is."

"We're in position to end up *dead*," Murray whined.

"We're not," Erica said. "Because SPYDER already thinks we're dead. So really, we're the last people on earth they're considering killing."

"Unless they discover they didn't really kill us all the first time around," Murray said. "At which point we will become the *first* people on earth they want to kill. Again. And every minute we stay here is another minute we're in danger."

"Not if we're careful," Erica said.

"Hey, guys," Mike interrupted. "I know SPYDER is really important and all, but I think there's something else that ought to be our primary objective: food. It's been a long day, and if I don't get something to eat soon, I'm going to implode."

"I second that," I said. With all our adventures, I had often been distracted from the fact that I hadn't eaten since the night before. But now I was starting to feel weak from hunger.

"Me too," Zoe agreed. Her stomach was grumbling so loudly I could hear it.

"And then a shower would be nice," Murray suggested. "I still have iguana poop in my hair."

"And we need to figure out where we're staying for the night," Mike added.

"All right!" Erica said, in a way that indicated she felt food, showers, and a place to sleep weren't nearly as important to her as they were to everyone else. "I'll take care of it." Her eyes flicked across the lobby to where the Farkles were now having a lemonade-chugging contest. "In fact, I know exactly what to do."

"What?" Murray, Mike, Zoe, and I all asked at once.

"Isn't it obvious?" Erica asked. "We're going to be Farkles."

FARKLES

Coco Loco Lounge
Aquarius Resort
March 29
1900 hours

No matter how hard I worked at honing my pow-ers of observation, Erica always made me look like an inatten-tive nimrod. This was the case with my friends as well. Even though we were all looking at the exact same view of the resort from the balcony, we hadn't *seen* what Erica had.

For example, there were a *lot* of Farkles at Aquarius.

It should have been clear as day. They were all wearing the same garish neon-yellow shirts; they couldn't have stuck out more if they were wearing those fruit-covered Carmen

Miranda hats. Farkles were everywhere: swimming in the ocean, strolling on the beach, basking in the sun, chasing iguanas through the landscaping, and splashing in the pool.

Not all of them were wearing their T-shirts, however. Most of the Farkles in the pool had left their shirts wadded up on their lounge chairs. No one was paying any attention to these, as they were all busy having chicken fights and playing rowdy games of Marco Polo. We were able to easily swipe five shirts as we walked through the pool area, then camouflage ourselves as Farkles.

High above us, on the patio around SPYDER's penthouse, Dane Brammage and other guards were still on patrol. But now, being kids worked to our advantage. There were many places where being a kid made you stick out (office buildings, hospitals, the Pentagon), but a family resort wasn't one of them. Instead, Aquarius was teeming with other kids. We easily blended in with them. After all, children rarely posed a threat to evil organizations—we were the rare exceptions—and SPYDER had good reason to believe that we had died by plane crash, missile blast, drowning, or crocodile attack that morning.

Still, we moved about with caution, trying to look like normal kids and not draw any attention to ourselves.

After acquiring our Farkle shirts, we focused on cleaning up. There were showers arrayed along the edge of the beach.

These were really for Aquarius guests to rinse the salt water and sand off themselves before polluting the swimming pools with it, but they worked perfectly well for us, too. We scrubbed off the layers of dirt, grime, and iguana poop, then dried ourselves with complimentary beach towels. Sure, we still ended up with damp shorts and underwear that way, but after the litany of things we had been through lately, moist boxers weren't so bad. (My underwear had been soaked so much that day, merely being moist was an improvement.) It felt fantastic to be clean again.

We were still hungry, though. There was poolside food service, but we didn't have any money—and even if we'd had some, the prices were outrageous. Getting hamburgers, fries, and drinks for all of us would have cost the same as a plane ticket home. I was giving serious thought to devouring the scraps off plates people had left behind when Erica revealed that she had a plan to feed us too:

Just before seven o'clock, as the sun sank behind the penthouse at the top of the hotel tower, all the Farkles began heading toward the Coco Loco Lounge, a large open-air restaurant next to the beach. It was a mass migration. The entire horde of them filtered into the room in their neon-yellow shirts, greeting one another heartily and happily recounting the events of the day. I was hesitant to enter, thinking there was no way we could all pass ourselves off as members of a family we hadn't been born into, but Erica advised us to act like we all belonged there and then she breezed through the door confidently.

It turned out I needn't have worried. There were even more Farkles than I had imagined—at least two hundred—and it seemed no one in the family could keep track of who everyone was. They were predominantly Caucasian, but through marriage (and possibly adoption) there was enough ethnic diversity to account for all of us. The mere fact that we had Farkle T-shirts was good enough to convince everyone that we belonged there.

The only two things all the Farkles seemed to have in common were exuberant personalities and massive family pride. Everyone greeted one another simply by yelling "Farkles!" followed by elaborate handshakes and bear hugs. We didn't get too far into the lounge before this happened to us. A hefty middle-aged woman in a billowing T-shirt opened her arms wide and screamed "Farkles!" at us.

To our astonishment, Erica opened her arms and screamed "Farkles!" right back.

Although I was well aware of Erica's talent for changing her personality to blend in, it still always caught me by surprise. Within seconds, Erica could become her complete opposite—and often, everything she hated about people in general. For example, she wasn't a fan of physical contact, even from friends, and yet, she now allowed the big woman to give her a hug that seemed to swallow her whole.

"All you kids are growing so fast, I can't keep track of who's who anymore," the woman told her. She had a Southern accent as thick as molasses. "Remind me who you all are again?"

"Why, I'm Ginny Farkle!" Erica exclaimed like this was common knowledge. "Lisa's daughter!"

The woman obviously didn't know who Lisa Farkle was, but she seemed embarrassed about it and did her best to pretend she did. "Ohhhh! Lisa! Of course! How is your mother?"

"Well, she's sad she couldn't make it this year," Erica replied. "But you know how her work can be sometimes."

"I sure do," the woman said supportively, even though she couldn't have possibly known this. "Well now, I'm your cousin Edna, in case you've forgotten. . . ."

"Cousin Edna, how could anyone ever forget you?" Erica asked, then pointed to Zoe, Mike, and Murray. "This here's my sister Sally, my brother Tim, and our cousin Ruprecht." She grabbed my hand and pulled me over. "And this guy here is George. He's not *really* family, but as far as we Farkles are concerned, he might as well be. So his folks said he could come on down here and spend spring break with us."

"Ohhh," Edna said, looking me over. "Now, Ginny, is this a boy who's a friend—or a boyfriend?"

"Edna!" Erica gasped. Somehow, she even made her face flush in embarrassment. "George is just a friend, that's all."

It was a completely dumbfounding performance. Partly because I was still in awe of Erica's chameleon-like personality, but also because Erica had established me as a potential boyfriend for her character. I had no idea why she'd done this when she could have simply passed me off as a random cousin, and the association made me blush too—only I was doing it for real, not as part of an act.

My friends were all surprised by this as well, but they barely had a chance to react before Edna declared, "Well don't just sit there, Farkles, give your cousin Edna a hug!" and grabbed us in her fleshy arms. For a moment, I was concerned we might all be suffocated in her grasp, but then a waiter passed with a tray full of drinks and Edna quickly released us to go after him. "See you later, kids," she announced. "I need to wet my whistle." Edna turned out to be the type of American who mistakenly believed the way to make herself understood to the hotel staff was to speak English very loud and slow, as if that would magically turn it into Spanish. "EXCUSE ME!" she shouted at the waiter. "CAN I HAVE A DRINK?"

The waiter proffered the tray and replied in perfect English. "Of course, Mrs. Farkle."

"MOOCH-ASS GRASSY-ASS, AMIGO!" Edna yelled.

Erica, Zoe, Mike, Murray, and I made a beeline for the buffet before any other Farkles accosted us.

I was so hungry, I probably would have eaten raw iguana entrails, but even so, the spread of food we found was a fantasy come true. Tables were piled high with the most delicious foods any teenager could ever ask for: hot dogs, burgers, tacos, pizza, french fries, nachos, chicken fingers, baby back ribs, and every fixing, condiment, and dip imaginable. There were tubs full of ice-cold sodas, a full bar for the adults, and a make-your-own-ice-cream-sundae station.

"Oh my God," Murray gasped. "There's bacon!"

Indeed there was. A pyramid of pig parts towered on a chafing dish. So much bacon was piled up, it was hard to believe there was a pig left alive in the Yucatán. Murray shoved two young Farkles aside, grabbed a handful of bacon, and crammed it into his mouth. His eyes rolled upward in ecstasy as he savored it. "This is soooo good," he moaned. "Oh, bacon, I've missed you."

"I thought you weren't eating like that anymore," Zoe said. "What happened to being the healthiest guy on earth?"

"That was before I knew SPYDER wanted me dead," Murray said sullenly. "What's the point of treating your body like a temple when it's about to get demolished by a wrecking ball? I'm not going to squander what might be the last meal of my life eating *vegetables*." He said this last word the way most people would have said "rat droppings."

I hated to admit it, but he had a point. I grabbed a plate and loaded it with everything I could, then started shoving food into my mouth.

Mike and Zoe were doing the same thing.

Erica wasn't. Even though she must have been famished, she still found a platter of crudités that had been completely ignored by all the Farkles and grabbed a handful of veggies.

"That's all you're eating?" Mike asked her. "We all nearly died today. Celebrate a little!"

"I am," Erica replied earnestly. "I'm having six ounces of baked potato with this. I haven't eaten a starch in six months."

"You're crazy," Murray informed her. "The only way I'm eating vegetables from now on is if they're deep-fried and then dipped in chocolate." His eyes suddenly lit up with inspiration. "What am I talking about? I could be dipping bacon in chocolate right now!" He hurried to the sundae bar and ladled hot fudge over his plate.

"Nice work getting us food," Zoe told Erica, between bites of cheeseburger. "Now what's the plan for finding us a place to sleep?"

Erica tossed her a credit card. "Go find a courtesy phone, call the front desk, and book five rooms with that."

Zoe flipped the card over. I caught a glimpse of the name on it: Edna P. Farkle.

I now understood why Erica had allowed herself to be bear-hugged by Edna. She'd been picking the woman's pocket.

Zoe frowned, having the same reaction to Erica's orders that I did. "I can't use this card! It's a crime!"

Erica lowered her voice so none of the Farkles would hear her. "No, a crime is whatever SPYDER is plotting. I'm merely asking you to do what is necessary for us to stop them. Booking a room with that card won't hurt Cousin Edna at all. When the charge shows up in a month, she'll contest it as fraudulent and won't have to pay it. Not that it'd matter to her anyway. Judging from the size of that rock on her ring, she has plenty of cash to spare. I'll bet she's bankrolling this whole Farkle Fiesta."

Zoe and I glanced toward Edna, who was now peppering a small Farkle child with kisses. Sure enough, she had a diamond on her finger big enough to choke a horse. Yet another thing Erica had noticed that I hadn't.

Even so, what she was asking for still didn't seem right. And Zoe was in agreement. "If Edna disputes the charge," she argued, "the hotel still will have to eat it. . . ."

"Serves them right for harboring a fugitive organization like SPYDER," Erica said coldly.

Zoe frowned, then handed the credit card back. "I'm sorry. It still seems wrong."

Erica took it and gave Zoe a stare full of disappointment in return.

"I'll do it!" Murray volunteered. "I don't have any morals at all!"

"That's why I don't trust you to do this," Erica said. "The moment I let you out of my sight with a credit card, you'll try to book a private jet to Rio."

Astonishment flooded Murray's bacon-grease-and-chocolate-sauce smeared face. Apparently, this exact thought had crossed his mind.

"I guess if you want something done, you have to do it yourself," Erica grumbled. She started out of the lounge, then turned back to Zoe and me. "Keep an eye on Murray, will you? If he tries to run, you have my permission to beat him senseless. You don't have a moral issue with that, do you?"

"No," Zoe said meekly.

"Good. Wait here until I get back." Erica stormed off to find a phone.

Murray happily returned to dipping bacon into melted chocolate.

Zoe sighed morosely. "She hates me."

"No she doesn't," I said.

"Well she certainly doesn't like me."

"You shouldn't take that personally. Erica doesn't like anyone."

"She likes *you*," Zoe said. "And she likes Mike, too."

"I'm not sure that's true," I said, and then wondered where Mike was. He was no longer beside us.

Instead, he was a few feet away, chatting up a young female Farkle. She looked about our age, she was pretty, and she seemed to be very attracted to Mike, fluttering her eyelashes and smiling coyly at him. "I did this zip-line today," she was telling him. "It must have been thirty feet above the ground. *Super* scary. But I did it anyhow, and it was incredible! How about you? Did you do anything exciting?"

"I was in a plane crash," Mike told her. "Also, I got attacked by crocodiles, fell into a cenote, and discovered a lost Mayan city."

The girl stared at him, stunned—and then burst into a fit of giggles. "Aw, you're teasing me, aren't you?"

"Maybe," Mike said.

"Are you really a Farkle?" the girl asked. "Cause I haven't seen you at any of these reunions before."

"I haven't made it to any," Mike said. "But I'm one hundred percent Farkle. I'm Tim."

"I'm Emma," the girl said.

"Let me guess," Mike teased. "Your last name's Farkle."

"Actually, it's Mathes. I'm only related by marriage. My stepdad's a Farkle." Emma took a step closer to Mike. "Which means we're not really related," she said meaningfully.

"How does he do that?" Murray asked, approaching us with a fully loaded plate from the dessert bar.

"Do what?" I asked.

"Attract women like that. I've got the hot new bod. And yet that girl's not coming after *me*."

Zoe eyed his plate warily. "Maybe it's because you're eating s'mores with bacon in them."

Murray had, in fact, combined bacon with chocolate, marshmallow, and graham crackers. And then he'd sprinkled gummy bears on top. "Don't knock it till you've tried it," he said. He attempted to take a bite, but the entire concoction collapsed in his hand, leaving him with a huge brown smear down the front of his Farkle Fiesta T-shirt.

"Yeah, it's hard to see why the girls aren't beating your door down," Zoe said sarcastically. "It looks like you wiped your butt with your shirt."

Murray didn't bother to argue—or to clean his shirt off. Instead, he returned to the dessert bar to rebuild his sandwich.

Emma Mathes was now flirting even more heavily with Mike, twirling a strand of hair around her finger. "Know who you kind of look like?" she asked. "That guy who's dating the president's daughter. Mike something or other."

"Yeah," Mike said. "I get that a lot."

I looked at Zoe and caught her looking at me. There was an awkward moment between us as we both realized we hadn't really been alone together since I'd learned that she liked me a month before.

It seemed that a mature person ought to address the situation and talk about it. But I *wasn't* a mature person. I was a thirteen-year-old boy. So I did my best to come up with something to avoid any serious conversation about our feelings. "Maybe we should get Mike away from Emma," I said. "Before he says something too glib and tanks the mission."

"Good idea," Zoe agreed. Though I got a sense she was as relieved to avoid a serious conversation as I was.

I walked over to Mike, grabbed his arm, and told Emma, "Sorry, but I need to talk to Tim. Family business." Then I yanked Mike back over to the nacho stand and told him, "Go easy on the flirting, okay?"

"I wasn't flirting," he said defensively. "I was just trying to blend in."

"It sure *looked* like flirting," Zoe said. "If you're not careful, you'll tank this mission. What if she realizes that you really are Jemma Stern's boyfriend?"

"I'm not her boyfriend," Mike said quickly.

"Probably not anymore," Zoe agreed, "now that you left the country and didn't even have the decency to tell her. You'd better call her and straighten things out."

"That's a guaranteed way to tank the mission," Mike

argued. "The Secret Service traces all her calls. How am I supposed to explain that I'm in Mexico all of a sudden?"

By the burger fixings bar, Emma Mathes crooked a finger at Mike, beckoning him to come back to her.

Mike held up a finger, signaling he'd be a little longer.

Zoe smacked him in the arm hard enough to make him wince. "No flirting!"

"All I did was signal her that I'd be back in a bit."

"You're not going to be back in a bit," Zoe told him. "You're not going to talk to her ever again. You need to keep your distance from that girl."

"But if I just ignore her, she'll think I'm a jerk," Mike protested.

"Great," Zoe said.

"Let me get this straight," Mike said. "You're angry at me because I blew off Jemma, but now you're going to be angry at me if I *don't* blow off Emma?"

"Exactly," Zoe said. "The less Emma wants to do with you, the better."

"I can't even make an excuse?" Mike asked. "Man, this is a real dilemma."

"Yes," I said. "An Emma dilemma."

"In addition to my Jemma dilemma." Mike suddenly noticed something behind Zoe and gasped with surprise. "Ashley Sparks!" he exclaimed.

"Don't change the subject," Zoe told him.

Mike pointed through the crowd. "She's here!"

Zoe and I both looked the way he was pointing. Outside the Coco Loco Lounge, beyond the sea of neon Farkle T-shirts, I saw a short, ponytailed girl wearing an extremely glittery spandex outfit. There were thousands of sequins on it, glittering in the moonlight. I only knew of one person who wore that many sequins.

"Mike's right," I said. "It's her."

Before enrolling at SPYDER's evil spy school, Ashley had been one of the most promising gymnasts in the United States. Unfortunately, she had barely missed the cut for the Olympic team (she still harbored a serious grudge against the judges) and had been so enraged about the injustice that she had turned to crime. At first glance, she didn't seem evil at all. In fact, she still looked a great deal like a professional gymnast. She was short and muscular, with a penchant for tight-fitting, sparkly athletic wear and glittery eyeshadow. She also had a chirpy, high-pitched voice that made her sound like an adorable cartoon character, even when she was threatening you with grievous bodily harm.

At the moment, Ashley didn't seem to be on any sort of important SPYDER mission. Instead, she was ambling along happily in the direction of the beach. Between her attractive looks and her glittery clothing, I didn't notice that there was someone else walking alongside her until Zoe gasped in surprise.

"She's with Warren!" Zoe exclaimed.

I shifted my attention to the person beside Ashley and realized that it was, in fact, Warren Reeves, our fellow classmate who had defected to SPYDER. It was hard to tell it was Warren, though. Not because Warren had changed a lot in the month since we'd seen him—but because Warren was incredibly easy to overlook. Warren's great (and frankly, only) talent at spy school had been his gift for camouflage. While this was partly due to his great skill with body paint, Warren naturally tended to blend into the background anyhow. There was a blandness about him that made him easy to overlook. Quite often, back at school, people had failed to notice Warren even when he was *trying* to be seen. The only things I had ever really observed about him were that he'd always had a grudge against me—and a crush on Zoe. Meanwhile, Zoe had failed to notice that crush herself, which had made Warren sullenly resentful and eventually led him to join SPYDER.

The last time we'd seen Warren, he'd been fleeing through the underground tunnels at the academy after betraying us. Ashley hadn't been too happy with him at the moment, as he'd botched her escape plan—but it appeared they had made up. The two of them seemed perfectly happy to be in each other's company. And . . .

"Oh, ick!" Zoe said. "They're holding hands!"

"No way!" exclaimed Murray, appearing beside us, holding a chocolate sundae with crumbled bacon on top. "That's not possible."

"Look at them!" Zoe exclaimed. "Glitter Girl and Chameleon are a couple."

That definitely seemed to be the case. Not only were the two of them holding hands, they were looking into each other's eyes as they walked with dopey, lovey-dovey expressions.

This was almost as astonishing as the discovery that Warren had betrayed us in the first place. Ashley might have been evil, but she had at least been fun to hang out with. When I'd first met her, I had found her friendly, cheerful, and extremely interesting. Meanwhile, Warren was . . . Warren. The human equivalent of soggy bread.

"Wow," Murray said, digging into his bacon sundae. "I *never* would have called that. It's like a swan going out with a rock."

"Should we tail them?" Zoe asked. "Maybe they're up to something evil."

"Looks like they're heading down to the beach to make out," Murray observed. "That's not evil. It's *disgusting*. I think I lost my appetite." He set his sundae down, then changed his mind. "Wait. It's back." He dug out a heaping spoonful and crammed it into his mouth.

"*You're* disgusting," Zoe said in a way that made any concerns I ever had about her liking Murray seem ridiculous.

Ashley and Warren were now well past the Coco Loco Lounge. They didn't appear to have seen us. But then, they weren't looking at anyone but each other.

I wondered if I had ever looked like they did while I was mooning over Erica. If so, I was retroactively mortified.

Ashley and Warren reached the beach and crossed the sand toward the water.

"I really think we should tail them," Zoe said. Though she was trying to hide it, something in her voice made me think this was about something else besides the mission. She wasn't jealous of Ashley, exactly, but seeing Warren mooning over someone else was obviously bothering her.

"Erica told us to wait here," I said. "If she comes back and finds us gone, she'll be upset."

"Erica isn't the boss of us," Zoe replied.

"She kind of is," I shot back. "She's a better spy than us, she has more experience—and frankly, I have no idea what we're supposed to be doing on this mission."

"We're supposed to be finding out what SPYDER is up to." Zoe pointed after Ashley and Warren. "And those are two SPYDER operatives right there!"

"There's no cover out on that beach," I said. "What if they see us tailing them? We'll reveal ourselves and screw up the whole operation. Then it won't only be Erica who's upset with us. It'll be the entire CIA."

"Then what's *your* plan, exactly?" Zoe asked, annoyed. "Sit here with the Farkles and stuff ourselves full of food all night?"

"That sounds good to me," Murray said.

"I just think we should wait until Erica gets back," I said.

"Ashley and Warren might be gone by then!" Zoe argued. "For Pete's sake, Ben, show some initiative! You're a good spy. You ought to be able to do things without worrying about what Erica will think of you for once!"

"I don't make all my decisions based upon what Erica will think," I said hotly.

"Yes you do," Zoe said. "You're more terrified of upsetting her than you are of SPYDER."

"That's not true," I said.

"Ha. You can't even say anything bad about her, even if it's the truth."

"Yes I could."

"Then do it."

"Fine. Erica can be cold and overbearing sometimes."

"She's also right behind you," Zoe said.

I yelped in surprise and spun around, mortified that I had just insulted Erica in her presence. To my relief, Erica wasn't there. Although a couple Farkle teenagers were now looking at me curiously. And Mike was snickering into his hand.

I spun back around to face Zoe, who was now smiling smugly.

"That wasn't funny," I said.

"It sure looks like you're terrified of upsetting Erica to *me*," Zoe observed. "The Ice Queen has way too much power over you than she ought to."

At which point, Erica stepped out of the crowd behind Zoe.

Zoe didn't notice. Instead, she kept right on ranting. "In fact, the Ice Queen has way too much power over *all* of us. . . ."

"Uh, Zoe," I said. "Erica's right behind *you*."

"You think I'm really going to fall for that?" Zoe asked. "Right after I got you with it? Fat chance. We all have to be able to stand up to Erica. Yes, she's a great spy, but she's a lousy human being. She has terrible people skills, she's mean, and she has the emotional range of a tuna fish sandwich. She doesn't care about anything except the mission, even if it means sacrificing her friends to do it."

"You're wrong," I said. In truth, Erica had used me to further a mission plenty of times, but I didn't want to upset her by saying this.

As it was, Erica was staring coldly at the back of Zoe's head. Although, I had no idea if she was angry or not. Erica always stared coldly at people. Zoe had also been right about her having the emotional range of a tuna fish sandwich. More or less. (Occasionally, when Erica had been drugged, she had revealed some emotional depth to me that she had managed to hide from others.)

"It *is* true," Zoe went on. "I know you like her, Ben, but she's practically a robot. A good team leader needs to care about more than just the mission. They need to care about the *team*. They need to understand people. And Erica doesn't. Which makes her leadership skills questionable at best."

"My ability to sneak up on people is quite good, though," Erica said.

Zoe wheeled around, saw Erica, and screamed. Even though she had just chastised me for being afraid of upsetting Erica, she obviously was too. In fact, her scream was so loud that several Farkles dropped their platters of food in surprise.

"It's nothing to be concerned about," Erica told the Farkles. "Cousin Sally here just heard the news about Cousin Hubert losing his arm in the wheat thresher."

The Farkles all nodded knowingly and went back to their business. Apparently, this was a true Farkle story that Erica had picked up from the crowd.

Still, Erica didn't trust them all to mind their own business. She grabbed Zoe by the arm and dragged her back to the buffet. Murray, Mike, and I obediently followed in their wake.

A good number of Farkles must have seen Murray dipping bacon into melted chocolate and decided it was a good idea, because they were now doing it. Others were experimenting with dipping bacon into caramel sauce, sprinkles, and nacho cheese.

Erica found a quiet spot far from any Farkles and doled out key cards to the rest of us. "These are for our lodging. Now, what's going on here?"

"We saw Ashley Sparks and Warren Reeves," I reported. "Zoe thought we should tail them, but I thought we should wait for you to get back."

"Oh, here's a fun fact," Murray added. "Ashley and Warren appear to be a couple."

He was obviously expecting Erica to register surprise. Instead, she barely showed any reaction at all. "That makes sense. She desperately craves attention, and he's so pathetic, he'll slavishly devote himself to anyone in return for the slightest bit of recognition. So if you think about it, they're perfect for each other."

Murray blinked at her, stunned. "How on earth can you know so much about other people's emotions when you don't have any of your own?" he asked.

"Which way were Ashley and Warren heading?" Erica asked.

"Down to the beach," Mike reported.

"I think they were just heading down there to make out," Murray said.

Erica looked at him curiously.

"A lot of people find moonlit beaches romantic," Murray explained. "Ask someone who's human. They'll explain it to you."

Erica ignored this and turned to Zoe. "You should tail them," she said.

"Ha!" Zoe said to me triumphantly. "Told you so!"

Erica looked to Mike. "You go as backup."

"C'mon, Romeo," Zoe said, grabbing Mike's arm and dragging him toward the beach. "We've got work to do."

"Have fun!" Murray said to them, then turned to Erica and me. "I'm gonna get something else to eat. I'm starving." He headed toward the dessert bar for round four.

"Why aren't *we* tailing Ashley and Warren?" I asked Erica. "I'm surprised you trust anyone else to do . . . well, anything, really."

"Ashley and Warren are small potatoes," Erica told me. "You and I have more important things to do."

"Like what?"

"Breaking into SPYDER's penthouse."

I gagged on a bite of hamburger. "You want to break in there? We've barely done any recon on the place! It's probably heavily guarded and filled with people who want us dead."

"We've done as much recon as we can. Breaking in is the only way to find out what SPYDER's plotting. In fact, we better go get ready."

"Now?! When are we going?"

Erica turned to me, her eyes gleaming with excitement. "First chance we get."

SLEEP DEPRIVATION

Luxury Villa 11
Aquarius Resort
March 30
0300 hours

Erica thought we should get some rest before infiltrating SPYDER's penthouse. Thanks to Edna Farkle's credit card, she had scored us some extremely nice accommodations: a luxury villa right on the beach. Erica claimed it wouldn't be conducive to our mission to have us all sharing a single room, and besides, this was the only lodging Aquarius had available. It was actually a house, one of a dozen on the resort property, for large (and wealthy) groups of people to stay in.

It was the kind of place you saw on the cover of glossy travel magazines. There were six bedrooms, seven bathrooms, a kitchen, a living room, a dining room, two balconies, four hammocks, and a private walled garden with a hot tub. The living room alone was nearly the size of my house. Thankfully, there was also a small laundry room, which we put to work right away cleaning our clothes. (There were incredibly plush complimentary robes for us to wear in the meantime.) The ocean was only a few steps across the sand from our door. There were beautiful paintings on the walls, a huge home entertainment system in the living room, and the bathrooms were all polished granite and gleaming fixtures.

My bed was the most comfortable I had ever lain on, the climate control system was set to the perfect temperature, and I could hear the soothing roar of the surf from my room. Unfortunately, I barely got a wink of sleep all night.

I was too keyed up about the mission. When I had originally signed up for Operation Tiger Shark, the plan had sounded far less dangerous: keep an eye on SPYDER and wait for the grown-ups to come do the dirty work. Yet here I was, about to actively infiltrate SPYDER's lair. Yes, Erica would be with me, and she had always been an incredibly competent partner, but SPYDER had a history of being several steps ahead of everyone, Erica included, and my previous attempts to infiltrate their lairs had always ended in disaster.

So I tossed and turned, plagued by visions of things going horribly wrong.

Erica had taken the room next to mine. I hadn't heard a peep from her after she'd shut the door around ten p.m., indicating that she was likely sound asleep. I figured she needed the rest. (After all, she had only pretended to sleep on the jet that morning, lulling the SPYDER operatives into thinking she had dropped her guard.) Then again, she might have still been wide awake, quietly plotting our infiltration. Whatever the case, it was clear she wanted to be alone.

Murray was downstairs in one of the smaller bedrooms. Erica had duct-taped him to the bed to make sure he couldn't run off during the night. Murray had briefly protested this, but then lapsed into a food coma and passed out cold. Evidently, consuming several pounds of bacon and chocolate after a month of trying to be healthy had taken a toll on him.

At eleven thirty, I heard Mike and Zoe return from their reconnaissance mission. Since I was still wide awake, I went downstairs to greet them.

They were checking out the villa, impressed. Mike already had the minibar open and was halfway through a ten-dollar can of Pringles. "Nice digs," he said appreciatively.

"Those are your bedrooms," I said, pointing them out. "Murray's in that one."

"I figured," Zoe said. "The snoring gave it away."

Indeed, Murray was snoring like a chain saw trying to cut through petrified wood.

"What happened with Ashley and Warren?" I asked.

"They didn't go down to the beach for anything romantic," Zoe reported. "There's a little pier down there, for scuba boats and such. Someone met them with a little dinghy and then took them out to that yacht."

"How long were they on it?" I asked.

"I don't know," Mike replied honestly. "We fell asleep."

Zoe wheeled on him, upset he'd revealed this. But she didn't contradict him.

"You fell asleep?" I repeated, failing to hide my annoyance.

"Sorry," Mike said. "But it's been a really long day, and, frankly, surveillance is *boring*. All we were doing was watching a yacht bob up and down on the waves in the dark. That's as dull as dull gets."

"So you don't know if Warren and Ashley are still on the boat or not?" I pressed.

"No idea," Mike admitted—to Zoe's deepening chagrin. "We were out cold for over an hour. That was plenty of time for them to come back."

I looked at Zoe accusingly. "This whole thing was your idea. You do realize what the whole point of surveillance is, right?"

"Obviously not," she said curtly. "I guess we can't all be amazing spies like you." With that, she stormed into her bedroom and slammed the door on me.

Mike gave me a disapproving look. "She was already upset at herself for blowing this. You could have gone a little easier on her."

I sighed. "Sorry."

"I'm not the one you need to apologize to. I'm gonna take another shower before bed. While I was asleep, I got a ton of sand down my pants." Mike shuffled off toward the closest bathroom, scratching his bottom. Sure enough, a cascade of sand spilled out down his pants leg and piled on the floor.

I knocked on Zoe's door. "Hey," I said through it. "It's Ben."

"I *know* it's you," Zoe replied from inside. "I'm not an idiot."

"Oh. Right. I'm sorry if I upset you. Can we talk?"

"Not now, Ben. It's late, and if it wasn't evident when I blew the surveillance, I'm really, really tired."

After that, I had little choice but to return to my room and try to go to sleep again.

Now not only did I have my mission to fret about, but I was also upset about how things were going with Zoe.

Before I'd known about her crush on me, Zoe and I

had always got along great. She'd been my best friend at spy school. But now, things were often awkward between us. It seemed to me that, a month earlier, I could have made a crack about Zoe blowing the surveillance and she wouldn't have taken it personally. She would have teased me back—or put me in a headlock until I begged for forgiveness. But she wouldn't have been hurt and angry.

Then again, maybe I was totally wrong about that. Maybe I had actually upset Zoe before, but hadn't realized it. I found myself wishing people were less complicated, like math. In math, you always knew what the right answer was. Pi was always 3.14159 no matter what, whereas you could say the same thing to the same person at different times and get two wildly different responses. She might think you were funny—or she might think you were an idiot. Or she might think you were the world's biggest jerk.

The hours ticked by. The villa was silent. Everyone else was asleep but me. I tried going out onto the balcony and watching SPYDER's yacht bob up and down on the ocean, since Mike had told me how soporific it was. It didn't make me tired at all. Instead, I found my head full of questions about SPYDER, which woke me up even more.

Who was sequestered on that yacht—and what did they want with Warren and Ashley? Was SPYDER plotting something nefarious again this time, or were they merely lying low? And if they *were* plotting something, what was it?

At three in the morning, I simply gave up. I pulled on my comfy robe and shuffled downstairs again, figuring I could at least watch some TV and distract myself for a while.

Someone else was doing the same thing.

Zoe.

She was also swaddled in one of the complimentary robes, though hers was so big on her, it made her look as if she'd fallen into a snowdrift. She had the TV on, but she'd kept the sound off to avoid waking everyone. She was watching Spanish CNN with subtitles.

This was an extremely awkward moment.

Finally, because I felt I needed to say *something*, I said the only thing I could come up with: "I thought you couldn't read Spanish."

"I can't," Zoe said. "But I can read French, and they're related, so I can kind of put things together. From what I can tell, two people drowned in a freak scuba accident."

I watched the TV for a few moments, reading the subtitles. "Actually, this says two people were eaten by a crocodile."

"Really? Oh. I guess I *can't* really put things together. Add that to the growing list of things I can't do. Like proper surveillance . . ."

"You're not that bad at it. . . ."

"Yes I am. I screwed up, didn't I? Like always. That's why I never get selected for missions like you and Erica. I have to sneak onto them. And then I fail miserably."

I started to contradict Zoe, but something on the TV caught my attention.

Zoe grew even more annoyed. "Ben, this is the part where you're supposed to say something reassuring, like *No you don't.* Or *We all make mistakes.* Or *I was an idiot for making you feel bad tonight.*"

"Sorry," I said. "It's just . . . The people who got eaten by the crocodile today . . . They were parachutists. According to the news, they landed in a lake and the croc got them."

Zoe forgot all about being irritated at me and grew worried instead. "Were they the pilots of our plane?"

"There wasn't enough left to identify them, but I'm guessing that's the case."

"So what do you think *really* happened? SPYDER killed them and fed them to the croc to make it look like an accident?"

"Probably. SPYDER doesn't like to leave loose ends. And Dane Brammage is here. His job is to get rid of loose ends. Like anyone causing trouble for SPYDER."

"So if SPYDER finds out we're alive, we'll end up crocodile chow too."

It wasn't a question. Zoe knew the answer as well as I did.

I changed the channel, looking for something lighter. All I could find was a rerun of some bizarre Spanish game show, but it was better than seeing footage of the gruesome fate of the agents who had betrayed us. I sank onto the couch beside Zoe without really thinking about it.

"Why do you like Erica?" Zoe asked suddenly. She no longer seemed frustrated with me. Facing your own mortality can have that affect. I got the sense this was a question she'd been wanting to ask for a long time.

Still, it caught me by surprise. "What do you mean?"

"I just don't get it. It's not only you. Every guy at school has a crush on her. I mean, I understand that she's beautiful and talented and all but . . . shouldn't there be more to it than that? Don't you guys ever think about a girl's personality? Because Erica doesn't really have one."

"You know that's not true."

"Fine. She has one, but it's not very pleasant."

"Erica's not that bad. You don't know her the way I do."

"True. But you had a crush on her *before* you knew her well, and back then, she was nothing except cold and mean and manipulative to you."

"No she wasn't."

"Ben, she consistently put you in danger to further her own agenda."

"Maybe, but her agenda was to protect our country."

"Would you listen to yourself?" Zoe exclaimed. "You're actually defending her for doing awful things to you! And no matter how much you think she's changed, she's *still* doing awful things to you."

"That's not true. . . ."

"Really? Think about *this* mission. Erica talked you into doing it, didn't she?"

I thought about that for a moment, then admitted, "Kind of."

"How?"

"She said it'd be easy. And maybe even fun."

"Ha!" Zoe laughed. "She manipulated you! She *never* thought this would be easy. I'll bet she was expecting this thing to go south all along."

"I don't think so."

"Then why did she fake being asleep on the plane all morning? She knew SPYDER was plotting a trap, and she brought you along as bait."

I stared at the TV for a bit, reviewing everything that had happened over the past day. To my dismay, I realized Zoe was probably right. Erica would have been willing to do anything to take down SPYDER, including walking into a double cross. But she knew the mission wouldn't happen without me, so she'd talked me into coming and hidden the truth from me.

"You know it's true, don't you?" Zoe asked.

"Okay, I admit that Erica has put me in danger a few times. But she has always saved me from that danger too. And her plans have always worked out."

"Oh yeah," Zoe said sarcastically. "This morning worked out perfectly. The whole part where we almost got blown up by a missile and eaten by crocodiles and then nearly died in the jungle couldn't have gone better. We were lucky to survive, Ben! Mike and I might have stowed away on that plane, but she *conned* you onto it. She risked your life for this mission."

"I don't think she imagined it would be this dangerous."

"Of course she did. Face it. Erica might be a great spy, but the mission is all she *ever* cares about. She is cold and ruthless, and she couldn't give a rat's patootie about anyone else—and yet all the guys at school fall all over themselves like a bunch of pathetic lapdogs whenever she's around." Zoe took a few moments to screw up her courage, then said, "I might not be anywhere near as good a spy as Erica, but I'm a much better person. I'm nice and I'm smart and I'm fun. So why don't guys like me more than her?"

"Warren liked you more than her," I pointed out.

"Yeah. And look how well that turned out. I'm not talking about Warren. . . ." Zoe trailed off, embarrassed about continuing the thought, but it was evident where it was going, even for someone as generally clueless about girls as me. She wanted to know why *I* had never noticed she was all those things.

But I didn't answer her right away. Because, while I *knew* Zoe was all those things, I was now struck, once again, by how pretty she was. And now she was sitting only inches away from me, in a fancy villa with the roar of the surf close by, bathed in the delicate glow of the TV.

I had only kissed one girl in my life, and that had been the very brief kiss with Erica when we thought a nuclear bomb was about to vaporize us. A kiss that Erica later claimed was merely to distract me from my imminent death.

At that moment, I very much wanted my second kiss to be with Zoe Zibbell. And I was quite sure she wanted me to kiss her. And I was additionally sure that a kiss without the threat of nuclear annihilation would probably be even better than the first.

But as much as I wanted to kiss Zoe, I didn't. I *almost* did. I leaned forward, then hesitated and pulled back.

I did it for reasons that I thought were right. And yet it immediately seemed to be the wrong thing to do. Zoe looked as though I'd offended her. "So you *don't* like me," she said.

"No!" I protested. "I do! But . . ."

"But you like Erica more."

"I didn't say that!"

"Then what's wrong with me?"

"Nothing!"

"Well, obviously something must be. Because you still seem hung up on Erica."

"That's not why I—"

"She's no good for you," Zoe interrupted coldly. "Her nickname is Ice Queen for a reason. If you want to keep pining away for her, I can't stop you—but I also can't keep hanging around, waiting for you to change your mind. I might not be as awesome or amazing as Erica, but I'm not chopped liver, either. Sooner or later, I'll get over you, and then I'm going to move on. And if it takes you that long to realize Erica is a no-go situation, it will be too late. Understand?"

"Yes," I said, hoping that I really did. "Um . . . Do you have any idea how long I have to figure this out?"

Zoe rolled her eyes in exasperation. "You mean, you want an exact timetable for my emotional state? I'm a human being, Ben, not a train station."

"I know," I said. Even though I really had been hoping for an exact timetable.

"Just know this," Zoe warned. "However strongly you feel about Erica, it doesn't go both ways. Maybe she cares a little bit about you, but she cares much more about being a spy. If she had to choose between saving your life or thwarting SPYDER, she'd thwart SPYDER."

"That's not true," I said hotly.

"Actually, it is," Erica said.

Zoe and I leapt to our feet, startled, and found Erica standing in the shadows by the stairs.

"How long have you been listening to us?" I asked.

"Long enough." Erica stepped forward. She was now dressed for action in her freshly laundered black suit and her utility belt. "Zoe is right, Ben. I've said it to you before, but evidently it hasn't sunk in: Friendships are a liability in the spy game, and an organization like SPYDER knows how to exploit them. Sooner or later, they'll try it. And when that happens, all of us need to be prepared to sacrifice the others for the greater good. That might sound awful, but if we can't do it, SPYDER will win."

"Told you," Zoe said to me under her breath.

Erica gave her an icy stare. "Sometimes you don't have the option to be a good person if you want to save the world," she said. Then she tossed me my clothes, fresh from the dryer. "Get dressed, Ben. It's time to get to work."

PREPARATION

Luxury Villa 11

Aquarius Resort

March 30

0330 hours

I considered the clothes in my hands. Erica had compulsively folded them perfectly so they looked like they had just come from the store. The mere thought of putting them on and going up against SPYDER filled me with dread. I looked to Erica. "We're going *right now*?"

"Statistically, this time of the night is the best for infiltrating an enemy hideout. Their guards will be bored and tired." Erica checked her watch. "Although, if you need a little extra time to get mentally prepared, I can spare ninety seconds."

I turned to Zoe. I still hadn't got the chance to explain why I hadn't kissed her. But I didn't have any idea how to even begin, let alone how to do it in only ninety seconds.

"Ticktock," Erica warned. "Time's wasting."

"You should go," Zoe told me.

So I slipped into the downstairs bathroom and dressed as quickly as I could, whacking my elbow on the sink twice in my haste. I also went to the bathroom. I had already gone a dozen times that night, but it always made sense to have your bladder bone-dry before a mission. I was back out the door and ready to go in a mere eighty-eight seconds.

Erica still seemed annoyed that I hadn't been faster. "Let's move," she said.

We exited onto the beach and worked our way down the hard-packed sand along the edge of the water. There was no moon visible, and we were far enough from civilization to be free of light pollution. Back in DC, we were lucky if we could see ten stars on a good night. Here, there were millions. The resort still had a few lights on, illuminating walkways so tourists didn't tumble into any of the swimming pools by accident, but those barely made a dent in the darkness. Across the resort complex, SPYDER's penthouse was merely an even darker shadow against the night sky. I couldn't see Dane Brammage or any of the other guards—but I knew they were up there.

Meanwhile, on the other side of us, the yacht was a similarly dark and lifeless shape out on the ocean.

Even though Aquarius had a very large staff, no one was awake down by the beach at that exceptionally early hour. Which was certainly another reason Erica had chosen to launch our mission then. There were no tourists, either. Even the Farkles, who had seemed to be a stay-up-late-to-party bunch, were nowhere to be seen, save for one in his early twenties who was passed out on the beach, snoring gently.

We arrived at the pier from which Warren and Ashley had caught the dinghy to the yacht. Nine motorboats of various shapes and sizes were moored to it, lazily rocking in the surf: two midsize, flat-bottomed scuba-and-snorkel cruise boats, two large fishing boats, and five smaller, sleeker speedboats. On the beach, not far from the pier, sat the activity shack. The shack was quite large but was designed to look run-down, like it was a quaint local business, with wooden walls that were slightly askew and a palm-frond roof, but all this was merely set dressing. Beneath it all, the shack was actually a thoroughly modern building, with plumbing and air-conditioning and a high-end security system that would have deterred most people.

Erica wasn't most people, though. She dismantled the alarm and picked both locks on the door in a mere forty-three seconds. Then she led the way inside, shut the door behind us, tossed me a penlight, and flicked on her own.

Inside, the shack didn't even pretend to be quaint. It was dull and utilitarian: cinder-block walls, cement floor, and fluorescent lights (which we didn't turn on). A big resort like Aquarius needed lots of sporting equipment: Long racks of it lined the walls and filled the interior. Our puny penlights only dimly illuminated a fraction of it all.

There were no guards on duty. Erica and I were alone and far from where anyone might overhear us. So I took the opportunity to ask the question burning inside me. "Did you really believe this whole mission with Murray was a setup from the very beginning?"

Erica sighed, like she was annoyed that I was squandering precious time with this, then said, "Of course."

I was stunned by the bluntness of her answer. "And yet, you talked me into coming along?"

"It wouldn't have happened without you." Erica started down an aisle of scuba gear. "And it was our best chance to get close to SPYDER."

"You said it was going to be easy!" I exclaimed. "You said it might even be fun!"

"Yes. I lied to you."

"Why?"

"Because if I'd told you the truth, you wouldn't have come."

"I could have been killed!"

"But you weren't. You're welcome, by the way." Erica grabbed a mesh bag designed for carrying scuba supplies.

"Welcome for what?" I asked. "Saving me *after* you put my life in danger in the first place?"

"No. For putting you in a position to help take down SPYDER. You can avenge every bad thing they've ever done to you *and* make the world a safer place. Most people never get the chance to make a difference like that. Very few spies even do. But we have it now, and we need to take advantage of it. So I'd really appreciate it if you could go find me a speargun."

"A speargun?" I repeated, more dully than I'd intended. I was thrown, not only by the sudden change of topic, but by the fact that Erica's argument had actually been convincing. It seemed I should be livid at her for manipulating me, and yet I had to admit she had a good point.

"Yes." Erica slung the mesh bag over her shoulder and headed off to find more gear. "Check the fishing supplies."

"Wouldn't it be better to have a *real* gun?"

"I doubt they stock real guns here. And even so, it's not for defense." Erica faded into the darkness before I could ask what it *was* for. Although, knowing Erica, there was a good chance she wouldn't have answered anyhow.

I stood there a while longer, reeling from our conversation.

I was annoyed at Erica for manipulating me, but equally annoyed at myself for letting her do it. I felt I should have been wiser about SPYDER's motives, or savvier about Erica, or a better spy in general. And as worried as I was about the upcoming mission, Erica had struck a nerve: I *did* want to take down SPYDER, make the world a safer place, and avenge every last thing they'd ever done to me. So I set off to find a speargun.

I passed all sorts of other gear: bundled-up volleyball nets; bins full of Frisbees and smashball paddles; supplies for bocce, cornhole, and badminton; and plastic tubs of snorkels and scuba masks soaking in disinfectant. Finally, I found the fishing gear. There was a staggering amount of it, indicating that fishing was a very popular pastime at Aquarius. Hundreds of fishing poles were racked along one wall, with shelves full of replacement parts beside them. Tackle boxes the size of suitcases lined the floor.

It was only now that I realized I had no idea what a speargun actually looked like. I hadn't ever seen one. It wasn't the sort of thing one came across that often in suburban Virginia. There had probably been one in a James Bond movie at some point, but my memories of those were hazy at best. Of course, I could have asked Erica what to look for, but that would have merely annoyed her and lessened her respect for me. So I poked around, hoping to find the right thing.

Eventually, I did—although I found plenty of wrong things first: water skis, pogo sticks, pool floats, a large gecko that had somehow got inside. The spearguns were hanging on the wall well to the side of the fishing poles. They looked like someone had mated a crossbow with a BB gun: long and thin, with a trigger at one end. The spears didn't launch with gunpowder, but a far more rudimentary elastic sling system. I grabbed what I suspected was the proper spear—a long silver shaft with a nasty barbed tip on the end—and slotted it into place to make sure everything was working properly.

"What's taking so long?" Erica asked, suddenly right behind me. If her ability to suddenly appear in broad daylight was occasionally unsettling, doing it in the dark-and-spooky shack was downright frightening. I yelped in surprise, accidentally pulled the trigger, and launched a spear across the room, where it butchered a volleyball. The ball exploded with an exceedingly loud bang that echoed through the room.

Erica glared at me in the darkness. "Given that this is a covert mission, it'd be nice if you tried to be quiet."

"It'd be nice if you tried not to scare the pants off me," I replied.

Erica snatched the speargun from my hands, then grabbed a few extra spears for it, which seemed to confirm that I'd at least found the right thing. In the time it had taken me to locate it, she had amassed a large amount of other supplies, which were all stuffed into the mesh gear bag. I spotted a spool of fishing line, some zip-line rigs, and a few rock-climbing harnesses. Erica also had an eight-inch fish-gutting knife newly holstered on her utility belt.

While the knife was disconcerting, it was the climbing harnesses that concerned me the most. "Are you planning for us to *climb* up to the penthouse?"

"*Can* you climb up to the penthouse?" Erica asked.

"Er . . . I don't think so."

"That kind of answers your question, doesn't it? I wasn't planning on it, though. The last thing I need is for you to get yourself into trouble while we're dangling eight stories up on the side of the building."

"So how are we getting all the way up to the penthouse?" I asked.

Erica dropped a large silk bundle onto the floor in front of me. "Isn't it obvious?" she asked. "We fly."

INFILTRATION

Manta Ray Bay
Aquarius Resort
March 30
0400 hours

The silk bundle Erica had found turned out to be
a parasail. When unwrapped, it was forty feet across and
a grotesque neon green—though, thankfully, you couldn't
see that in the night. A harness for two people was attached
in the middle. It was designed for an instructor to take out
first-timers, so one person was directly behind the other. That
was good news, as it meant Erica and I could use it together,
but we still needed a third person to get us into the air.

Which was where Mike came in.

Mike knew how to drive a motorboat. His family had one. It wasn't anything fancy, but it worked. On summer weekends, they took it down to Chesapeake Bay to go water-skiing.

While Erica unfurled the parasail on the pier and organized her gear, I ran back to the villa and woke Mike. I didn't even have to explain the entire mission for him. I only got as far as "Erica and I need you to drive a boat for us" before he said "Sure thing" and hopped out of bed.

Mike and I were back at the pier less than six minutes after I'd left. Erica already had the parasail rigged up and attached to one of the speedboats. She tossed Mike the keys to it as he approached, then gave him explicit orders as to what she wanted him to do.

Mike didn't question anything. He simply saluted and hopped behind the wheel of the boat.

Erica helped me get into the harness, slung the mesh gear bag over her shoulder, then strapped herself in behind me and gave Mike a thumbs-up. Mike unmoored the boat from the pier, turned on the ignition, and pushed the throttle forward. The boat sped away, and the coil of rope connecting us to it quickly unspooled into the water.

Due to the way the harness worked, Erica was pressed right against my back. When she spoke, she barely had to whisper, as her mouth was right next to my ear. "Careful," she warned calmly. "There's going to be a slight jerk as we take off."

Three seconds later, the last of the rope played out, and then the whole line snapped taut.

As was the case with many of the things Erica said, "a slight jerk" turned out to be an understatement. It felt as though I was in a car wreck, but in reverse. Instead of slamming to a stop, my body was suddenly yanked forward at great speed. My head whipped back so fast, I might have smashed Erica's nose if her head hadn't also done the same thing. We were instantly jerked off the pier and into the air. Luckily, the parasail billowed out behind us just as quickly. Instead of dropping into the water, we were now yanked backward almost as violently as we had been yanked forward a second earlier. The sail caught the air, and we rose upward so fast, my ears popped. Normally, parasails only went up twenty to thirty feet, but Erica had tied several tethers together. Before I knew it, we were ten stories above the water, the motorboat so far below us, it looked like a bathtub toy.

I was surprised to find that, despite dangling from a thin piece of fabric high above the ground, I wasn't that afraid of falling to my death. Though this was probably because there were so many other things to be afraid of at the moment: being captured by SPYDER, being killed by SPYDER, screwing up the mission in front of Erica. Compared to infiltrating an enemy hideout, parasailing was quite peaceful and almost relaxing.

I had been concerned that the motorboat's sound might draw attention, but between the roar of the surf and the wind rustling the palm trees along the shore, the beach was surprisingly noisy, and the thrum of the motor was swallowed up. From our high vantage point, we couldn't even differentiate its sound from the ocean's—which was hopefully the case for any guards stationed at the penthouse as well. Even so, Erica had instructed Mike to keep his distance from the yacht anchored offshore. Instead, Mike paralleled the beach in the opposite direction, then hooked a sharp turn and headed back for the pier.

There were two extremely simple controls for the parasail: cloth handles that Erica could yank on, tugging us left or right. Erica pulled on the left-hand one, and we made a graceful curve in the air, dropping in behind the boat as it raced back toward the resort complex.

When the boat reached Aquarius once again, Erica whipped the fish knife from her holster and cleanly sliced through the tether, cutting us free. The line dropped away into the ocean below.

Parasailing no longer seemed quite so peaceful or relaxing. My entire body tensed in preparation for confronting SPYDER.

Erica pulled on the left handle again, harder this time. We veered inland, soaring over the outer reaches of the resort. Darkened villas and swimming pools swiftly passed far beneath my feet. Ahead of us, the main pyramid of the central building loomed.

The penthouse remained shrouded in darkness. The balconies were impossible to make out—as were any guards who might have been patrolling them.

"Are you sure the guards won't see us?" I asked.

Erica replied, "It's a little bit late to be asking that now, don't you think?"

"There's still time to abort," I said, then thought to add, "Isn't there?"

"The guards aren't going to be anything to worry about," Erica told me. "They're watching a sleeping resort for the two hundredth night in a row. Nothing's happened in all those previous nights. They probably assume nothing's going to happen tonight, either. Especially at this hour. If anyone's even on patrol, they've probably nodded off by now."

That made sense—and yet it seemed counter to the whole idea of guarding a hideout. If you got hired as a guard, you knew you were signing up for exceptionally long periods of boredom. For this reason, the job tended to attract dim-witted thugs, people who *liked* the idea of not having to do anything for eight hours at a stretch. Or worse, sadists who were so excited to do harm to someone, they sat up all night, eagerly scanning the skies for any incoming enemies that they could kill.

We homed in closer, passing over the Coco Loco Lounge. Mike's boat was now far enough away that it had disappeared into the night.

A light flicked on in one of the windows of the penthouse.

It was only a single lamp, but in the pitch-black night, it was almost blinding.

Erica stiffened behind me, apparently surprised that someone at SPYDER was awake.

Whoever had turned it on wasn't looking out the window, though. And they seemed to be the only person awake in the complex. By now, we were close enough that I could make out distinct shapes on the balcony. I could see the tufted forms of potted palms, the mushroom caps of patio umbrellas—and a great deal of gymnastics equipment. Located away from the railing, where we hadn't been able to see it from below, was a set of uneven bars, a pommel horse, a balance beam, and a trampoline.

"Looks like Ashley's keeping in shape," Erica observed.

There was also a guard on the balcony. A big, imposing slab of muscle. However, as Erica had predicted, he was asleep, slumped in a deck chair by the railing.

He didn't even stir as we drifted ten feet over his head. We crossed above the rest of the balcony, then came to the roof of the penthouse. Erica dropped us down perfectly atop it, then dug in her heels. We came to a pinpoint stop, and the parasail collapsed behind us.

Since the roof of the penthouse was the highest point at Aquarius, and thus couldn't be seen from anywhere else at the resort, no one had made any attempt to beautify it. It was an ugly, flat expanse of tar paper, dotted with ventilation ducts, water pipes, and industrial-size air conditioners. The air conditioners were humming busily, easily covering the sounds of our arrival. We detached ourselves from the harness, but when I went to bundle it up again, Erica shook her head and said, "Don't." Given the noise of the A/C units, she could speak normally without fear of being overheard.

Even so, I whispered back. "Why not?"

"In case we have to leave in a hurry."

I considered the parasail wadded in my hands. "You mean . . . we'd jump off the building?"

"How did you *think* we'd be leaving? The elevator?"

"Er . . . ," I said. Because, up until that moment, I had been so concerned about how we were getting into the penthouse, I hadn't given any thought to how we'd leave it. Taking the elevator might have been reckless, but it still seemed infinitely safer than jumping off a building and hoping that the parasail deployed fully enough on the way down to prevent us from splatting onto the pavement.

"Relax," Erica told me. "That's only the backup."

"What's the primary?" I asked.

"This." Erica removed the speargun from the mesh bag and calmly fired it off the roof.

At some point while I'd been fetching Mike, she had affixed a spool of fishing line to the spear. The line spun out behind the projectile, which disappeared into the darkness and impaled something in the far distance that I couldn't see. Given that whatever it hit didn't scream in agony, I assumed it wasn't human.

"That's our *primary* escape route?" I asked, aghast. "Going down a fishing line?"

"Calm down. It's eight-hundred-pound test line. You can land a marlin with it. It ought to hold us just fine." Erica calmly sliced through the line with the gutting knife and then efficiently tied it to a standpipe.

"*Ought* to hold us?" I repeated. "You just cut through it with your knife!"

"I don't recall either of us having knife blades for hands." Erica didn't put the knife back in its sheath. Instead, she found a large ventilation duct, jabbed the blade under the edge of the grating, and pried it up. The grating easily popped free, and Erica deftly caught it before it clattered onto the roof.

She pressed a finger to her lips, indicating there should be no more arguments from me, then lowered herself through the hole into the ventilation system.

I reluctantly followed her. The ventilation system was pretty much the *last* place I wanted to go, but I wasn't about to let Erica do this solo. A cardinal rule of being a spy was that you never let a partner go anyplace dangerous alone— and a cardinal rule of being partners with Erica was that if you didn't follow her plan, you would lose her respect.

The ventilation duct was cramped and claustrophobia inducing. Erica could barely fit inside it with the gear bag slung on her back. We had to move by wriggling along with our arms folded beneath us. I was staring at Erica's feet, which turned out to be the one part of her body that didn't smell fantastic. Plus, SPYDER had the air-conditioning cranked to eleven, so arctic air blew through the ducts, refrigerating us.

Every once in a while, we would come to a slatted grating that allowed us a peek into the room below it. Erica paused at each, scoping out the rooms before silently moving on. Thus, I arrived at each only after she had already been there.

The first looked down into the bedroom of Ashley Sparks. Ashley was asleep, though she was having a terrible dream. She writhed back and forth restlessly under the sheets, murmuring, "That's not fair! I stuck the landing! I stuck the landing!"

The next room was also a bedroom, although the bed appeared to be empty—at first. It was only after I had stared at it for a few seconds that I realized Warren Reeves was actually in it. Even while asleep, he naturally camouflaged himself. His pale skin blended in perfectly with the white sheets, and he slumbered without sound or movement.

Next came the bedroom for Dane Brammage. While Warren seemed lost in his bed, Dane was way too big for his. His feet jutted past the end, his huge shoulders extended the width of it, and the whole piece of furniture was buckling beneath his bulk. While Dane was sound asleep, he still seemed primed for action. I got the impression that, if need be, he could snap awake instantly, ready to kill or maim anyone who warranted it. His presence so disturbed me that I froze, looking down at him for way too long. When I finally pried my attention from him, Erica had disappeared.

I scuttled along as fast as I could to catch up with her—although that wasn't very fast. For a few, desperate moments, I feared that she might have left the ventilation system altogether, abandoning me in the ceiling.

But then I rounded a corner and found her. She was several feet ahead of me, and she must have taken a different route to this point, because she was now turned in my direction, so I could see her face, not her feet. There were two gratings looking down into the room below us. Erica was on the far side of the first, while I was arriving at the second.

Light beamed up into the duct from the room below, sliced into thin beams by the gratings. This was obviously the room that we had seen the light come on in during our approach. The sounds of a conversation filtered up into the duct as well.

I stopped at the closer grating and peered down through it into the room below.

If my spine hadn't already been freezing, a chill would have gone up it.

Joshua Hallal sat directly beneath me.

Joshua had once been one of the most promising students at spy school, but he had switched sides to become one of the most promising evildoers at SPYDER. He was only five years older than me, but he had been a true evil prodigy, quickly working his way up through SPYDER to become one of its highest-ranking members. (There were others above him, but I—and the CIA—didn't know their identities yet.) He was cruel, he was dangerous—and worst of all, he had a big grudge against me. While running away from me after I had thwarted his plans the previous summer, he had been horribly disfigured. That hadn't really been my fault, but he still blamed me. He had lost a leg, an arm, and an eye in the incident.

The room below me was the dining room for the penthouse suite, but it was being used as more of a conference room. Joshua sat at one end of the dining table with three items before him: a stack of important-looking documents that were too far away for me to read, a phone, and a small, sleek device with a single red button on it.

It had been seven months since I'd last seen Joshua, back at SPYDER's evil headquarters. He had fled those before they had blown up. I had no idea where he'd been in the interim—although I could guess at least a small portion of that time had been spent at a hospital. Before, Joshua's missing hand had been replaced with a hook, which was scary but not very practical. Now, that had been exchanged for something much more high-tech: a prosthetic metal hand. There was no fake skin on it; instead, it seemed that pains had been taken to show off how nonhuman it was. It was skeletal in its design. The metal had been precision sculpted and polished until it gleamed. Although it was far less medieval than the hook, this new version was even more menacing. It lay flat on the table below me, one finger tapping against the wood. That simple motion, and the rhythmic *tap, tap, tap,* was terrifying.

Joshua seemed well aware of this. It appeared that he was

doing his best to terrify the other person in the room with him.

I had been so focused on Joshua, I didn't even notice the other man until he spoke. He was sitting at the opposite end of the dining table. He was considerably older than Joshua, in his fifties, I guessed, and not nearly as frightening. In fact, given that he was attached to SPYDER, he was about the least frightening person I could have ever imagined. He was meek and twitchy, his skin moist from nervous perspiration, his eyes nearly obscured behind thick glasses. It was hard to tell how tall he was, as his posture was stooped and cowering. He was on the phone, speaking to someone else in an anxious, stuttering style that betrayed an air of permanent embarrassment. There was a slight English accent in his voice.

"Is that . . . well . . . I mean . . . has it happened, then?" he stammered. "Are we . . . or you . . . er . . . what I meant was . . . then it's done?" He waited a moment, then nodded agreement, even though the person on the other end of the line couldn't possibly see him doing it. Then, after an uncomfortable pause, he realized he needed to actually give his agreement out loud. "Oh . . . right. That's good, then . . . isn't it? Okay . . . yes . . . right . . . if you say so. Well then . . . good-bye." He hung up, mopped his brow, and looked skittishly toward Joshua. "Celeste has arrived in Ushuaia."

"Good," Joshua said. And yet, somehow even that single

word was ominous enough to make the man at the other end of the table cringe.

"So . . . ," the other man said, almost apologetically. "Since the . . . ah . . . the goods have been . . . well, delivered . . . and that's . . . er . . . the, uh, the . . . well, the last batch . . . then you . . . if it's no imposition, really . . . you see, I uh . . . well, there's the matter of . . . the matter of payment due. Which would be . . . ah . . . two billion dollars."

I looked up at Erica, shocked by this amount. She didn't budge at all and continued peering down through the grating, but I still got the sense the sum of money had caught her by surprise as well.

Rather than answer the other man, Joshua reached up with his good hand and toyed with something that hung on a thin chain around his neck. With many people, this wouldn't have been threatening at all, but like everything Joshua did, it somehow seemed malicious. I couldn't see what the object on the chain was, but the mere activity of Joshua stroking it made the nervous man shift even more uncomfortably in his seat.

After a few seconds, the phone on the table by Joshua buzzed with a text. Joshua let the object on the chain fall back beneath his shirt, picked up the phone, and read the message. "My source in Ushuaia confirms Celeste's arrival and says everything looks to be in order with her."

"Good!" the nervous man exclaimed. "Then you will . . . er . . . ah . . . um . . ."

"Issue payment? That seems only right. After all, you have provided our organization with exactly what we wanted, Mr. Lee."

I looked up at Erica once again, even more shocked now. Erica was looking at me, prepared for this.

That's Paul Lee? I mouthed silently.

Erica nodded curtly, then returned her attention to the conversation below.

So did I, although I was having trouble believing the high-strung, unimpressive man facing Joshua Hallal could possibly be the Paul Lee I had heard about before. That man, according to Erica, was one of the world's most ruthless arms dealers, a criminal she had described as "real scum of the earth." I had envisioned someone cruel, conniving, and equally as menacing as Joshua Hallal, quite likely with a bald head and a nasty scar across his face, and also possibly with a Maltese cat in his lap, which he would stroke in an intimidating fashion. (I admit it, I had imagined that he looked exactly like Blofeld from the James Bond movies, which was stereotyping.) Instead, Paul Lee was a wretched, squirming milquetoast.

He looked at Joshua now and smiled weakly, revealing a mouthful of teeth that appeared to have never been subjected to any sort of dental hygiene. They were crooked and brownish and no two pointed in the same direction. "Right, then. So let's . . . if it's okay with you, we could . . . er . . . I mean, the funds . . . well, they . . . the transferring thing could happen . . . ah, well . . . Would now be good?"

"No," Joshua said.

"Excellent!" Paul Lee said cheerfully, and then frowned as he realized that Joshua hadn't said anything to be cheerful about. "Er, wait. Did you . . . was that . . . did you say no?"

"Yes."

Paul Lee's rheumy eyes blinked moistly behind his thick glasses. "But . . . but . . . you . . . well, you owe me . . ."

"Two billion dollars?" Joshua finished. "Yes, we do owe you that. And as I said, issuing payment only seems right. But as you may recall, Mr. Lee . . . We here at SPYDER are evil. We *never* do what is right." With his good hand, he produced a gun from underneath his jacket and aimed it across the table.

Paul Lee started in fear, then tried to compose himself. He didn't do a very good job. He was fidgeting so nervously, he almost smacked himself in the face several times with his own hands. "But I, er, I thought . . . that, uh, well . . . I mean, I suspected that . . . Point is, I wouldn't do that. . . . Well, you see, this is why I brought . . ." He gave up on explaining himself and yelled, "Dane! I need you!"

There was a great deal of noise from the room we had just passed. As I had suspected, even in sleep, Dane Brammage was prepared for action. Through the ventilation system, I heard the pained groan of his bed as he sat up in it, the thud of his enormous feet hitting the floor, and then pounding as he raced through the hall. He burst into the dining room, a gun clenched in his hand. He would probably have been terrifying if his pajamas hadn't been decorated with baby ducks.

His arrival gave Paul Lee an unusual burst of confidence. "You kill me," he told Joshua, "and Dane kills *you*."

Joshua didn't appear the slightest bit concerned about this. In fact, he seemed amused. "Sorry to say this, old chap, but Dane here isn't as loyal as you thought. Turns out, it was a lot cheaper to buy him off than it would be to pay you that two billion."

Dane shifted slightly, so his gun was now pointed at Paul Lee as well. If he was embarrassed about switching sides, he didn't show it. His expression remained as implacable as always.

I wouldn't have thought that Paul Lee could have looked more pathetic than he already did, but he now proved me wrong. He shrank even smaller in his chair and began quivering in fear. His speech, which had barely been functional at normal times, now became completely unintelligible.

"Urk," he gibbered. "Murm . . . phlepthhh . . . yarp . . ."

I looked at Erica, worried.

She met my gaze coldly and gave me the same slight shake of her head that she had given me on the street during the robbery two days before. The message was the same: Don't get involved.

"Here's something else you'll find interesting," Joshua was telling Paul Lee gleefully, really enjoying himself. "Remember that two billion we already paid you to get this deal going? Well, we've had access to your Swiss bank account the entire time. If you care to check it, you'll see that we've taken our money back. And the rest of your money as well. After all, you won't be needing it when you're dead."

Paul Lee gawped at him. It seemed that he wanted to say something insulting, but in his fear and rage, he couldn't even form words.

I watched the entire scene play out below in horror. In my gut, I knew Erica was right: We shouldn't get involved. We were supposed to be on a reconnaissance mission, finding out what SPYDER was plotting. We had one great advantage over them: They thought we were dead and thus had no reason to suspect that we were even at the resort, let alone lurking in the ventilation system above their heads. But if I did anything stupid—like trying to save Paul Lee—I would instantly give away that advantage. And I would be putting myself in direct and grave danger to boot. Danger that I was completely unprepared to handle.

However, the alternative was idly sitting by and watching a man die. An evil man, yes. A man who probably would have happily ordered my own death, in fact. But he was still a human being.

Despite all my adventures with the CIA, I had never seen anyone die before. I *thought* I had seen men die, but both those men—Joshua and Dane—happened to be alive and well in the room below me, so maybe that didn't count. In any case, I hadn't enjoyed witnessing what I thought were their deaths, and, thus, I was really, really sure that I didn't want to witness this one.

I looked back at Erica again.

She was frowning menacingly at me, really wanting me to get the picture. *No,* she mouthed silently.

Paul Lee was in a terrible state now. He was trembling so badly, his glasses were jouncing up and down on his nose, and his standard sheen of sweat was now a tidal wave. If Joshua didn't shoot him soon, he would probably die from dehydration. He made a desperate attempt to say something, but couldn't even manage a real word. "Flommenflirk!" he yelled at Joshua accusingly, then seemed to realize that hadn't been what he was hoping for at all. "Gimpgrackle!" he tried again. "Pudwhanger!"

Joshua laughed, finding this all very amusing. "Are you trying to insult me?"

"Klumblebarf!" Paul shrieked. "Zingofloom!"

Joshua clucked his tongue. "As much as I'd like to stay here all night, listening to you try to speak coherently for once, I have lots of things to attend to. So . . ." He looked to Dane. "Take care of him, will you?"

Dane raised the gun in his hand toward Paul.

Erica glared at me, a final warning to stay where I was.

I glanced down through the grating, knowing that trying to stop Dane would be idiotic, rash, reckless, foolish, imprudent, and insubordinate. Not to mention it would also probably be completely ineffective, and I'd only get myself and Erica killed.

But I did it anyhow.

AQUATICS

Penthouse Suite

Aquarius Resort

March 30

0430 hours

Before I even knew what I was doing, I punched
the grating out of the vent below me, then swung through
the hole and launched myself at Dane Brammage.

The first two steps of this process went surprisingly well.
The grating fell out easily, and I swung through the hole with
an agility I wasn't even aware I had.

The third part didn't go nearly as smoothly.

From the look on Dane's face, I could tell that I had
caught him by surprise. My whole plan was to slam into him,

knocking him off-balance and keeping him from shooting Paul Lee. After that, I hadn't really prepared anything. My plan was basically "Hope that Erica comes to my rescue."

I slammed right into Dane, as intended, but I didn't knock him off-balance. He was simply too big. Instead, he stayed firmly rooted to his spot while I glanced off him harmlessly and wound up sprawled on the dining table.

I *did* manage to scare Paul Lee half to death with this maneuver, though. As he was already severely stressed out, my sudden appearance pushed him over the edge. He screamed in terror and collapsed to the floor, unconscious.

Dane looked at me, his face muddied with confusion, as though he was trying to place where he'd seen me before while at the same time trying to grasp where I'd come from. This distraction was what kept him from shooting at Paul Lee, rather than anything I had done to him physically.

Joshua Hallal wasn't nearly as thrown. "Ripley!" he yelled, quickly piecing together that 1) I wasn't dead and 2) I'd been spying on him. He sprang from his seat and pointed his own gun toward me.

I was still flat on my back in the middle of the dining table, with nowhere to hide.

Luckily, Erica did come to my rescue. She punched out her own grating and swung through the hole, with even more finesse than I had done. She held on to the edge of the ventilation duct and drove her feet right into Dane's face.

Even though Erica wasn't any bigger than me, her attack was much more effective. Dane didn't fall, but he did get knocked off-balance. He stumbled backward and slammed into Joshua, which might not have been too bad if Dane had been a normal-size person. For Joshua, however, it was like getting hit by a truck. He was bowled off his feet. And the shot he intended for me went wide, ricocheting off a decorative vase and shattering the window.

Joshua landed on the floor in a heap, a murderous glint in his eye. He still had his gun clutched in his hand, and he would have squeezed off another shot at me . . .

Had Erica not nailed Dane with a flying roundhouse kick to the face. The bodyguard's musculature might have been impressive, but it also made him top-heavy. He had already been struggling to regain his balance from Erica's first kick; the second now sent him reeling. He tripped over Joshua's prone body and came crashing down right on top of Joshua himself.

Joshua barely had time to scream before he was flattened beneath Dane's bulk.

Erica gave me a disdainful glare. Obviously, there was a lot she wanted to say to me, none of it good, but there wasn't time for that. She raced to the end of the table, hoisted Paul Lee to his feet, and yelled, "Help me get him out of here!"

I rolled off the table and grabbed the other side of Paul's body. Luckily, the arms dealer was even scrawnier than he looked; he didn't weigh as much as several sixth graders I knew, and we were easily able to prop him up between us. He was still unconscious, so we had to drag him from the room together.

Behind us, at the other end of the table, Dane was struggling to get back to his feet. However, that wasn't easy for a man built like a sequoia tree. Joshua Hallal was writhing around beneath him on the floor. "Get off of me, you idiot!" he shouted, although he was muffled beneath Dane's mass, so it sounded more like "Bed offa knee, new bibbidit!"

Erica and I raced out the door and found ourselves in a gourmet kitchen, filled with an astounding array of appliances and cooking utensils, given that most people who stayed there probably just ordered their meals from room service. "Take Paul," Erica ordered, then shifted all his weight to me and grabbed every blade out of the knife block.

Ahead of us lay the bedrooms. A door opened, and another bodyguard stormed out. This was the guy who I had seen on the balcony when we'd first arrived at the resort. He was built similarly to Dane, muscles on top of muscles. He had a gun in his hand—but only for a few seconds. Erica flung a carving knife at him that spiked his pajama sleeve to the wall and made him drop his weapon in surprise. She rapidly threw three more knives, pinning his other limbs to the wall, and then whacked him on the head with a waffle iron just for good measure.

Next to me, Paul Lee regained consciousness. "Am I still alive?" he asked blearily, and we hurried through the kitchen.

"Yes," I told him.

"Oh good," he said. "I'm not, er . . . a fan of being dead."

"That makes two of us," I said.

Ahead of us, several more bedrooms, which probably all held enemy agents, lay between us and our escape route. So I took evasive action. A sliding door led out onto the wide patio that surrounded the penthouse. I shoved it open and dragged Paul through it.

Back inside, another bodyguard had emerged from a bedroom, but Erica quickly took him out with a well-aimed panini press.

A series of thumps and muffled yelps of pain from the dining room indicated that Dane was still trying to get back on his feet, to the great dismay of Joshua Hallal beneath him.

Out on the porch, the warm, humid air was a relief after the heavily air-conditioned penthouse. There was a profusion of potted plants arrayed around a private rooftop pool, Jacuzzi, and sundeck, as well as Ashley Sparks's gymnastics equipment.

A fourth bodyguard came thrashing through the jungle

of potted plants. This was the guy who'd been asleep on the balcony as we'd drifted over his head. He had been roused by the commotion and now looked groggy, embarrassed, and angry. He burst between two ficus trees behind us, preparing to open fire—

When Erica sailed through the sliding door and body-slammed him. The bodyguard tumbled into a large, exceptionally thorny cactus and howled in pain. He immediately forgot all about us and flailed about, trying to pry the prong-laden cactus sections from his body.

"Egad," Paul Lee said. "That was, er . . . quite something."

Erica took the gear bag she'd been hauling around off her shoulder and threw it to me. "Get harnessed up!" she ordered.

"Aren't you coming?" I asked, with a lot more worry in my voice than I'd intended.

"I have something to deal with first."

"What?"

A penthouse window shattered as a small, incredibly muscular body dove through it. The body curled into a ball in midair, flipped over twice, and stuck the landing.

"Her," Erica answered.

Ashley Sparks was awake and ready for action. She stood between Erica and me, wearing spangled pajamas and a look of abject hatred.

"I should have known you jidiots wouldn't have enough sense to stay dead," Ashley sneered. Ashley had a thing for combining two words into one. "Jidiot" was "jerk" plus "idiot," a favorite of hers—or at least one that she used for me an awful lot.

Ashley had her own personal fighting technique, an impressive combination of martial arts and gymnastics that rivaled even Erica's prodigious skills. I knew I wouldn't stand a chance against her, so I kept running, doing my best to pull Paul Lee along with me.

Erica attacked before Ashley could follow us. Ashley tucked into a defensive posture, deflecting Erica's flying kick, and the two of them launched themselves into a fight that probably would have been extremely impressive if I'd had the time to stop and watch it. I didn't, though.

As Paul Lee gained more and more consciousness, he was becoming harder and harder to move. His naturally skittish personality was returning, and he was now dragging his feet and flailing his arms. "Oh my," he said. "What is . . . Are we . . . Who are . . . ?"

"I'm rescuing you," I said, fearing that if I waited for him to actually finish a thought, I might die of old age.

"How?"

"I'm still working on that." We stumbled past the end of the penthouse suite and arrived at the far end of the balcony.

The fishing line that Erica had fired earlier stretched over the edge and angled downward, so thin it was almost invisible.

To the east, daylight was peeking over the horizon, providing just enough illumination for Paul and me to see exactly how big the drop over the balcony railing was. Ten stories, straight down into a large, wide concrete expanse.

I opened the gear bag and found a tangle of zip-line harnesses inside. I pulled one out and thrust it into Paul's chest. "Get this on."

"Oh no," he gasped, realizing what I intended to do. "You can't . . . I mean . . . we won't . . ."

"It's either this or staying behind," I said, quickly slipping into my harness. Zip-lines had proven surprisingly useful in the spy game, and I could practically suit up for one in my sleep. "Your odds for survival are a lot better with me, though."

"But . . . ," Paul protested. "I . . . well . . . the thing is . . . Aaaaahhhh!"

His scream of terror came as a human form suddenly materialized from almost out of nowhere. Warren Reeves had emerged onto the patio. Or maybe he had been on the patio all along. With Warren, it was always hard to tell. His pajamas had blended perfectly with the brown stucco walls of the penthouse, allowing him to get the jump on us.

"Ripley!" he shouted. "You're not going to thwart us this— Aaaaahhhh!"

His scream wasn't one of terror so much as surprise and pain. In his haste to attack, he hadn't noticed the fishing line stretched across his path. It caught him in the face and clotheslined him, knocking him flat on his back. His gun flew from his hand and sailed over the balcony railing, leaving him sprawled and helpless on the floor at my feet. His attitude instantly shifted from aggressive to cowardly. "Don't hurt me!" he mewled.

Fighting had never been my strongest talent at spy school. In fact, I had been one of the worst in my class. But Warren had still been worse than me, inevitably getting the lowest grade. In Introduction to Self-Preservation, I had often tried to be paired with him so that I could make myself look a tiny bit better. Now I simply pulled out another zip-line harness and swaddled Warren with it, binding him like a tuna snagged in a fishing net.

Meanwhile, Paul Lee continued blathering beside me. "I can't do . . . uh, this. . . . It's . . . I mean, the splatting . . . I just . . . um . . ."

"Oh for crying out loud." I grabbed the harness from him, whipped it around his shoulders, and clipped the carabiner over the line. It wasn't anywhere close to the proper way to put the harness on, but I figured it would still work in the short term.

"What are you . . . ," Paul yammered. "How dare . . . er . . ."

A shot rang out, and a sliding glass door near us instantly collapsed into shards. Dane Brammage was on his feet again and charging down the hall toward us, a gun clutched in his hand. For a man the size of a rhino, he moved with surprising speed.

There was no more time to listen to Paul Lee dither. I shoved him over the railing. The carabiner held tight, his harness cinched around him, and he skimmed down the fishing line, screaming the whole way.

I quickly locked my own carabiner over the line and leapt after him.

There was a sickening drop for a second as the line bowed under my weight. But then it yanked taut, and suddenly, I was racing down through the morning air behind Paul Lee.

As the day brightened around us, I could now see where we were heading. The line was at least a hundred yards long, and the spear at the end was embedded in the wall at the very top of the fake pyramid where the waterslides ran.

Although I was moving quickly, it still didn't seem fast enough. The ground was disturbingly far below me, and there were lots of people who wanted me dead close by. I craned my neck around to look behind me, then immediately wished I hadn't.

Dane Brammage was at the railing, aiming his gun my way.

And then he wasn't. Something large clobbered him on the head. It looked vaguely like a potted geranium, but I couldn't quite tell from my vantage point. Dane dropped out of sight, and then Erica sprang over him, hooked her own harness to the fishing line, and dove off the balcony.

The line jounced unnervingly as Erica's weight hit it, but in front of me, Paul Lee was almost at the end, which meant I was almost down myself.

However, I now had to pass over the worst part: the shark tank. The enormous aquarium was several stories tall, wrapping around the fake pyramid, and to my dismay, it was open at the top, revealing dozens of large, torpedo-shaped bodies slicing through the water beneath me. Should the line have snapped then, I would have been breakfast.

Thankfully, it held. Ahead of me, Paul Lee reached the end of the line. Unfortunately, the man made no attempt to brace himself for the finish and simply smacked into the wall with a resounding thud. "Ouch!" he cried. "I mean . . . ow . . . er . . . oof."

He also didn't think to unclip himself so he could get out of the way before I arrived. I did my best to prepare myself, but I'd been expecting to hit a wall, not an arms dealer. I slammed right into him, producing yet another round of pained expressions.

I unclipped my carabiner and then Paul Lee's. He immediately collapsed into a pile on the ground. "That was . . . I mean . . . ugh . . . I didn't care for . . ."

"We're still not safe," I informed him.

As if to drive this point home, a few bullets pocked the temple wall close by. Dane Brammage was back on his feet on the balcony and had opened fire again. He was trying to hit Erica, but she was moving too fast for him to get a proper bead on. Eventually, Dane's gun clicked empty, and, in frustration, he must have decided to simply take out Erica the old-fashioned way: by pummeling her. He unwrapped the harness I had bound Warren with, looped it over the fishing line, held on tight with both hands, and jumped.

His added bulk was enough to nearly rip the spear from the wall. It wobbled ominously, but held. Dane's weight also made him move down the line much faster than any of us had, though. He quickly bore down on Erica like a freight train.

As Erica got closer, I saw that she hadn't come through her battle with Ashley unscathed. She had welts and slashes on her arms and legs, and there was a smear of what might have been either blood or red glitter on her forehead. "Clear the way!" she shouted.

Paul Lee didn't listen. He kept staring at her dumbly, still completely useless. I had to hook my hands under his armpits and yank him out of the way as Erica came hurtling in. She bent her legs for impact, jounced off the wall, unclipped her carabiner, and dropped to the ground, all within a second.

Dane Brammage was only ten seconds away.

Two other bodyguards arrived at the balcony. They had somewhat recovered from Erica's attacks—one still had a piece of cactus jabbed in his scalp at a jaunty angle, while the other's face was imprinted with a distinct waffle pattern—and they were desperate for revenge, guns clenched in their hands.

Erica pulled the fish-gutting knife from her utility belt. It glinted in the first rays of the sun.

Dane's face furrowed in concern. It occurred to him that, in his haste to pursue Erica, he had made a terrible mistake.

Erica lifted the blade over her head and slashed through the fishing line.

It snapped and recoiled, whipping back toward the penthouse balcony with such force that it took out the two bodyguards. Meanwhile, Dane Brammage suddenly found himself hanging on to nothing but air. His momentum kept him sailing toward us—but he didn't quite make it onto the ledge and plummeted into the shark tank below. He cannon-balled so hard that a plume of water thirty feet high exploded out—along with one very startled young mako shark—drenching Erica, Paul Lee, and me. Down in the tank, the water churned, though whether this was the sharks attacking

Dane or Dane attacking the sharks, I couldn't tell. We didn't have time to stick around to find out.

The two bodyguards had recovered—and the third one, who sported a large welt courtesy of the panini press, had joined them. They opened fire on us again.

There was only one way to go. I flung Paul Lee onto Montezuma's Revenge before he could protest, then dove on after him. Erica came right behind us.

We rocketed down the flume, careening through the shark tank, which was roiling with activity. I thought I caught a glimpse of Dane punching a tiger shark in the face, but we were soon well past it, spinning through the corkscrew loops. Paul Lee screamed the whole way, until the floor suddenly seemed to drop out from under us and we plunged down into the pool of water at the bottom. All in all, as ways to escape professional killers went, it was rather fun.

Erica and I emerged from the water, dragging a spluttering Paul Lee between us, only to find two pool-maintenance workers staring at us in surprise.

"Um," one said. "The rides aren't open yet."

"Sorry," I said. "We just couldn't help ourselves."

Thankfully, the flume was designed so that the exit pool was on the opposite side of the fake temple from the penthouse, preventing the bodyguards from shooting at us anymore. We sloshed out of the pool and raced through the water park, once again dragging Paul Lee between us. The man was stubbornly refusing to be any help at all. By now, I was wearing out. My initial adrenaline rush had subsided, I had a stitch in my side, and my waterlogged shoes squelched with every step I took. But still, Erica and I pressed on, going as fast as we could, wanting to put as much room between us and SPYDER as we could.

This was the first time Erica and I had had a spare moment to talk since the dining room, and she promptly laid into me. "What the heck were you thinking?" she shouted as we ran past the wave pool. "This whole mission is toast!"

"We couldn't just let him die!" I argued.

"Of course we could! He would have done the same to you!"

"Maybe not."

"There's no maybe here. The man is a scumbag. One less scumbag in the world would have been a good thing. And you just had to save him!"

A few different responses popped into my head. It seemed to me that saving anyone's life, even a bad person's, should have been the right thing to do. And maybe there was even something positive about rescuing Paul Lee: Perhaps the man could be of use to us, which would justify the risks we had taken. But I was too cowed and winded to make any serious arguments at the moment. All I could manage was "I'm sorry."

Erica responded with a scowl.

We hustled past the wave pool and found ourselves back at the activity shack. Mike had returned the boat to the pier and had the engine idling. He gave us a wary look and shouted over the motor, "Did something go wrong?"

"No," Erica shouted back. "*Everything* went wrong."

A bullet ricocheted off a coconut tree ahead of us.

In the sky above us, the very parasail we had used to get to the penthouse was now drifting downward. Ashley Sparks and Joshua Hallal were harnessed into it, Ashley in front and Joshua behind. Apparently, they had BASE jumped from the roof. Joshua had a gun in his real hand, while steering with his robotic one.

If any of us had possessed a gun, they would have been easy targets. But we were unarmed. A machete was stuck in a stump close by, where some employee had been using it to husk coconuts, but a machete wasn't much use against a gun. We had no choice but to take cover. On the wide expanse of beach, our only option was a rack of scuba tanks, laid out for an early-morning dive. Erica and I dove behind it while Paul Lee thumped face-first into the sand beside us and whimpered.

Joshua fired again. The bullet pinged off the metal tank by my head.

From the air, Ashley taunted, "Nice try, schmoozers!"

which I figured was a combo of "schmucks" and "losers." "But there's nowhere to run! You're screwed!"

Indeed, it seemed that we were. Joshua and Ashley would soon be in a position where they had a direct shot at us. Or, if Joshua simply hit one of the scuba tanks just right, it could explode and tear us all to shreds, since the air inside was under intense pressure. . . .

Which suddenly gave me an idea.

Before I could even think twice about it, I leapt from my hiding spot and raced the few steps toward the stump with the machete. Geysers of sand erupted as bullets hit the ground around me. I snatched the knife from the stump and doubled back, quickly calculating the angle of the tanks in the rack and the drift of the parasail.

Then, at just the right moment, I brought the blade down on the pressure valve of a tank.

The valve snapped off cleanly, and the air inside erupted through the hole. The tank took off like a rocket, blasting off from the rack and barreling right toward the parasail.

Ashley reacted a little faster than Joshua, unsnapping the straps that held her. She dropped from the chute just as the tank sailed right over her head . . .

And hit Joshua dead-on. It slammed into him with such force that it tore him right out of the parasail and carried him another several yards. He crashed down into a swimming pool and sank to the bottom.

Ashley dropped twenty feet to the ground and stuck the landing in the soft sand beneath a coconut tree. She watched what happened to Joshua, then wheeled on us with a murderous gleam in her eye. "You jidiots are going to pay for that!" she screamed.

Erica grabbed the machete from me and whipped it at Ashley. To my surprise, it sailed several feet over Ashley's head, not coming anywhere near her, and thunked harmlessly into a lawn chair in the distance.

Ashley seemed equally surprised that Erica had missed her, and quickly found the most antagonistic response possible. "Ha!" she laughed. "Nice throw, loser! You missed me by a mile!"

"I wasn't aiming at you," Erica said coldly.

At which point, the clump of coconuts that she *had* been aiming at dropped out of the tree, their stems cleanly severed, and whacked Ashley on the head.

"Youch," Ashley said—a combo of "yeow" and "ouch"— then passed out in the sand.

I turned to Erica, feeling rather pleased with myself. "That worked out pretty well."

Erica glowered back. "Nothing about this mission has worked out remotely well at all, thanks to you. We still don't know what SPYDER is up to, our element of surprise is gone, they're on the hunt for us, and now we're stuck with this blithering idiot." She pointed accusingly at Paul Lee.

He lifted his head from the sand and said, "Well now . . . I, uh . . . you see . . ."

"Shut up," Erica told him, then grabbed the collar of his shirt and yanked him to his feet. "Come on. We need to get to safety, fast." She looked to Mike and nodded.

He saluted her, threw the motorboat into gear—and then inexplicably leapt onto the pier, allowing the boat to speed away across the ocean without any of us in it.

I gawked at this, then turned to Erica, so astonished that I practically became Paul Lee for a moment. "Wait . . . we're not . . . um . . . uh . . . we're not taking the boat?"

"I'd have thought that was obvious," Erica said.

"Then where are we going to hide?" I asked.

"The last place they'll ever think to look," Erica replied.

LYING LOW

Luxury Villa 11
Aquarius Resort
March 30
0500 hours

"Let me get this straight," I said to Erica, trying to remain calm. "SPYDER knows we're alive. They want all of us dead. They're combing the entire Yucatán Peninsula looking for us. And you think the safest place to be is at the very same resort where they're holed up?"

We had returned to our villa with Paul Lee, who now lay on the couch in our living room, curled up in the fetal position and whimpering, shaken from the morning's events. Mike was taking a shower while Zoe was ordering room service. Murray was still sound asleep. I was freaking out.

Erica's plan was that the boat Mike had set loose would provide a distraction: SPYDER would think we had set off across the ocean and would waste valuable time chasing the boat down. By the time they found it empty, they would figure we'd fled somewhere else. The wasting-valuable-time-chasing-the-boat-down part seemed to have worked. From our villa, we had watched SPYDER's thugs race down to the pier, commandeer the resort's scuba boat, and head off to sea. The question at hand now was: Once SPYDER realized they'd been duped, where would they think we had gone?

The villa had been designed for privacy, with walls and landscaping blocking the windows, but we had drawn the shades anyhow, just to be on the safe side. We were also trying to speak as quietly as possible, which was hard to do when I was on the edge of panic.

"SPYDER only knows we're alive because of you," Erica said to me angrily. "I'm doing everything I can to keep us that way."

"Then shouldn't we get as far away from here as possible?" I asked.

"That's exactly what SPYDER would expect us to do."

"No, that's what a *normal* evil organization would expect us to do," I argued. "But SPYDER isn't a normal evil organization. They would expect us to do the opposite of what anyone else would expect us to do."

"And they know we know that," Erica insisted. "So therefore, they'd actually expect us to do the *opposite* of the opposite of what anyone else would expect us to do—which would be running away. Which is why we're now doing the opposite of the opposite of the opposite of what they'd expect us to do—which is staying right here."

I slumped into a chair. Now, in addition to being panicked, I was also so confused that my brain hurt.

"Look," Erica said as patiently as she could. "Joshua and Warren both went to spy school with us. They know the CIA operates on a shoestring. Warren was there in Colorado for Operation Snow Bunny when they put us up in that fleabag motel. They don't think we could afford a single room at a luxury resort like this, let alone a private villa that costs several thousand dollars a night. Once SPYDER realizes that boat was a decoy, they'll have to decide where to focus their hunt for us. SPYDER might be a powerful organization, but it's still small. They have limited manpower, and they can't look everywhere. They might start hunting for us in the surrounding jungle, or maybe some of the nearby resorts, but they won't look here. Not right away, anyhow."

"Not right away?" Zoe echoed, hanging up the phone

with room service. "That means that sooner or later, they *will* search here."

"Yes," Erica conceded. "But we've still bought ourselves some time to figure out what they're up to."

"And we're just supposed to stay holed up in this villa until then?" I asked.

"I can think of a lot of worse places," Erica replied. "Though maybe we won't need much time at all." She turned to Paul Lee and demanded, "What's SPYDER up to?"

The arms dealer looked up at her, startled to have been spoken to. "Oh . . . uh . . . well, you see . . . I . . . er . . ."

Erica sighed heavily. "Paul Lee, we have two days, at most, to thwart these guys. So it'd be really helpful if you could complete a full sentence before then."

Paul Lee frowned, chastened. But then he concentrated, as though it took extreme focus for him to get more than four words out at once. "I don't know what they're up to."

Erica glared at him. "We nearly got ourselves killed ten times over just now rescuing your sorry butt. The least you could do is not lie to us."

"I . . . er . . . I'm not . . . uh . . . lying," Paul stammered.

"Joshua wasn't going to kill you merely to save himself a few billion dollars," Erica said. "He also needs to get rid of you because you're a loose end. SPYDER saves a load of money *and* keeps their secrets. It's a win-win for them."

I suddenly had a realization. "That's what they were doing with Vladimir Gorsky at the White House!"

Erica nodded knowingly, as though she'd already put this together. But Zoe didn't catch on as fast. "What are you talking about?"

I explained, "When SPYDER bombed the White House, it wasn't only the chairman of the Joint Chiefs and me that they were trying to kill. Gorsky was there too. He's another big-time arms dealer with connections to SPYDER. I saw him—and he seemed to know his time was up. SPYDER must be getting rid of every arms dealer they've worked with."

Paul Lee uncurled himself and sat up on the couch, looking even more stunned than usual. "They uh . . . er . . . they bought arms from Gorsky, too?"

Erica returned her attention to him. "Why is that so surprising? You had to know they worked with lots of different dealers."

"Yes," Paul said. "But . . . er . . . I, well . . . you see . . . they uh . . . they bought a *lot* of arms from me."

Despite her cold facade, I could tell that Erica had grown very intrigued. "Exactly how many are we talking about?"

"Megatons," Paul replied. "Enough to wipe New York City off the map. Several times over."

"They're going after New York?" Zoe gasped.

"I don't know," Paul said for the second time. "I only meant that, er . . . well, that's what I, uh . . . sold them enough to, ah . . . do."

"And this woman, Celeste, that you told Joshua about?" I said. "Where was she delivering them?"

Paul didn't answer right away. He simply shrank on the couch, looking like a three-year-old who'd been caught coloring the walls.

Erica sat on the coffee table across from him. "I know you're thinking about lying to us right now," she said. "It's in your best interests not to do that. You are only worth anything to us because you know valuable information. Meanwhile, SPYDER wants you dead. So if you don't want us to wrap you in duct tape and leave you on their doorstep, you'd better start telling us what you know right now."

Her threat worked. Paul Lee cracked like an egg. "Celeste isn't a, uh . . . a woman. She's a, uh . . . a cargo ship."

"An entire cargo ship?" Zoe asked. "Loaded with weapons?"

"*Nuclear* weapons," Paul clarified. "Delivered, um . . . well, to Ushuaia. It's the, uh . . . well, it's . . ."

"I know what it is," Erica interrupted, then looked to us. "It's a city at the southern tip of Argentina. The southernmost city on earth."

There was a computer terminal in the room for guests. Zoe ran to it and brought up a map of Ushuaia. It was all the way down at the end of South America, surrounded by the islands of Tierra del Fuego. "Doesn't look like there's anything significant within a thousand miles of it," Zoe observed.

I asked Paul Lee, "Why on earth is SPYDER sending that much weaponry down there?"

"I, uh . . . I keep telling you . . . I, er . . . I don't know." Paul looked to Erica plaintively. He really seemed to be telling the truth.

Erica appeared to think so too. "You sold an evil organization enough weaponry to wipe out millions of people and you didn't even bother to ask why they needed it?"

"Er . . . ," Paul stammered meekly. "Well . . . I . . . um . . . ah . . . er . . . no."

"How did a pathetic excuse for a human like you ever get to be so powerful?" Zoe asked.

"His daddy gave him the company," Murray said, wandering in from his bedroom. His hair was a rat's nest, and his eyes were bleary. He had thrown a complimentary robe over the boxer shorts he'd slept in but, unfortunately, hadn't bothered to tie it tightly, so we all had an unrequested view of his mostly naked body. Amazingly, what had been highly toned and well-muscled was already beginning to show signs of the wreck it had once been. His ramrod posture had been replaced by his old slouch, and his stomach was bulging pregnantly from all the food he'd consumed the night before.

"I thought I taped you to your bed," Erica said.

"You *did*," Murray agreed. "But Zoe cut me loose."

Erica shifted her icy gaze to Zoe. Before she could ask why, Zoe offered an answer. "I had to. He woke up after you left for the mission and needed to use the bathroom. I told him to hold it, but he said he really had to go. When I wouldn't cut him loose he . . . yodeled."

"Yodeled?" I repeated, thrown.

"At the top of his lungs," Zoe went on. "He has the worst singing voice on earth, and he knows it. It was horrible. He wouldn't stop until I cut him free."

"I had to go *very* badly," Murray explained. "I think I had something like eight sodas last night. And three milkshakes."

Erica glared at Zoe even more icily than usual. "My great-great-grandfather once withstood three months of torture in a Confederate prison and didn't crack. And you cut a prisoner free after a few minutes of *yodeling?*"

Murray apparently didn't want Zoe to get into deeper trouble, so he came to her aid. He cocked his head back and yodeled at the top of his lungs.

It was worse than I could have ever imagined. Fingernails being dragged down a chalkboard had nothing on Murray's yodeling. Paul Lee screamed in horror and curled into the fetal position again.

Erica only made it a few syllables before yelling, "Stop!"

Thankfully, Murray stopped. Blessed silence fell back over the room.

"I owe you an apology," Erica told Zoe. "That ought to be banned by the Geneva Conventions as cruel and unusual punishment." She looked to Murray. "If you ever so much as *think* about yodeling again, I'll forcibly remove your voice box with my bare hands."

"Duly noted," Murray said, then asked, "Is there breakfast? I'm starving."

"It's coming," Zoe said. "I just ordered it."

"Is there bacon?" Murray asked hopefully.

"You want *more* bacon?" Zoe asked. "You ate three pigs' worth last night!"

"With SPYDER after us, our time left in this life is limited," Murray replied. "I'm going to enjoy every last second of it." He opened the minibar and grabbed several bags of candy.

I sat beside Erica on the coffee table and resumed our interrogation of Paul Lee. "You inherited the arms business?"

"Er . . . ," Paul began. "I, uh . . . well . . ."

"Let me answer this. It'll be faster." Murray crammed half a Snickers bar into his mouth. "Paul's family goes way back in illegal arms, the same way Erica's family goes way back in the spy biz. Only while Erica's family has been a bunch of Goody Two-shoes for the past ten generations, Paul's family has been on the dark side." He looked to Erica. "You're both legacies. And as you know, when that's the case, there's a lot of pressure to keep the business in the family—even when talent skips a generation."

"Right," Paul agreed, and then realized that he should have been insulted. "Hey! I'm not . . . uh . . . so bad. . . ."

"Yes you are," Murray said. "You screw up the orders for SPYDER all the time. You deliver the wrong number of weapons, or the wrong size—or the wrong weapons altogether. Last year SPYDER ordered two nuclear warheads from you, and you shipped us thirteen ground-to-air missiles. The only reason SPYDER has stayed in business with you is your accounting skills are worse than your organizational skills. They've been underpaying you for years."

"They have?" Paul said angrily. "Why those . . . those . . . those . . ."

At this point, Mike entered from his bedroom, freshly showered and dressed in his pilfered Farkle Family shirt. He looked far more rested and refreshed than all the rest of us put together. He stopped and considered Paul Lee, who was still struggling to come up with the third word of his sentence.

"Pinheads?" he suggested. "Jerks? Schmoes? Scum-sucking slimebuckets?"

"Slimebuckets!" Paul agreed triumphantly. "Er . . . yes! That's exactly what they are!"

"You're just as bad as they are," Zoe told him. "SPYDER might be a bunch of murderous, sadistic scuzzballs, but they wouldn't be able to do what they do if you hadn't sold them the weapons to do it."

Paul blinked at her sadly, like he was hurt by the accusation. "If I, er . . . if I didn't sell my, um . . . my weapons . . . well . . . er . . . they'd just find, uh . . . someone else to buy from."

"That doesn't make what you do right," Zoe informed him.

Paul didn't have a response to that. He could only nod meekly.

Mike grabbed a bottle of orange juice from the minibar. "Here's what I don't get: Even if SPYDER stole the money they gave Paul back from him, they're still laying out billions of dollars for these schemes. But none of their schemes has paid off lately. Ben and Erica have thwarted them all. SPYDER ought to be in the red for all that. But they seem to be as flush as ever. How can that be? How do they still have so much money?"

"Insurance," Murray replied.

Even Erica seemed surprised by this. "Are you saying that SPYDER insures their evil schemes?" she asked.

"Of course." Murray poured an entire bag of M&M's into his mouth. "They'd be idiots not to."

"So . . . ," I began, trying to get my head around this, "there's actually evil insurance?"

"More or less." Murray stored the M&M's in his cheeks so he could talk, making him look like a chocoholic chipmunk. "Though the insurers themselves probably don't think of it that way. To them, it's just business. We show them a business plan, they do a risk assessment, and if they like the odds, they make the deal. And they almost always make the deal. Before you came along, Ben, a SPYDER scheme was regarded as very low risk. So the payouts SPYDER has received for your thwartings have been quite high. In fact, SPYDER has made money on their failures. So, I guess they owe you some thanks for that."

I stiffened at this. The idea that my defeating SPYDER would still have brought in profits for them was revolting.

Erica put a calming hand on mine. "Don't get upset. Whatever they've made in insurance is certainly only a fraction of what they would have made if their schemes had been successful." She turned to Murray. "And now that they're on a zero-for-four losing streak, I'm sure the insurance companies don't see them as low risk anymore. In fact, I'd be surprised if they could line up any for this latest scheme."

Murray swallowed a lump of chocolate thoughtfully. "That's possible, I guess. I haven't been around SPYDER HQ much lately, given that you guys arrested me, but I do know it wasn't so easy for them to get their last scheme insured. And you definitely screwed that one up."

"Which is another reason why they need to kill off all their arms dealers," Zoe concluded. "They don't have the funds to cover all their costs."

"They're still laying out big bank for this job, though," Mike said.

"True," Erica agreed, a smile spreading across her face. "But if they don't have insurance this time, they're taking all the risk themselves. So if we thwart them now, they might not have the funds to bounce back."

"You mean we could destroy SPYDER once and for all?" I asked, starting to smile myself.

"It's possible," Erica answered. "Without money, they won't be able to fund another scheme—and more importantly, they won't be able to run very far. Assuming they even get away from us in the first place."

"I like this," Mike said approvingly. "I like it a lot."

"Aren't you forgetting something?" Zoe asked. "We can't thwart their scheme until we know what it is."

Mike waved this off casually. "I'm sure Ben can figure it out." He turned to me. "Any ideas?"

"None," I confessed.

"No big deal," Mike said supportively. "I'm sure you'll get it sooner or later. We just need to review a bit. What do we know so far?"

Zoe pointed to Paul Lee. "Captain Pantywaist here sold a cargo ship full of serious weaponry to SPYDER and shipped it down to southern Argentina."

"Um," Paul Lee said quietly. "Er . . . ah . . . not exactly."

"You didn't ship it to southern Argentina?" Erica asked.

"Er . . . no. I mean, I . . . uh . . . I did. But . . . ah . . . it wasn't, um . . . it wasn't only one ship."

Erica's gaze bored into him. "How many ships was it?"

Paul shrank in fear. When he spoke, it was so quiet, I could barely hear him. "Three."

"Three?" Erica exclaimed. "You sold *three* entire ships full of nuclear explosives to SPYDER?"

"Um . . . yes."

"And that's only the weapons *you* sold them," I said. "They bought from Vladimir Gorsky, too—and maybe others as well."

Zoe returned her attention to the map of southern Argentina on the computer. "What on earth could possibly be worth using that much nuclear power on? There's nothing around there but mountains and sea."

"There's guanacos," Murray said helpfully.

"What the heck's a guanaco?" Zoe asked.

"It's a relative of the camel," Murray explained. "It kind of looks like an anorexic llama. From what I understand, the pampas down there are full of them."

"And you think SPYDER wants to nuke them all?" Zoe said. "What good is a whole bunch of vaporized guanacos?"

"Suppose they only nuked *one*," Murray said ominously. "What if they focused all that nuclear energy on it? If a single irradiated iguana could turn into Godzilla, just imagine what a giant guanaco would look like. It'd be terrifying!"

Zoe gave him a withering look. "The only terrifying thing about this plan is that you actually think it's possible. Godzilla never existed!"

"But maybe he could," Murray countered. "Or worse . . . Guanacazilla!" He gave a roar that was probably supposed to be half llama, half monster, but it sounded more like an angry hamster.

We all considered him for a moment.

"Moving on," Erica said. "Does anyone have a suggestion that isn't completely idiotic?"

"Ha ha," Murray said petulantly. "You mock me now, but we'll see who's laughing when there's a thirty-story guanaco running rampant through Buenos Aires."

Paul Lee leaned close to me and whispered, "Has he . . . uh . . . had some sort of . . . um, brain injury?"

"No," I replied. "This is how he was born, I think."

"The lower tip of South America is awfully narrow," Mike observed, staring at the map. "You think that much explosive could sever it from the mainland?"

"What good would that do?" Zoe wanted to know.

"Maybe SPYDER could create their own country," Mike said.

"They'd also render it completely uninhabitable from all the radiation," Zoe said. "And it'd be full of radioactive mutant guanacos."

Mike sighed, then looked to me. "How about you, Brainiac? Any ideas?"

"Maybe they just want to blackmail every country on earth," I said.

"You mean, they threaten to nuke everyone unless they cough up the money?" Erica asked.

"Yes," I answered. "It's your basic James Bond villain plot from the early movies, but it could still work. It's a variation on what they were planning last time, except now, instead of controlling the U.S. nuclear arsenal, they have their own."

Erica nodded gravely. "That's the best I can come up with too. The biggest problem with threatening to nuke people is getting hit by the fallout yourself, but Ushuaia's an awful long way from almost everywhere else." She looked at Paul Lee. "Did you ever hear of SPYDER plotting something like this?"

"They never . . . well . . . tell me . . . er, anything. . . . You see, they, well . . . they just ask for things, and . . . ah . . . I provide them."

Erica frowned in frustration, then looked back to me. "We should have just let Joshua kill this guy. He's useless."

"He gave us crucial information about the amount of weapons he shipped," I argued.

"We could have learned that on our own," Erica said dismissively.

I was about to argue that there should have been some merit to saving *anyone's* life, no matter how awful they were, but Zoe seemed to sense this and spoke up quickly to prevent any quarreling. "Let's assume SPYDER *is* plotting to blackmail everyone on earth with nukes. Isn't it about time that we alerted the CIA? We're still only students. We can't take SPYDER down by ourselves."

"We have before," Erica said.

"This time, we might not be so lucky," Zoe said. "Don't you think we could use some help?"

"I never said we didn't," Erica replied.

There was a knock at the door. "Room service!" a pleasant female voice announced.

"Finally!" Murray exclaimed, tossing aside a wad of empty candy wrappers. "I'm starving!" He ran toward the door and flung it open before I could protest that this might not be the smartest thing to do with SPYDER around.

Indeed, the woman at the door was not hotel staff. She was in her forties but looked much younger, and she wore slightly more formal dress than your typical tourist: a collared polo shirt, a nicely pleated skirt, and sensible shoes. Instead of carrying trays of food, she had a large suitcase.

Murray froze when he saw her. "Hey!" he demanded. "Where's my breakfast?"

The woman socked him in the face.

Murray reeled backward. "Okay, no tip for you," he said, then collapsed on the floor, unconscious.

Paul Lee screamed in fear again and ducked under the coffee table.

Mike and Zoe both went on guard, worried about the sudden intruder.

In contrast, I couldn't stop smiling. I'd had the pleasure of meeting the woman before, and she had quickly become one of my favorite people.

The woman stepped over Murray's prone body, dragging her suitcase behind her. "That's for trying to kill my daughter," she informed the unconscious teen in a clipped British accent, then brightened when she saw me. "Hello, Benjamin! Such a pleasure to see you again!" She threw her arms open wide. "Come here! Give me a hug!"

"Mike, Zoe," I said, "I'd like you to meet Erica's mother."

REUNION

Luxury Villa 11
Aquarius Resort
March 30
0530 hours

"It's a pleasure to meet all of you," Catherine Hale told my friends, then gave me a warm hug. The kind of hug that made me feel that all my problems were going to be taken care of. "Ah, Benjamin," she sighed. "It seems you've gotten yourself into a spot of trouble yet again."

Erica's mother worked for MI6, the British intelligence service, although Erica was the only one in her family who knew that. At first glance, Catherine looked as prim and proper as a servant at Buckingham Palace, but in truth, she could kick some serious butt.

"Yes," I admitted. "I guess I have."

Catherine released me from her grasp, then opened her arms wide for Erica. "I have a hug here for you, too. Or is that not the sort of thing you care to do in front of your friends?"

Erica's cheeks turned a very faint shade of pink. Whenever she was around her mother, she tended to act more like a teenage girl than at any other time. "Mom," she said coolly, "I invited you here to help with the mission, not to embarrass me."

"I *am* here to help with the mission," Catherine said. "The embarrassment just comes with having your mother around, I suppose. Benjamin, be a dear and help me with this, will you?" She nodded to her luggage.

I picked the bag up and found it much heavier than I was expecting. I lugged it to the coffee table and was about to drop it there when Catherine said, "Oh, you might want to be cautious with that. There's a few explosives in there. We don't all want to get blown to smithereens now, do we?"

Mike and Zoe, who were still trying to get their minds around the fact that Erica's mother had appeared, now shifted their attention to the luggage and stared at it warily. Neither had said a word since Catherine's arrival.

I set the bag down on the coffee table as gingerly as I could.

"I thought you said we couldn't call for backup," I said to Erica.

"I said we couldn't call the *CIA*," she corrected. "Way too many double agents there. Look what happened with our pilots on the way down here. Plus, SPYDER is certainly keeping tabs on my father and grandfather. But I don't think they know about Mom."

"Of course they don't," Catherine said. "I hate to toot my own horn, but virtually no one on earth knows of my position, even within MI6 itself." She pointed a perfectly manicured finger at Mike and Zoe. "It's a measure of how grave the situation is here that you've been made party to this information. If I get any sense that you're about to ruin my secret, well . . . I'm afraid I'd have to take rather stern measures to protect it."

Even though Catherine sounded like the nicer, sweeter sister of Mary Poppins, there was an undercurrent of menace to her voice. Mike and Zoe both gulped fearfully.

"You two don't say much," Catherine observed. "Are you always quiet as church mice, or has my arrival flummoxed you?"

"The second one," Mike answered. "We're very flummoxed."

"Yes," Zoe agreed. "It's just that . . . I've known Erica for years, and I never realized she even *had* a mother."

Catherine laughed. "Did you think she hatched from an egg?"

Now Zoe turned pink from embarrassment. "Of course not. But . . . Erica's never mentioned you. Ever. Although, given that she's barely ever spoken to me unless we were on a mission, I guess that shouldn't be so surprising."

"Erica does tend to be a bit tight-lipped where I'm concerned," Catherine said. "I hate to be stereotypically British, but do you have any tea? I had a very long flight, and I'm knackered."

Mike hurried into the kitchen. "Hot tea, coming right up! Any type in particular?"

"English breakfast if you've got it," Catherine replied. "Though orange pekoe will work in a pinch."

Paul Lee emerged from his hiding place under the coffee table. Or perhaps he had emerged quite a while earlier and I simply hadn't noticed him. Paul had such an absence of personality he was easy to miss. He now did his best to make himself presentable, however, smoothing his hair and straightening his rumpled shirt. Evidently, he was already smitten with Catherine. "Er . . . ," he said nervously, extending his hand as graciously as he could. "Ah . . . hello. I'm, uh . . ."

"I know exactly who you are, Mr. Lee," Catherine said disdainfully. "And I know exactly what you've done. Forgive me if I don't shake your hand, but you are one of the most putrid, vile, despicable excuses for a human being that has ever existed, and the mere thought of having physical contact with you makes my skin crawl."

Paul meekly withdrew his hand. "Oh . . . er . . . um . . ."

"What's SPYDER up to?" Catherine demanded.

"He doesn't know," Erica said, before Paul could begin stammering again. "He's been completely useless."

"Figures." Catherine sighed, then glanced toward where Murray was regaining consciousness on the floor by the front door. "Do you have anything to contribute? Or have you been useless too?"

"Murray?" Zoe laughed. "If you look up 'useless' in the dictionary, you'll find a photo of him."

Murray staggered to his feet, clutching his swollen jaw, and looked curiously at Catherine. "Apparently I missed something here. Who are you, exactly?"

Erica desperately signaled us not to say anything, but Zoe missed it and said, "She's Erica's mother."

"No way!" Murray looked to Erica and grinned. "You came from a flesh-and-blood person? I always figured you'd been assembled at some sort of spy factory."

Mike returned to Erica's side, bearing a steaming cup of tea. "Here you go, Ms. Hale."

"Why thank you, Michael. What a gentleman you are."

Catherine gave him a coy smile. "Handsome too. If I were back in spy school, I'd have my sights set on you."

"Mother!" Erica gasped, mortified. "Please don't flirt with my classmates!"

"That wasn't flirtation," Catherine said, taking a sip of tea. "It was observation. There's a difference."

Murray sprang onto the couch by Catherine's side. "Enough talk about Mike. Let's talk about Erica. What was she like as a child? Do you have any embarrassing stories about her? Or better yet, embarrassing photos? Ouch!" Murray yelped as Erica seized his ear in a vise grip and twisted hard. "There's no need for physical violence! I'm just being friendly."

"Yeah, right." Erica dragged Murray off the couch and shoved him toward the kitchen. "Keep your distance from my mother."

Paul Lee slipped into the gap on the couch that Murray had left, trying his best to be debonair and failing miserably. "Ms. Hale, er . . . I fear that you, um . . . may have gotten the wrong . . . er, idea about me. . . ."

"You keep your distance from me as well," Catherine told him. "Or I'll let Erica rip off your kneecaps and make castanets with them."

Paul paled and slunk away.

"Now then." Catherine took another sip of tea. "Do we have any intel at all?"

"SPYDER is holed up in the penthouse suite at the hotel," Erica reported. "As of now, we know that Joshua Hallal is there, along with Ashley Sparks, Warren Reeves, and possibly four bodyguards."

Catherine arched an eyebrow. "*Possibly* four bodyguards?"

"Dane Brammage fell into the shark tank earlier this morning," Erica explained. "He might have been eaten alive, but knowing him, we can never assume his death."

"It's conceivable that he ate the sharks," Mike suggested.

"There weren't any other SPYDER officers?" Catherine inquired. "Joshua Hallal still isn't that highly ranked. He wouldn't be running this show all by himself."

"I figured that as well," Erica said. "However, if there were any other SPYDER officers in the penthouse, we didn't see them. Unfortunately, our reconnaissance mission ended before we had a chance to make a complete sweep because *someone* thought it'd be a good idea to rescue this piece of garbage." She pointed at Paul Lee.

Catherine sighed. "Erica, Ben's decision might have been rash and reckless, but it wasn't necessarily bad. I suspect Mr. Lee here hasn't been completely useless."

"That's right!" Paul Lee announced. "I've only been, er . . . *mostly* useless. Oh." He frowned as he realized how that had sounded.

"He did give us some intel," I added. "He's shipped three

entire cargo ships full of nuclear weapons to Ushuaia, Argentina, for SPYDER."

Catherine did the most refined spit take I had ever seen, daintily spewing a mouthful of tea into a fine mist. "Three entire cargo ships? Oh my."

Erica said, "We expect that SPYDER intends to use Ushuaia as a base to threaten the rest of the world with nuclear annihilation."

"Right." Catherine set her teacup down thoughtfully. "Mr. Lee, are you aware as to whether or not SPYDER has any missile-launching facilities in Ushuaia?"

"Er . . . no," Paul said. "I didn't, ah . . . sell them anything like that . . . um . . . only the, ah . . . the missiles themselves."

"It's very hard to launch nuclear missiles without an intricate system of silos or launch platforms," Catherine observed.

"SPYDER could have bought that stuff from another dealer," Erica told her. "Paul isn't the only scumbag they've made arrangements with."

"We're relatively sure they bought arms from Vladimir Gorsky, too," I put in. "And then they tried to kill him at the White House."

"Along with you and the president and the chairman of the Joint Chiefs of Staff," Catherine recalled. "And Gorsky hasn't been seen since. Until this morning, at least."

Everyone perked up at this, intrigued. Even Erica was

uncharacteristically caught off guard. "This morning?" she repeated. "Where?"

"Right here," Catherine replied. "At the breakfast buffet at the Coco Loco Lounge. I saw him while I was on my way over here—although I wasn't quite sure it was him until this very moment. He's lost some weight, dyed his hair, grown a beard, and gotten a tan. Also, he was wearing sunglasses and the most horrid Hawaiian shirt."

Erica sprang to her feet. "If here's here, then we need to find him!"

"We will, dear," Catherine said calmly. "In good time. Let's not be rash about this. Given his tan, I suspect he's been at this hotel for quite a while already. At least two weeks. My guess is, he tracked SPYDER down here himself and is looking for revenge. Can anyone here hack into the hotel's database?"

"Oh, I already did that," Zoe said.

"Really?" I asked. "When?"

"This morning while you were out on your mission." Zoe returned her attention to the hotel computer and entered a few commands. "You think I just slept that whole time? I have things to contribute. I got straight A's in Intro to Hacking last semester, and this hotel's security has more holes than a golf course. There." She finished typing with a flourish. "What do you need?"

"A list of all guests and their rooms." Catherine picked up her teacup again and carried it to the computer.

Zoe's fingers flew across the keyboard until the computer displayed a long list of names. "Ta-da!" she announced.

"Excellent," Catherine said. "Now, let's check out the pricier rooms. Gorsky isn't one to travel economy."

"Here you go." Zoe typed in a few more commands.

Catherine only had to look at the screen for a few seconds before her eyes lit up with recognition. "Ah! Here we are. Luxury Villa Twenty-Three! Under the name of Benito Cacciatori. That's one of Vladimir's secret aliases. He likes to pretend he's Italian. Thinks it makes him seem sexy."

"That villa's right down the beach from ours," Erica observed. "We passed it this morning."

Catherine returned to where her luggage lay on the coffee table and unzipped it. "Gorsky will certainly have bodyguards with him. We need to be prepared for trouble."

She flipped open the suitcase. Inside, in addition to her normal clothing, there were weapons: guns, knives, a few pounds of explosives—as she'd warned—along with some more medieval items like nunchucks and a mace. In addition, there were several ammunition belts, plastic baggies full of bullets, two timers, and a device with a large red button that looked awfully familiar.

"What's that?" I asked, pointing to it.

"Um," Catherine said, reddening slightly. "Those are my undies. Sorry, I should have packed them separately."

"I mean next to your undies," I said, turning red myself. "The device with the big red button."

"Oh, that!" Catherine laughed and picked it up. "This is the latest technology in long-range detonation. The T-38 Boombox from MegaCorp. Most of the old detonators relied on radio waves, but this uses satellite feeds so you can remotely blow up anything from anywhere on the globe."

"I think Joshua Hallal had one of those in the penthouse," I said.

"Really?" Catherine asked. "That's intriguing. Are you sure?"

"Not a hundred percent," I admitted. "There was a lot going on at the time."

"That's what he had all right," Erica said. "Exact same make and model." She pointed to one of the guns. "Can I borrow this, Mom?"

"Of course, sweetie," Catherine said. "And take some knives, too, just in case."

Erica selected a few knives and set about holstering them onto her utility belt.

"How'd you get all that onto an airplane?" Mike wanted to know.

"Oh, I didn't fly commercial," Catherine replied. "I

borrowed a private jet from a friend and flew myself down here. Didn't want to make any waves." She suddenly smacked Murray on the wrist as he inched closer to the suitcase. "Back off, you miscreant. Those are only for children who behave themselves."

"I was just looking," Murray whined, massaging his hand.

Catherine turned to me apologetically. "Benjamin, I hope you understand. . . . Good sense forbids me from allowing you to carry a weapon as well. No offense."

"None taken," I said. I didn't even want a weapon, for fear that I'd accidentally shoot someone on my own team. In fact, I felt nervous even being near the suitcase at all. "Can you launch a missile with a detonator like that?"

"I suppose you could," Catherine replied. "Although detonators are usually used for, well . . . detonating things. Like explosives." She picked up a smaller device that looked similar to the detonator, but without the button. "You attach one of these receivers—or two or three, or as many as you'd like, really—and when you press the big red button, they all send an electronic burst which sets off the explosions. I wonder what Joshua had one for . . . ?"

"Why do *you* have one?" Zoe asked.

"Or a mace?" Mike added. "And . . . are those hand grenades?"

"Oh, you never know what will come in handy on a mission," Catherine replied cheerfully. "I once defeated a splinter cell of a radical terrorist group with only a slingshot and a bag of marbles. Ah, memories." She sighed wistfully, then shook it off and returned her attention to the present. "Come to think of it, a grenade might come in handy today." She plucked one out of the suitcase, along with two guns, which she quickly tucked into holsters hidden beneath her skirt.

"I'm ready whenever you are," Erica said, grabbing several more things from Catherine's suitcase. She spoke with the eagerness a normal girl might have used to discuss going on a horseback ride with her mother, rather than chasing down an international arms dealer.

"Very well," Catherine said. "Here's the plan: Zoe and Michael, stay here and keep an eye on both Murray and Paul."

Zoe began to protest, but Catherine interrupted her. "I know it sounds like a lame babysitting job, but it's not. Keeping an eye on these men is crucial to this mission, and I give you both my full permission to keep badgering them to see if they can tell you anything else about what SPYDER is plotting. Can you handle that?"

"Yes," Mike and Zoe agreed.

"Good," Catherine said. "Benjamin, you'll come with

Erica and me. We'll handle the guards, but I want you there when we ask Gorsky why he's here. You're the best of any of us at seeing the connections and putting together what SPYDER is up to."

"All right," I said, wishing I had the same confidence in my own abilities that Catherine did.

"Enough delegating," Erica said impatiently. "Can we go?"

"After breakfast," Catherine said calmly. "You know how I feel about going on missions with an empty stomach. I've had more maneuvers fail because someone was hypoglycemic and cranky than anything else."

Erica groaned, exasperated.

There was a knock at the door. "Room service!" someone called.

Mike cautiously peered out the window and confirmed that it was actually room service this time and not someone looking to attack us.

"Let's have a good meal," Catherine said, "and then we'll go confront Gorsky and get to the bottom of this once and for all."

"Fine," Erica agreed sullenly, disappointed she had to wait any longer.

As for me, I wasn't quite as excited. In fact, I was quite sure that, despite being ravenous, I wouldn't be able to eat a thing. Even though Catherine and Erica, who were perhaps the two most competent spies I knew, were with me, I was still very nervous about our upcoming mission. The day's previous mission had gone badly enough, and now SPYDER knew we were alive and close by.

No matter how confident Catherine and Erica were, I couldn't shake the feeling that this wasn't going to work out well.

And it was going to work out even worse than I'd feared.

INFORMATION EXTRACTION

Luxury Villa 23

Aquarius Resort

March 30

0700 hours

Vladimir Gorsky's villa was even nicer than ours.
It was newer and bigger and had a larger private garden,
which I got a nice tour of as we infiltrated the compound.
Catherine figured Gorsky wouldn't fall for the old trick
where we knocked on the door, said "room service," and
then popped him in the nose when he answered. "He knows
SPYDER wants him dead," she explained. "So he'll have his
guard up."

She was right. In Gorsky's case, this meant having two

Russian men the size of silverback gorillas protecting him at all times. However, neither of them was any match for Catherine and Erica.

The first was on patrol in the private garden. Catherine sprang onto him from the top of the wall and rendered him unconscious with some masterful martial arts moves in less than five seconds. She handed me some zip ties, and I dutifully bound his arms and legs behind his back. I might not have been much of a fighter, but I was getting pretty good at tying up unconscious bad guys.

The second guard was watching TV. The first had left the sliding glass door to the garden open when he went on patrol, so all Catherine had to do was fire a sedation dart through it. The second guard winced as it hit him in the neck, then slumped unconscious in his chair.

We could hear water coursing through pipes in the walls, indicating that a shower was running upstairs. We could also hear the cries of what sounded like someone in horrible pain.

"Do you think he's torturing someone?" Erica whispered.

Concerned, Catherine focused on the noises a bit longer, then sighed with relief. "No. That's just Gorsky singing in the shower." She grinned and led us up the stairs to the master suite.

Gorsky's singing got louder and more painful as we approached. It wasn't quite as bad as Murray's yodeling, but then, Murray had been *trying* to sound bad. Gorsky was just naturally awful.

The master suite's door was locked, but Erica jimmied it quickly.

The suite was a wreck. Gorsky had obviously been living there for weeks, during which he hadn't allowed a cleaning crew inside. This might have protected his privacy, but hygienically, it was a disaster. The man was a slob. Dirty clothes were strewn over every conceivable surface. Piles of filthy dishes moldered on the floor, attracting hordes of insects. A cockroach the size of a mouse was making off with an ancient pizza crust.

Given that Gorsky was an arms dealer, there were also a lot of weapons lying haphazardly around the room. Semi-automatic weapons were piled on a chair, a flamethrower rested on the unmade bed, and a pair of grotty boxer shorts dangled off the business end of a grenade launcher.

The bathroom door was also locked. As Erica went to jimmy it, Catherine raised a hand, looking a bit embarrassed. "Darling, while this is an opportune time to get the jump on him, you might want to avert your eyes. The man probably isn't showering in his clothes. . . ."

"I'll do my best, Mom," Erica assured her, then picked the lock.

We all stepped inside. Gorsky was in the glassed-in

shower, butchering "'O Sole Mio" and lathered up so thickly that he looked like a sheep. Thankfully, between the lather and the steamed-up glass, his nether regions were hidden from our view. He was so busy cleaning himself, he didn't notice our arrival right away. A gun sat on the vanity within arm's reach of the shower door. Catherine calmly picked it up, then pointed it at Gorsky.

"*Che bella cosa!*" Gorsky sang in a voice that made me want to run screaming from the room. "*Na jurnata 'e sole . . .* Aaugh!" He screamed in surprise as he finally noticed us. The bar of soap shot from his hand, caromed off the wall, and clocked him in the head before falling to the floor. Gorsky lunged for his gun, only to realize it was now pointed at him, then recoiled in shock and promptly slipped on the soap. He gave another scream as his feet went out from under him, and he landed flat on his back with a wet thud on the shower floor.

"Hello, Vladimir," Catherine said pleasantly. "How long has it been? Two years?"

"Uh . . . ," Gorsky said, trying to gather his wits, then launched into desperate, mangled Italian. "My name-o es notta Vladimir. Me Benito Cacciatori!"

"Oh for Pete's sake, Vlad, I'm not an imbecile," Catherine said. "Now drop the moronic Italian routine and tell me what you're doing here, or I'll shoot your toes off."

Gorsky took a moment to consider his options, then realized he didn't have any. We had caught him defenseless and naked. "Could I at least have a towel to cover myself?"

Catherine grabbed a washcloth instead and lobbed it over the top of the shower glass. "That should work."

"Oh come on!" Gorsky cried.

"If you answer my questions honestly, I'll get you something bigger," Catherine said. "Believe me, we want to be in this situation even less than you do."

Gorsky didn't seem pleased, but he was in little position to argue. He clapped the small towel over his privates like a loincloth and struggled back to his feet. The shower was still going strong, and he kept it on, probably so he could stay warm; if he turned it off, he would have been left soaking wet in the air-conditioned marble bathroom. "I'm not up to anything," he informed us. "I am merely here on vacation." Though his voice was inflected with a Russian accent, his English was perfect. Far better than his Italian had been. Despite his embarrassing position, he was handling himself as well as could be expected. I got the sense that he was far smarter and more competent than Paul Lee. Although there were probably hamsters who were smarter and more competent than Paul Lee.

Catherine clicked her tongue in disappointment. "I'm trying to be reasonable here, Vlad, and yet you're still lying to me. Frankly, it's quite aggravating. I'm tempted to truss you like a Thanksgiving turkey and go let SPYDER know you're here. I doubt they'd be nearly as nice to you as I'm being right now."

Gorsky gulped, his bravado quickly fading. "All right," he said weakly. "Let's not do anything rash here."

"Then start talking," Catherine told him.

"I have a bone to pick with SPYDER, all right?" Gorsky said. "They stiffed me on a huge deal and tried to kill me—along with that kid." He pointed to me. "They destroyed my business when they didn't pay me. *Nobody* does that to Vladimir Gorsky. So I tracked them down here, and I'm going to get my revenge. On *all* of them."

"All of them?" I repeated, before I could help myself. "You mean you know who everyone at SPYDER is?"

Gorsky wiped some steam off the shower glass so he could get a good look at me. "No, I don't know all of them. I'm not sure anyone does. They're very secretive at SPYDER. But I'm working on it. Or I *was* until you guys showed up. I'll tell you what: You let me go, and I'll handle them for you. You won't even have to get your hands dirty."

Catherine ignored this offer. "Who runs the organization?"

Gorsky shrugged. "Some guy they only refer to as Mister E. I don't know his real name. I've never seen him. All I know is, he's out on that yacht anchored in the bay."

"Warren and Ashley went out to the yacht last night," Erica told her mother. "Guess they were meeting with him. Or at least relaying a message to him from Joshua."

I flashed back to a night seven months before, when I had been sneaking around SPYDER's compound in New Jersey. On that night, I had heard Joshua talking to someone high-ranking in the organization, although I hadn't been able to see them. I had only heard the voice. *Was that the mysterious Mister E?* I wondered. Had I been that close? Or had it been someone lower in the organization?

Catherine never took her eyes off Gorsky. "Do you have names for any of the other members?"

"Of course I do." Gorsky sounded offended. "What do you think I've been doing down here the last two weeks, playing shuffleboard? I've been doing research. Lots of it."

"So give them to me," Catherine said.

"I gotta get out of the shower to do that. They're all written down in a safe place."

"You don't remember them all?" Catherine asked.

"I wrote them down so I wouldn't have to remember them," Gorsky replied.

"Is all of SPYDER's top brass here right now?" Erica inquired.

"Not quite," Gorsky asked. "But most of the leadership is on that yacht. There's not that many of them. They run a very tight operation. You guys mind if I get out of the shower? I'm getting waterlogged in here."

"Answer a few more questions first," Catherine said.

"Aw, come on," Gorsky pleaded. "I'm pruning up in here. Look at this!" He held up a hand to show that, indeed, his fingertips were puckered like raisins.

Catherine ignored this. "What did you sell to SPYDER?"

"Girl Scout cookies," Gorsky said defiantly. "They're suckers for the Thin Mints."

"You're very funny," Catherine said. "I think I'll call SPYDER now and have them come down to this villa so that they can have a good laugh with you." She reached for the house phone by the toilet.

"Wait!" Gorsky cried, then sagged defeatedly. "I sold them planes."

"Planes?" I asked. "Not weapons?"

"No. Although they *were* military planes. Russian army surplus. Antonov An-124 Ruslans."

"How many?" Erica asked.

"Only two. Which ought to be plenty for anyone. Each one of those things is big enough to move a herd of elephants."

I was suddenly struck by a very bad feeling. I had dealt with SPYDER enough times to begin to understand how they worked—and what they might be up to. "How far can those planes fly?" I asked.

"A couple thousand miles, easy," Gorsky replied.

I sat on the toilet, feeling queasy. My breakfast was threatening to make a return trip through my digestive system.

"I know that nauseated look," Erica said. "You know what SPYDER's up to, don't you?"

"I *might* know," I corrected. "It's only a guess."

A tense moment passed.

"Don't just sit there, building the suspense," Erica snapped. "Tell us what it is!"

I said, "SPYDER just shipped a huge amount of weaponry down to the tip of South America along with two planes big enough to haul it all wherever they want. Now, Ushuaia is pretty far removed from most of the rest of earth . . . except for one place. It's the jumping-off point for most tours to Antarctica."

Catherine, Erica, and Gorsky all stared at me, considering this. Catherine spoke first. "Benjamin, are you suggesting that SPYDER is going to nuke Antarctica?"

"Worse. I think they're going to *melt* it."

"They couldn't . . . ," Erica said. "Even with all the nukes in the world . . ."

"But they could get the process started," I said. "There are ice sheets the size of entire countries around the edges of Antarctica. If just one of those slides into the sea, that alone would be enough to raise ocean levels worldwide by a few inches. If a few of them go at once, we're talking several feet of ocean rise. Any city located on the water anywhere in the world would be drowned. Last September, SPYDER was looking to get rich by destroying the infrastructure of New York City and then getting paid to rebuild it. Well, this wouldn't just hit New York. It'd hit Miami, Rio, San Francisco . . ."

"Beijing," Catherine said. "Djakarta, Mumbai . . ."

"Cairo," Erica continued. "Tokyo, Amsterdam . . ."

"The Bahamas!" Gorsky gasped. "Oh no! I just bought a house right on the water there! It will be ruined!"

"Serves you right for working with SPYDER," Erica snarled.

I looked to Catherine. "Joshua had one of those fancy detonators from MegaCorp in the penthouse. You said it could trigger explosives anywhere on earth. If they used the planes from Gorsky to drop all the nukes somewhere on Antarctica, then detonated them, they'd cause an insane amount of chaos and mayhem."

"The last shipment of those nukes arrived in Ushuaia this morning," Erica reminded us. "It would only take a few hours for SPYDER to fly them to Antarctica, and then they'd be good to go."

"Meaning we don't have much time to stop them," Catherine concluded. She grabbed a full-size towel and tossed it over the glass to Gorsky. "Dry yourself off and get dressed. If you want to save your vacation home—or any place on earth, really—then we're going to need your help. No more dilly-dallying. It's time to get your revenge on SPYDER."

Gorsky turned off the water and gratefully wrapped the towel around himself.

Catherine turned to Erica and me. "I'll stay here with him and work out a plan. Go get the others and bring them back here."

"The others?" Erica asked. "They'll only slow us down. And so will this guy. We can handle this by ourselves."

"No we can't," Catherine told her. "Sweetheart, you have a lot of wonderful qualities, but humility isn't one of them. Other people are not always liabilities. More often than not, they can be assets, and right now we need every asset we can find." Erica started to protest, but Catherine cut her off. "That's my word and it's final. I'm your superior officer on this mission, and more importantly, I'm your mother. I've given you an order. I expect you to follow it."

This was as sternly as I had ever heard Catherine speak. Given Erica's reaction, this might have been the case for her as well. She immediately backed down. "All right, Mom," she said, and then ducked out of the bathroom.

I followed her. In the living room, Gorsky's thug was waking and discovering he was bound like a rodeo calf. He shouted something angry in Russian at both of us, but we didn't stop. We raced right out the door, heading back to our villa—and nearly ran right into Emma Mathes and a small herd of Farkles. Today, they were all wearing matching neon-pink Farkle Family Fiesta T-shirts.

"Hey!" Emma shouted at me. "I need to talk to you!"

"Now's not the best time." I sidestepped her and ran down the path from the villa.

"I know you're not Farkles!" Emma shouted after us. "And I know who your friend really is: Mike Brezinski!"

I stopped in my tracks, concerned. So did Erica. I looked back at Emma and signaled her to keep her voice down.

She ignored this and beamed proudly. "That's right. He's the boyfriend of the president's daughter. Or the ex-boyfriend now. There was a whole story about him on CNN this morning, with photos and everything, about how he's disappeared and hasn't been returning Jemma's calls and now she's all heartbroken and stuff. And I realized it's the same guy I met last night, not just some guy who looks a whole lot like him. And he hasn't gone missing. He's just come down to Mexico for spring break and didn't even have the decency to tell his girlfriend about it!"

"Listen," I said in a hushed voice. "You have to keep quiet about this. It's very important. You can't tweet it or post it or even tell anyone he's here."

A look of concern crossed Emma's face. "Even your friends?"

The nausea I had felt since figuring out what SPYDER was planning suddenly grew much worse. "Which friends?"

"Well," Emma said, "I was at the breakfast buffet when I saw the news this morning. So I started telling all my cousins that Mike Brezinski had crashed our reunion the night before, posing as a Farkle. And then these two friends of yours came up and said they'd been looking all over for him."

"What did they look like?" Erica asked, sounding worried too.

"The girl was short and had sparkles in her hair. And the guy . . . he uh . . ." Emma frowned. "Hmmm. I can't really remember anything about him at all. He kind of blended into the background."

"What did you tell them?" Erica demanded.

"That you guys were all staying somewhere at the resort." Emma now looked worried herself, feeding off the concern she sensed from us. "That was okay, wasn't it? I mean, they said they were good friends of all yours."

Rather than waste any more time, Erica simply turned and ran back toward our villa. I dropped in behind her.

"Hey!" Emma shouted after us. "If Mike's really not interested in the president's daughter anymore, tell him I'll be on the beach volleyball courts this afternoon!"

"Even if she did tell Ashley and Warren we were here," I said to Erica hopefully, "that doesn't mean SPYDER could find us. There are thousands of rooms here."

"But I booked *ours* with Edna Farkle's credit card," Erica said. "Last night. If Zoe could hack the resort computer, so could SPYDER. And if they knew we had crashed the reunion, they'd only have to check the rooms booked to Farkles. . . ."

We rounded a copse of coconut trees and caught sight of our villa up ahead. It only took one glance for my worst fears to be confirmed:

SPYDER had found my friends. Dane Brammage was dragging Mike and Zoe out the front door. He had survived the fall into the shark tank. His arms and legs were covered with bite marks, but that hadn't slowed him down; he was still as imposing as ever. He was holding Mike and Zoe by the scruffs of their necks, moving them about as easily as rag dolls. Mike and Zoe were both doing their best to fight back, but they were no match for the behemoth.

Behind them, two of SPYDER's other thugs followed. One had Murray, while the other had Paul Lee. Paul Lee was blubbering in terror while Murray was trying to cut a deal.

"There's no need to be so rough," he was saying. "I'm on your side—and I have been all along. I was only *pretending* to be a prisoner here to find out what the CIA was up to. . . ."

The thugs saw us the moment we saw them. Erica and I dove into the landscaping. Erica had her gun out before we even hit the ground.

But instead of shooting at us, the thugs simply backed through the door of our villa, dragging their captives with them. Dane slipped out of the line of fire, but left Zoe standing in the doorway, his massive hand clenched around her neck. "Drop your weapons and give yourselves up!" he yelled to us in his odd, singsong Dutch accent. "I'll give you to the count of three, and then I'll snap her neck!"

Zoe tried her best to put on a brave face, but she was obviously terrified. She knew Dane wasn't bluffing.

I looked to Erica, worried. She was crouched in the plants, gun in hand, looking for a shot at Dane Brammage that didn't exist.

"One!" Dane shouted.

Erica frowned in frustration. I knew what was going through her mind, because I knew Erica all too well. If we gave ourselves up, we were done for. SPYDER would win. The only way we could survive to beat them was to sacrifice our friends. And Erica had told me, over and over again, that she had no place for friends in her life. They could only be liabilities.

Like they were right now.

"Two!" Dane shouted.

If we wanted to prevent SPYDER from melting Antarctica and causing worldwide chaos, we needed to abandon our friends, run away, and regroup. Even *I* knew that. As much as I hated to admit it, this was a situation where Erica was right and I was wrong. Our friends would die, but if we didn't defeat SPYDER, thousands of other people—if not millions—would suffer too.

"Three!" Dane shouted. "Time's up! You asked for this!"

Zoe screamed in pain as he squeezed her neck.

"Stop!" Erica shouted. "We give up!" To my astonishment, she leapt from the cover of the landscaping out into the open, holding her hands—and her gun—high above her head.

Dane must have lessened his grip on Zoe's neck, because she stopped screaming. She was now looking at Erica with astonishment, as stunned as I was that she was sacrificing herself.

"*Both* of you need to give yourselves up!" Dane yelled from the villa. "That means you, Benjamin! And drop your weapons!"

I emerged from the landscaping into the open beside Erica, who let her gun clatter to the ground.

"*All* your weapons!" shouted Dane.

Erica sighed, withdrew the knives she had sheathed under her belt, and dropped them to the ground too.

"Very good!" Dane yelled. "Now approach the villa very slowly with your hands up. And don't try anything funny— or your friends will die."

Erica did exactly as he ordered. I did too. We started down the pathway toward our villa with our hands raised high.

Ahead of us, Zoe's face was a jumble of emotions. Relief that she wasn't dead. Concern that she'd allowed herself— and now us—to be captured. And a good amount of shame, given that Erica had done exactly what Zoe had said she would never do: sacrifice herself for her friends.

"Thanks," I said to Erica.

She didn't answer me. Instead, she muttered under her breath, "Stupid conscience. I *hate* it."

Then the two other thugs emerged from our villa and took us captive.

DETONATION

Penthouse Suite
Aquarius Resort
March 30
0900 hours

"Benjamin Ripley," Joshua Hallal said. "And Erica Hale. It's such a pleasure to see both of you again."

We were all on the penthouse patio. Joshua was having a late breakfast: a platter of fruit and cottage cheese. He held a green-colored smoothie in his metallic hand, which glinted in the morning sun.

"I'm not being sarcastic when I say that, mind you," Joshua continued. "I really am excited to see you both. Because you caused me quite a bit of trouble here this morning. You thwarted a perfectly good murder—and you got hotel management upset with me as well. I had to spread a lot of pesos around to get them to stop asking questions and keep the police away. Like the thousands I'm laying out weekly for this place isn't enough. But now, here you are again. Only, this time, you're my prisoners. And rest assured, I am going to make you pay not just for this morning's trouble—but for *all* the trouble you two have caused my organization." He grinned cruelly as he said this, his one good eye alive with excitement.

Erica and I were seated in patio chairs across the table from Joshua. Three thugs loomed behind us, guns aimed our way to ensure we didn't try anything stupid, while Dane Brammage stood beside Joshua.

Now that I was closer to Dane, I had a much better look at what the sharks had done to him. He had taken quite a beating. In addition to all the bite marks, he was missing several pieces of his body, including the lobe of his right ear, the tip of his nose, and the pinky finger on his left hand.

If any of this pained him, he didn't show it. A normal person would have spent weeks recovering in the hospital after a shark attack, but Dane had just slapped some bandages over the wounds and gone back to work as though this were a routine day at the office. He was either incredibly tough or really doped up on painkillers.

Murray, Mike, and Zoe were all sitting in patio chairs behind Erica and me. It felt like Joshua had purposefully given them worse seats to the show he was putting on. Paul Lee was slumped in a fourth chair, whimpering pathetically.

Meanwhile, Ashley Sparks was working out on her gymnastic equipment close by, doing loops and twirls on the uneven bars. I suspected that Warren was also around, although I couldn't see him anywhere. Most likely, he was wearing something green so as to blend in with the forest of potted plants.

"I am going to make you suffer physically," Joshua told Erica and me. "But before that, I'm going to revel in your failure. This time, you are not going to thwart my plans. Instead, you are going to watch me succeed." He raised his good hand and snapped his fingers.

Dane produced the T-38 Boombox detonator and placed it in Joshua's outstretched hand.

Joshua grinned wolfishly. "I suppose you're wondering what my plans even are this time."

"No," Erica said. "Ben figured them out again. As usual."

For the first time since we had been seated on the patio, Joshua's smile faded. "That's not possible."

"You're using all the planes Vladimir Gorsky sold you to drop all the nukes Paul Lee sold you on the Antarctic ice cap," Erica said. "Then you're going to use that detonator to set them off, melting enough ice to raise the world's sea levels several feet, causing worldwide chaos. After that, you'll come in with all your construction companies and make billions fixing the infrastructure."

Joshua lost his cool. He turned on his thugs. "How do they know that? Who let that information slip?"

"No one did," Murray told him. "Ben just figured everything out on his own like he always does. I told you that you can't fool that kid."

Joshua glared at me, annoyed his surprise had been ruined. "There's no way you could have figured it out. It was just a lucky guess."

"No it wasn't," I said, realizing this was getting under his skin. "Honestly, it wasn't even that hard to figure out."

"It's a pity Ben works for the other side," Murray said, then added, "As for me, I'm on *your* side, Joshua. And I have been all along. So any time you want to free me, I'll be happy to do your bidding—"

"There is *one* thing I don't understand," I said, cutting Murray off. "Why go through all the trouble and expense to do this when it's happening anyhow? The planet is already heating up due to human behavior. And humans aren't doing what's needed to stop it. The ice in the Antarctic is already melting. The seas are going to rise and cause all this trouble anyhow."

"But they're not going to rise fast enough," Joshua said. Now that he once again knew something I didn't, he quickly shifted back to his pompous, cocky self. "Yes, the world is heating up, but it's happening way too slowly if we want to profit off it now. Humans suck at preparing for the future. No one wants to spend their taxes on preventing something that's going to happen to their grandchildren. All anyone cares about is themselves at the present. If you want the government to pony up the big bucks, you need a crisis *now*. So we're creating one."

"Millions of people might die because of what you're doing," Zoe said angrily. "And hundreds of millions will lose their homes or businesses. Entire cities will be destroyed. And you're doing all this just so you can make a fortune rebuilding everything?"

"Of course not," Joshua said, offended. "We're also going to make a killing in real estate."

"How?" I asked before I could stop myself.

Joshua burst into laughter. "My goodness. It appears the great Ben Ripley isn't quite as brilliant as we thought. He doesn't know *everything*."

"He's still way smarter than *you*," Zoe challenged.

"I highly doubt that." Joshua languidly waved a hand in the direction opposite the beach. "Tell me, Ben, what do you see over there?"

We were at the highest point for miles, so I had a view in every direction, although it was partly blocked by some potted plants and Ashley's gymnastic equipment. While the thin strip of land along the coast was lined with resorts, to the west, across the two-lane highway, there was a great, unbroken expanse of greenery.

"A jungle," I said.

"A jungle?" Joshua asked disdainfully. Like I'd said something stupid. "That's where you come up short, Ben. You only see jungle, whereas I see *opportunity*."

Mike stared at him blankly, then said, "You probably ought to be wearing a hat. All this sun has cooked your brains."

I finally grasped what Joshua meant, though. "All these resorts are going to be flooded when the sea rises."

"Exactly!" Joshua's eye lit up with excitement. "Right now, most people think that huge swath of jungle is useless. The beach is over here. All they have there is snakes and mosquitoes and humidity. That land is barely worth anything. I should know. SPYDER and I own most of it. We bought it for a song."

"But once the sea rises," Erica said, putting everything together, "all the resorts on this side are ruined. They get swallowed by the ocean, and suddenly you have a ton of beachfront property."

"Admittedly, it's not ideal beachfront," Joshua said,

looking awfully pleased with himself. "You'll have all the ruins of the old resorts within sight, but the guests won't complain. Tourists want to be next to the water, not in it. Resort companies like this one will be lining up to take that brand-new coastline off our hands. And this isn't the only place we've invested. We bought land throughout the tropics all over the world. We'll make trillions."

"My God," Murray gasped. "That's brilliant."

Erica gave him a scornful look.

"Face it," he said. "It *is*."

Erica shifted her scorn to Joshua. "You'll never get away with this."

"Oh, but we will." Joshua picked up a raspberry with his steel hand and popped it into his mouth. "You're in no position to stop me. The CIA is clueless as usual. Who else is there?"

As if in response to this, the phone in the suite began to ring.

Now it was Erica's turn to smile. "I'd answer that if I were you."

Joshua's good mood faltered slightly. He looked to Dane. "Get it."

Dane dutifully ducked inside and answered. *"Ja?"* He listened for a bit, then came back outside, flipping the phone to speaker. "She says she wants to talk to you."

"Hello, Joshua," Catherine Hale said. "Call off your plans. Right now."

"Is that your mother?" Joshua asked Erica tauntingly. "You called your mommy for help?"

For a moment, I was surprised that Joshua knew about Catherine at all, but then I realized that much had happened between Joshua and Erica before I arrived at spy school. Erica had had a crush on Joshua, and she'd been younger and possibly even a bit naive. It was possible she'd told him plenty of secrets that he could now use against her.

Erica didn't say anything. But her glare grew even colder.

"Don't talk to my daughter that way," Catherine told Joshua. "In fact, the only people you should be talking to at all are the ones who can call this whole sordid plot of yours off."

Joshua raised an eyebrow. "And if I don't?"

"Then I'll blow up your yacht with all your friends on it. I have a grenade launcher aimed at it right now."

Joshua swiveled in his chair, turning from the jungle to the ocean. SPYDER's yacht bobbed on the azure water.

"That's an awfully big target," Erica informed him. "Mom won't miss."

"So she's here?" Joshua asked.

"That's right!" Zoe cried triumphantly. "And she has your bosses right in the crosshairs!"

Joshua stared at the yacht. His real hand moved to his chest, and once again, he absently fiddled with something on a chain around his neck. That morning, I hadn't been able to see what was on the chain. But now, I could.

It was a silver key. There was something odd about it, though. It looked almost normal, but not quite. As though it would open a type of lock I had never seen before.

Joshua never looked at the key. He didn't even seem to realize he was playing with it. Instead, he kept his eyes locked on the yacht. He appeared to be considering whether or not Catherine was lying to him.

And then, to my surprise, he started laughing.

Judging from the looks on their faces, Zoe and Mike were surprised as well. Meanwhile, Erica remained cold and placid.

Joshua returned his attention to the phone and said, "Catherine, be my guest."

There was a pause before Catherine spoke again, now sounding somewhat confused. "I'm sorry. What was that?"

"I said, 'Be my guest,'" Joshua repeated. "Do you honestly think blowing up my bosses is a threat to me? I don't need them anymore! They've already done all the work. With them gone, that's a lot fewer people for me to split the money with. You'd be doing me a favor!"

There was another pause. It was brief, but it gave the

impression Catherine had been caught off guard and wasn't quite sure how to play this. "Joshua, if you think I'm bluffing, I'm not. . . ."

"I certainly hope you aren't!" Joshua chuckled. "If you don't kill those guys, I'll have to do it myself."

"Fine," Catherine said. "I warned you."

There was a sudden explosion from the beach. Even though it was quite far away from us, it was still loud enough to rattle Joshua's plate on the table and make all of us jump. All of the windows at the resort rattled too.

A rocket-propelled grenade blasted off the patio of our villa and screamed across the water toward the yacht.

Joshua reflexively turned toward it, as did Dane and the other bodyguards—and me and Zoe and Mike and every other person at Aquarius. It's basic human nature; when someone fires heavy artillery close by, you automatically look that way, partly because big explosions grab your attention, and partly because you want to make sure that the heavy artillery hasn't been aimed at *you*.

One person didn't look toward the beach, though. Instead, Erica Hale saw her opening and sprang at Joshua Hallal. In a split second, she had snatched a paring knife off the table and swung it toward Joshua's throat.

But before she could make contact, something very fast and sparkly slammed into her.

Apparently, Ashley Sparks hadn't been distracted by the grenade either.

The grenade itself was still racing across the water.

Ashley and Erica crashed down onto the patio table, which splintered and collapsed beneath them. Joshua's fruit plate sailed into the air and splatted on Dane's face.

I leapt from my chair, planning—or at least hoping—to give Erica a hand. But before I could even get to my feet, I felt the cold steel of a second knife, this one pressed against *my* throat.

"Don't even think about it," Warren hissed in my ear.

I hadn't even seen him, but a quick glance over my shoulder explained why. Warren wasn't merely wearing camouflage gear; he had painted every inch of his skin and festooned himself with leaves and flowers so that he blended perfectly into the jungle of potted plants on the patio. He'd even gone so far as to dangle an orchid from one ear.

I reluctantly sank back down in my chair. I might have been able to beat Warren in a fair fight. In fact, he was one of the *only* people I could have beat. But I didn't stand a chance against the knife.

Meanwhile, things weren't going much better for anyone else. Zoe and Mike had also attempted to back Erica up, but by now Dane and the other bodyguards were no longer distracted by the grenade and had aimed their guns at us.

"Stop!" Dane warned, wiping a large dollop of cottage cheese off his nose. My friends had no choice but to obey him.

Erica was straddling Ashley amid the shards of the patio table, her fist cocked, ready to deliver a devastating punch to the face. She should have been able to beat Ashley one-on-one, but that was no longer the situation. The rest of us all were on the wrong ends of weapons. Erica reluctantly gave up the fight and raised her hands in surrender. "I'm stopping," she said. "Don't hurt anyone."

Ashley promptly took advantage of the situation and sucker punched Erica. Sucker kicked, really. She whipped her sturdy gymnast's legs up, bucking Erica off and sending her sprawling.

Out at sea, the grenade flew past the yacht, missing it by mere inches, then exploded in the ocean beyond, sending up a geyser of turquoise water.

"Ha!" Ashley laughed. "She missed!"

"I did not," Catherine said over the phone, sounding offended. "That was a literal shot across the bow. The next one leaves that yacht—and your superiors—in very tiny pieces."

"Go right ahead," Joshua replied. If this was an act, he was giving an Oscar-worthy performance. He really didn't seem to care for his superiors at all.

Out on the yacht, everyone was far more concerned for their own well-being. A dozen people were scrambling for their lives, racing across the decks to where the helicopter was parked on the roof. I was too far away to see anyone clearly, though; they were only silhouettes against the glare of the sun on the water. They looked like ants swarming an upturned anthill.

Around the resort, none of the guests quite knew what to make of all this. Most everyone with a view of the ocean was simply watching the events unfold. Many were applauding, having mistaken Catherine's attack on the yacht for some sort of midmorning fireworks. A few resort security people milled about uneasily, unsure what to do. The greatest security risk most of them had ever faced was probably pool crashers; confronting someone armed with a grenade launcher was well above their pay grade.

"I am not joking about this," Catherine warned Joshua, though her voice wavered tellingly. Joshua had called her bluff. I knew she wasn't about to kill all those people, no matter how evil they were. "I know there must be someone on that yacht you care about."

"No. In all honesty, I'm far more upset about the fruit plate your daughter ruined." Joshua turned on Erica and pointed to the scattered remains of his breakfast, finally showing some emotion. "Look what you did! That cost me seventeen dollars! I'm telling you, what they charge for room service at this place is criminal."

On the yacht, the heads of SPYDER piled into their helicopter. The rotors began to spin.

Erica strained to shout even though Ashley had knocked the wind out of her. "Mom! Blow them up before they escape! And then take out this penthouse too! Before Joshua can set off those bombs!"

Warren gulped behind me. Ashley, Zoe, Mike, and Murray all paled in fear as they realized this was Catherine's best option for defeating SPYDER. Perhaps her only one.

I might have paled a bit myself.

"Um, Erica . . . ," Murray said. "We're *in* the penthouse."

"Our lives are worth less than the future of the earth," Erica told him.

Joshua broke into laughter again. "Erica," he chided, "do you know your mother at all? She doesn't have the nerve to take out all those bad guys, let alone to kill her own daughter, no matter what's at stake."

"I'm willing to do whatever it takes to save the lives of millions of people," Catherine warned.

"Yeah, right," Joshua said, then hung up on her.

Another phone rang. This one was in Joshua's pocket. He fished it out with his good hand and answered it. "Hey. Are we good to go?"

I couldn't hear the person on the other end of the line too well, but it sounded as though they said, "One minute."

Joshua's laptop computer had tumbled to the ground when the patio table broke. Dane picked it up and held it open for him. A satellite image of Antarctica was on the screen. A series of red blips lit up across it as the receivers for various bombs came online. A counter displayed sixty seconds counting down to zero.

Joshua kicked aside some shards of the patio table and found his detonator. He picked it up, humming happily as more red lights came on across Antarctica.

On the yacht, the helicopter took to the air and skimmed across the water, whisking the leaders of SPYDER to safety.

Catherine Hale did not blow it out of the sky. But then, that might have been because she'd reoriented her grenade launcher toward us.

Mike looked to Erica worriedly. "Do you think she'll really take us out?"

"She *should*," Erica said quietly.

Warren looked to Zoe. "I've always loved you," he said. "I just wanted you to know before we die."

Zoe looked even more disturbed by this than she did about potentially dying. "Oh, ick," she said.

Meanwhile, Ashley's eyes flared with rage. "You love *her*?" she screamed. "I thought you loved *me*!"

Warren backed away fearfully, realizing he'd just made a big mistake. "Um . . . well . . . I really like you."

I glanced around the patio uncomfortably. I wasn't crazy about dying, but if I had to go, hearing Warren deal with his romantic problems was pretty much the last way I wanted to spend my final seconds. The last time I had thought I was going to die, Erica had kissed me, which was an infinitely better experience.

I looked toward Erica, wondering if maybe she was going to lunge across the patio and kiss me again. Even with all our friends and enemies around.

She wasn't even looking at me. She was staring intently at Joshua, looking for her chance to attack him and wrest the detonator away.

Which, come to think of it, was probably what I should have been doing, rather than getting all wrapped up in my own romantic issues.

There was no way Erica could get to Joshua, though. Dane and the other bodyguards still loomed over her. If she so much as twitched a muscle in Joshua's direction, they'd flatten her.

And despite my best efforts, I still couldn't get romance off my mind. I realized Zoe was staring at me, watching me watch Erica. I looked her way, and we locked eyes. I could tell she was upset that I'd looked to Erica first and not to her, which made me realize that maybe she'd been hoping that I would have spent my last few seconds alive kissing *her*, rather than pining for Erica. Now she seemed to realize that I'd realized this, and things grew even more awkward than before.

Which was also not a great way to spend my final seconds on earth.

Murray took a piece of bacon from his pocket and crammed it into his mouth. It was greasy and had lint stuck to it, but he didn't care.

"Murray!" Zoe gasped. "Where'd you get that?"

"From the buffet last night," Murray replied. "I always like to keep some bacon handy for emergencies like this. If I'm going to die, at least I'm going to die happy."

Warren and Ashley were still bickering.

Paul Lee was curled in the fetal position in a patio chair, gibbering in fear.

And Joshua was watching us all, laughing at us, his thumb poised over the big red button on his detonator.

My potential last minute on earth wasn't going very well at all.

Then I caught Mike looking my way.

"Hey," he said. "If this is the end, I'm glad we got to be friends."

That made everything better. Not much, but enough.

"Me too," I said.

Erica suddenly sprang at Joshua. She didn't have a chance, but she wasn't going to just sit still.

Dane Brammage was ready for her. He caught her in the chest with one of his huge arms and sent her flying. She skidded across the patio and crashed into a potted palm tree.

The counter on the computer clicked to zero. The final red lights came on in Antarctica.

Catherine Hale hadn't fired a grenade at us. We were all still alive.

"I told you she wouldn't do it," Joshua said.

And then he pushed the button on the detonator.

HIGH-TECH ELECTRONICS

Penthouse Suite

Aquarius Resort

March 30

0930 hours

I cringed, expecting something horrible to hap-pen. Beside me, Mike and Zoe did the same thing.

Nothing horrible happened, though.

Joshua Hallal's cockiness shifted to annoyance. He pressed the button on the detonator a few more times. Then he pounded on it with his fist.

Dane looked at him curiously. "Isn't it working?"

"If it was working, this satellite image of Antarctica would have just lit up like a disco ball!" Joshua pointed to his computer. "Do you see anything like that happening?"

On the computer, Antarctica looked exactly the same as it had for the past few minutes.

"Did you put fresh batteries in the detonator?" Dane suggested.

"Of course I did!" Joshua snapped. "Do I look like an amateur to you?"

"I'm just asking," Dane said. "There's no need to be a jerk about it."

Joshua pounded the button more times, taking out his frustration on it. He no longer looked like a suave and debonair evil genius. Instead, he looked more like my father trying to get the universal TV remote to work. "Stupid detonator!" he roared. "How am I supposed to blow up Antarctica when all my tech is crap?"

"Maybe you should stop punching the button," Ashley suggested. "Before you break it."

"It's already broken!" Joshua screamed. "Lousy piece of garbage! I don't understand! It was working just fine when I tested it yesterday. . . ." He trailed off as a thought occurred to him.

The exact same thought occurred to me. It had seemed rather suspicious that the detonator didn't work at the very moment Joshua needed it to. Lucky, for sure. But still suspicious.

And, for that matter, it had also seemed suspicious that Dane Brammage had been able to knock Erica for a loop the way he had. Erica might not have been able to overpower him, but it seemed unlikely that she would have ever let him beat her to a punch. . . .

Unless she wanted him to.

I spun around toward where I had last seen Erica.

She was no longer there. Instead, she was on the far side of the patio, about to slip over the border wall, the *real* detonator clutched in her hand.

Catherine Hale had owned the exact same detonator as Joshua. Erica had taken several things out of her mother's luggage earlier that day. Apparently, one of them had been the detonator. And then she'd swapped it out while pretending to attack Joshua Hallal. Which meant she hadn't surrendered to SPYDER to save our friends at all; she had merely wanted SPYDER to *think* that so she could get close enough to switch the detonators. This time, she'd been one step ahead of SPYDER, rather than SPYDER being one step ahead of us.

Unfortunately, Joshua had figured Erica's plan out as quickly as I had. He aimed his metal hand at her, and I heard something click ominously inside it.

"Erica!" I yelled. "Look out!"

Erica dove to the floor as Joshua fired. It turned out his

metal hand was also a weapon. A small explosive charge rocketed out of his palm. It missed Erica by inches and blasted a gaping hole in the wall right where she had been a second before.

"Holy cow," Mike gasped. "Talk about being heavily armed."

Erica scrambled behind a potted ficus tree for cover. It was the only thing close by, but it didn't look big enough to protect her from another attack by Joshua.

Joshua aimed his hand at her again.

Zoe lunged at him. She was much smaller than him, but she was surprisingly strong for her size. She knocked him off his feet as a second explosive launched from his palm, bowling him into Dane, who also lost his balance and fell on the other bodyguards. All the bad guys went down in a heap. Joshua's shot went far wide of Erica and blew up Ashley's trampoline instead.

Ashley shrieked in horror.

Dane's gun tumbled from his grasp and slid across the floor. Mike snatched it and ran.

Zoe was right behind him.

I started to follow, but Warren sprang into my path, clutching his knife, still resembling the world's angriest topiary.

Before I even could think about what I was doing, I punched him in the face. Maybe my self-defense classes were finally starting to sink in. Or maybe I needed an outlet for all my anger at Warren for his betrayal. Whatever the case, it was a good, solid punch that my professors would have all been proud of.

"Ouch!" he whined, and then dropped like a sack of potatoes.

Behind us, Murray Hill hadn't moved. Even though SPYDER had tried to kill him, he was staying by Joshua's side.

Paul Lee hadn't moved either. This wasn't because he had chosen sides, however. He simply appeared incapable of making a decision to run or not.

Joshua and his bodyguards were struggling to their feet. Mike might have had Dane's gun, but they still had plenty of other weapons.

I spotted the real detonator lying on the patio by the hole in the wall. Erica had dropped it while diving for her life. A few steps ahead of me, Zoe saw it too. She raced to pick it up.

But Ashley got to her first. She slammed into Zoe, wailing like a banshee. Both girls tumbled across the patio. The detonator skittered across the ground . . . and through the hole in the wall. It sailed off the penthouse level and tumbled out of sight.

Mike came to Zoe's rescue, yanking Ashley off of Zoe and flinging her into the remains of the trampoline. We all followed Erica around the corner of the penthouse suite as Joshua and his bodyguards opened fire on us again.

A long, narrow stretch of patio ran along the penthouse. Erica snatched the gun from Mike and ordered, "Get downstairs and secure that detonator! I'll hold the others off!"

"But . . . ," I began.

"Just do it!" Erica yelled with such vehemence that I knew I'd better save my breath.

I glanced over the wall as I ran onward.

The detonator was lying on a scenic walkway at the base of the building ten stories below. It seemed to still be intact—and therefore possibly still functional. A group of people in neon-pink T-shirts was standing around it. Farkles.

"Don't touch that!" I yelled, but I was too high up for them to hear me.

One of them bent down and picked it up anyhow.

Ahead of us was a door marked EMERGENCY EXIT. Our current situation seemed to qualify as an emergency. We burst through the door into a stairwell and raced downward as quickly as we could. Our entry triggered the alarm, which clanged loudly.

From above us came the sound of gunfire and another loud blast from one of Joshua's palm-launched explosives.

"How many of those do you think he's got?" Zoe asked breathlessly.

"There can't be too many left," I said. "That hand wasn't big enough to hold very many."

"You don't think he's got extras?" Mike asked.

None of us dared to ask what we were *really* worried about: Could Erica possibly hold off everyone else long enough for us to escape—and survive herself?

We reached the bottom of the staircase in less than a minute and barged through the fire door to find ourselves on the scenic walkway that we had seen from above. The spot where the Farkles had all been gathered around the detonator was only a few feet away from us, but the crowd—and the detonator—was all gone.

"Lousy Farkles," Zoe cursed under her breath.

Around us, three separate groups of Farkles were heading off in different directions, one toward the water park, one toward the lobby, and one toward the beach. There was no way to know which one had the detonator. There wasn't time to work out a plan, either. We simply split up, each racing after a separate group.

Mike headed for the beach. Zoe headed for the water park. I headed for the lobby.

From behind us, in the stairwell, I heard what sounded like someone very big tumbling downward in a very painful fashion. I could only hope it was Dane.

I raced along the scenic walkway, leaping over a few

wayward iguanas, and skidded into the lobby. A large clump of Farkles was headed out toward the front drive, where it looked like they were about to begin an ATV tour. A dozen mud-splattered ATVs were idling there, while a mud-splattered tour guide was telling them how epic their morning's adventure was going to be.

Meanwhile, Emma Mathes stood at the front desk, holding the detonator.

"Is there a lost and found?" she was asking. "I found this outside and it looks important."

"That's mine!" I yelled, far louder than I'd intended. I was too amped on adrenaline to modulate my voice. I raced across the lobby and rudely grabbed the detonator from Emma.

There was a cry and a thud from the lobby behind me. Dane Brammage and Joshua Hallal were chasing me and had bowled over a hapless Farkle grandmother in their haste.

I didn't think they would open fire on me in front of a bunch of tourists, but I didn't wait around to find out. I dodged through the crowd of Farkles and out into the front drive.

There was only one option for escape. I jumped onto the lead ATV, gunned the engine, and sped away.

"Hey!" the tour guide yelled after me. "You're not allowed to use that unless you sign a waiver first!" He then yelped in surprise as Dane Brammage casually swatted him aside. Dane and Joshua stole two more ATVs and set off after me.

A rugged, twisting ATV track peeled off the main drive and led into the jungle around the hotel. I veered onto it.

Unfortunately, I had never driven an ATV before. Evasive Driving classes at spy school didn't start until we were sixteen, and even then, they focused on normal things like cars and motorcycles. Meanwhile, the track twisted like a snake and was filled with gnarled roots, large chunks of limestone, and belligerent iguanas. I did my best to avoid as many obstacles as I could, but then an iguana the size of a schnauzer lurched in front of me, and I lost control while trying not to pancake it. I skidded off the track, crashed through a cheap wooden fence, and suddenly found myself racing through the water park.

I emerged underneath a tangle of waterslides. Six tubes twirled around one another like a serving of spaghetti, accessed by a five-story tower and supported by a spindly framework of metal beams. Even though it was rather early in the morning, dozens of gung-ho teenagers were already in line at the top of the tower, eager to get some rides in before the crowds showed up. Quite a few were recognizable as Farkles, wearing their neon-pink shirts, which were now sopping wet after a few rides.

I swerved through the support beams, splashing through

murky puddles of water that had sloshed out of the slides. Joshua and Dane followed me, although Dane was having even more trouble controlling his ATV than I was. Since he weighed as much as a baby elephant, the ATV didn't corner well with him atop it. He banged off several of the supports, severely bending each one, until the entire structure began to buckle under its own weight. The metal shrieked ominously, and the tubes trembled like Jell-O in an earthquake. The teens waiting for the slides realized they needed to bail out quickly. While many stampeded back down the stairs, others launched themselves onto the slides en masse, resulting in six separate clumps of humanity careening downward at once. None of this was good for the structural integrity of the ride.

With a final groan of rending metal, the whole thing crashed into the plunge pool, creating a tidal wave that swept a contingent of Farkle mothers into the lazy river.

Joshua Hallal barely escaped being crushed by detouring directly through a smoothie shack. Meanwhile, a large chunk of waterslide came down right on Dane's head. A normal human would have ended up in a coma, but Dane shook it off as though he'd merely been beaned with a baseball.

The water park erupted into chaos. The walkways quickly clogged with panicked tourists.

I did my best to avoid them, while behind me, Dane and Joshua showed no such courtesy. They sped right at the guests, forcing them to dive into various pools for cover. Patio furniture and seventeen-dollar fruit plates were crumpled beneath their wheels.

I was wondering how I was ever going to shake these guys when I heard a familiar yell. "Ben! Heads up! Incoming!"

Zoe Zibbell was racing down a zip-line toward me with something long and shiny slung across her back. The zip-line ran low to the ground, designed to drop swimmers into the main pool. I swerved under it, and Zoe deftly dropped onto the ATV in the seat behind me. "Looks like you could use some help!" she announced.

"Is that a speargun?" I asked, nodding toward the object slung over her shoulder.

"Yes!" she proclaimed excitedly. "I got it from the activity shack. I was hoping for a machine gun, but they didn't have any of those, so we'll have to make do!" She plunged a spear down the barrel, then wrapped an arm around me to steady herself as she aimed back at Dane. "Try not to make any sudden movements now!"

That was far easier said than done. Ahead of me, sunblock-smeared tourists were running every which way. Dozens had crashed into one another and were now sprawled on the lido deck. As Zoe took aim, a small child raced across my path, forcing me to swerve into a shallow kiddie pool.

I plowed through it, sending up a spray of water that was probably 50 percent toddler urine.

Zoe's shot went wide, missing Dane and puncturing an inflatable water slide in the kiddie area instead. With a flatulent blast of air, the slide promptly deflated, withering into a candy-colored pile of latex.

"We need to get out of this park or someone's going to get hurt," Zoe warned, then thought to add, "besides us."

"I'm working on it," I told her. Not far ahead, I spotted a four-wheel-drive road with a spindly gate stretched across it and a RESTRICTED ACCESS sign. A security guard slumped in a plastic chair beside it, sound asleep. I swerved that way, flattening the gate beneath my thick tires.

"Much better." Zoe locked in another spear, then swiveled around and fired.

This time, her aim was spot-on. The spear pegged one of Dane's front tires, which burst like a popped balloon. The ATV dipped forward and plowed into the turf, catapulting Dane into the main pool. His enormous body plunged into the water like a depth charge, dousing dozens of tanning teenage girls.

Now only Joshua Hallal remained on our tail. He veered onto the four-wheel-drive road behind us, glaring at us hatefully with his one good eye.

"I need to explain why I didn't kiss you this morning," I told Zoe.

"Now?" she gasped.

"There hasn't been a good time since then," I said. "And given that we might die soon, I didn't want you to die thinking I don't like you. Because I do. I think you're amazing."

"Really?" Zoe locked another spear into place.

"Yes!" I splashed through a large puddle that soaked both of us in brown glop. "You're smart and beautiful and you're a really talented spy, and I'm an idiot for never noticing it before."

"You really are," Zoe agreed. "So why didn't you . . . ?"

"Because I think Erica might be right about how relationships mess everything up. If something started between us, what would Erica think? Or Mike? Or Catherine?"

"What's it matter what anyone else thinks?" Zoe shifted her weight to take aim at Joshua.

"It matters because we're all on a mission together! We have to work as a team, and things like jealousy can ruin that. Look what happened with you and me and Warren! He went to the dark side because of you! And you and I hadn't even kissed or anything."

"Not everyone's a whack-job like Warren!"

"Even so, relationships can be a problem."

"I get that, but still . . . Hold steady now."

That was a tall order on an ATV, but I steered over as flat a piece of road as I could. I felt Zoe's arm tighten around me as she steadied herself to fire. . . .

And then the world shook. Joshua had fired another explosive, which detonated only a few feet from us, tearing a date palm to shreds. The concussion of the blast sent us skidding wildly, caroming off a tree on the opposite side of the road. The speargun flew from Zoe's grasp, tumbled to the ground, and was crushed beneath the wheels of Joshua's ATV.

Joshua grinned evilly and raised his hand toward us, planning for another shot.

I cut hard to the right just as he fired. The explosive roared past us, close enough that we could feel the heat, and then blew up a stand of coconut trees. The coconuts then rocketed through the air at disturbing speeds, given that they all weighed as much as bowling balls, crashing through the vegetation like incoming meteors.

The roar of another engine cut through the air behind us. Murray Hill had joined the chase—and he had acquired an even bigger, more souped-up ATV than we had. It was faster and far more rugged than ours, which was good for Murray, because Murray was the worst driver I had ever met. When we'd been at evil spy school together, he could hardly back a car out of the driveway without getting into an accident. Now he barely seemed to be in control of his ATV at all, banging off trees on both sides of the road and going right over every obstacle in his path, rather than around them.

None of them stopped him, though. They were all flattened beneath his massive wheels.

Thus, he was bearing down on us quickly. I had already feared it would be nearly impossible to ditch Joshua and his explosive hand, but now, with Murray and his juggernaut of an ATV in the mix, escaping the bad guys no longer seemed to be a likely option. I needed to think of something else, and I needed to think of it fast.

If that wasn't bad enough, a crowd of Farkles appeared directly in our path.

The road widened into a large clearing with dozens of ATVs parked along the sides. The Farkles were all clustered in the center, their fluorescent shirts blinding in the bright sunshine. For some reason, even though they were in the middle of the jungle, they all carried snorkels and diving masks. Instead of scattering out of our way, they remained in a clump like a bunch of startled cattle and desperately signaled that we needed to stop before we ran over them.

Only, I *couldn't* stop. Because if I did, Joshua and Murray would catch up to me, kill me, and then destroy Antarctica. So I signaled to them even more desperately that they needed to move.

I didn't have a chance to look back at our pursuers. Zoe was doing that for me. Now she shouted in my ear, "Joshua's going to fire again!"

Which meant I had to change direction. Only, I couldn't do that, either, as we were surrounded by ATVs, and any abrupt changes in direction would merely result in us crashing into one of them. So I had no choice but to go forward and hope that the Farkles would disperse and that Joshua would misfire.

At which point, I suddenly realized *why* the Farkles all had snorkel gear in the middle of the jungle. The revelation was equally terrifying and exciting, because it meant there might be a way out of my predicament—but it was going to be dangerous.

I gunned the engine and raced forward at top speed.

The Farkles finally seemed to grasp that I wasn't going to stop. Now they scattered like chickens, everyone going a different direction at once, desperate to get out of my way.

I took the detonator and flung it as high over my head as I could. It sailed a good twenty feet up into the sky.

"What are you . . . ?" Zoe started to ask, but she didn't get to finish the thought, because I wrapped my arms around her and dove off the ATV.

We hit the ground hard and rolled over each other through the dirt until we came to a painful stop, Zoe splayed on top of me. Our faces were only inches apart, and if the fate of the world hadn't been in the balance, it might have been a potentially romantic moment. But the fate of the world *was* in the balance, and, as such, there were many other things to concentrate on.

As I'd hoped, my seemingly desperate and potentially stupid decision to throw the detonator in the air had distracted Joshua for a few key seconds. He had forgotten about shooting us to focus on the detonator instead.

He had also forgotten about watching the road ahead of him.

As the last of the Farkles scattered out of the way, they revealed what they had all been clustered around: the entrance to a cenote. A gaping hole sat smack in the center of the clearing, ten feet in diameter. A ladder descended into it to give the tourists access, but other than that, it was a straight drop down into the cave below.

Our ATV plunged right through the hole, taking out the ladder on the way. I couldn't see into the cenote from my angle on the ground, but given how long it took before I heard the ATV crash, I could deduce it was approximately a fifty-foot drop to the bottom.

Joshua was still watching his precious detonator instead of the road in front of him. It was far too late when he finally saw the hole dead ahead. His remaining eye went wide in terror, and then he bailed out. Only, he didn't have enough time. His own inertia kept him tumbling behind his ATV. It dropped through the hole, and he went right in after it.

Almost.

At the last second, he snagged a tree root with his metal hand. Instead of falling into the cenote, he wound up dangling from the rim of it.

"Help!" Joshua yelped. "Somebody help me!" Now that he was in trouble, he sounded like Paul Lee usually did: timid, meek, and scared.

Zoe and I raced toward the cenote, but Murray beat us there. He parked his ATV on the edge and clambered off it. The several pounds of bacon he had consumed since arriving in Mexico had already taken its toll on him. Even though it was only a few steps to where Joshua dangled, Murray was winded by the time he got there. I might have been able to take him in a fair fight, but Murray never fought fair. Instead, he aimed a gun at us. "Stay right there!" he warned.

Zoe and I froze. We were on the far side of the hole from Murray and Joshua, close enough to see into the cenote, but too far away to do anything.

Joshua hung from the root directly below where Murray stood, clinging on for dear life with his metal hand. Far below him was a small island of rock surrounded by clear water. The ATVs had crashed onto the island, and the fall hadn't been good to them. It was evident that falling wouldn't be good for Joshua, either.

Somehow, Joshua had managed to catch the detonator

as he'd fallen into the hole. Thankfully, his grip wasn't great on it—he only held the antenna between two fingers of his good hand—so he couldn't push the button. But he had still prevented it from smashing on the rocks below. Which was a problem for us. Joshua had a more pressing problem, however: His metal hand was slipping off the roots.

"Murray!" he exclaimed. "Quick! Help me up!"

Murray looked down at him and grinned. "What's it worth to you?"

"You're negotiating with me?" Joshua squawked. "Now? My life is on the line!"

"What better time is there to negotiate?" Murray asked. "I expect you'd do exactly the same thing. So tell me . . . what's your life worth to you? Fifty percent of what SPYDER is about to make on this deal?"

"That'd be billions of dollars!" Joshua cried. Even as he said it, though, his fingers slipped a little more.

"You're running out of time," Murray told him.

"You dirty rat!" Zoe yelled at Murray. "Don't you realize how many people will die if this happens?"

"Can it," Murray warned, then looked back down at Joshua. "I'm waiting."

"Fine!" Joshua exclaimed. "If you help me out of here, I'll give you fifty percent of everything we earn!"

"You promise?" Murray asked.

"I promise!" Joshua said. "Now help me!"

Murray lay flat on the ground and reached down toward Joshua with his right hand, keeping the gun trained on us with his left.

Joshua's hand slipped a little bit more on the roots. "Hurry," he whined.

"There's just one problem with this deal," Murray told him.

"A problem?" Joshua asked, even more fear creeping into his voice.

"Your promises aren't worth squat," Murray said coldly. "You tried to *kill* me, Joshua. And that's not the first time you've double-crossed me. So I'm sure that, even if I *did* save you right now, you'd only double-cross me again."

Joshua shook his head wildly. "No! Not this time, Murray! I swear it!"

"Sorry," Murray said. "The trouble with being evil is that no one can trust you. And you're as evil as they come, pal. So you deserve what's coming to you."

The roots Joshua was hanging on to snapped. Joshua screamed in terror and dropped into the darkness.

Zoe and I quickly averted our eyes, but even the sound of Joshua hitting the bottom was enough to make us wince.

"Owwwwwww!" he wailed. "My leg! I broke my other leg! And my other arm!"

I realized I was holding Zoe's hand again. I figured I had grabbed it at some point during our tense standoff, but I didn't remember doing it. I didn't bother letting go, and neither did Zoe.

I chanced a look into the cenote. Joshua was alive, but in bad shape and serious pain. Though I found it very hard to feel bad for him. He was now bawling like a toddler.

A few feet away from him, the detonator was in several pieces, busted on the rocks from the fall.

"I *hate* you!" Joshua yelled up at us. "I hate you all! You have thwarted my plans for the last time, you hear me? Revenge will be mine!"

"Aw, put a sock in it," Murray said.

And then three dozen commandos emerged from the trees, aiming their guns at us.

BARGAINING

Blue Moon Cenote

Somewhere in the jungle

Quintana Roo, Mexico

March 30

1000 hours

I could tell by their uniforms that the commandos were from the Mexican army.

The Farkles, who had all been on the edge of panic throughout the entire ordeal, promptly freaked out. Most dropped to their knees and begged for mercy, but quite a few simply passed out. Edna Farkle was one of the few who kept her wits. "WE ARE NOT CRIMINALS!" she announced at the top of her voice. "PLEASE DO NOT SHOOT US, MUCHACHOS!"

The commandos didn't say a word. However, they did appear a bit confused. It seemed they had been expecting something more formidable than a bunch of Farkles.

"Whoa whoa whoa!" a familiar voice yelled. Cyrus Hale raced out of the jungle, dressed in army fatigues himself, waving his arms desperately to get the commandos' attention. "These are not the bad guys!" he explained in perfect Spanish, then pointed to Zoe and me. "These are our agents."

The leader of the commando squad looked to him curiously. "Them? They are children."

"Junior agents," Cyrus corrected, then pointed at Murray. "Him, I'm not so sure about. Keep your eye on that one."

The commandos all shifted their guns toward Murray.

Murray quickly dropped his. "I come in peace," he said in English.

Behind Cyrus, Alexander Hale emerged from the trees, along with Erica. Erica was in surprisingly good shape, given that she had fought several opponents that morning. There were a few bruises on her arms, but otherwise, she might have just spent a day at the beach. I noticed relief in her eyes when she saw I was alive—and then what might have been a tiny flicker of annoyance when she saw Zoe and I were holding hands.

Zoe caught this too. She immediately released my hand

and tried to act like she'd never been holding it in the first place.

Alexander looked as dapper as usual, in a bespoke three-piece suit, which was completely the wrong choice of clothing for the jungle. The patches under his armpits were already soaked with sweat. "Hello, kids!" he said, waving to Zoe and me. "You can relax! The cavalry has arrived! We've got everything under control!"

"It was already under control!" I exclaimed, unable to suppress my exasperation. "Where were you guys five minutes ago when we needed you?"

Alexander assessed the situation and realized that it was, in fact, under control. "Oh," he said. "Well, we had a little problem . . ."

"Getting into the country," Cyrus said quickly. "It's not easy to arrange an incursion into a foreign nation on short notice. Especially when you're trying to keep it a secret from your own agency."

"Plus, Dad got lost on the way here," Alexander said.

"I wasn't lost!" Cyrus snapped.

"Face it, you were," Alexander chided, then looked to us. "He always refuses to use the GPS in the rental cars. . . ."

"Any technology like that can be easily corrupted by enemy agents!" Cyrus argued.

"Anyhow," Erica said, before they could continue

bickering, "Late or not, they're here now. I updated them on SPYDER's plans while en route, and our friends from the military here have taken Ashley, Warren, Dane, and the other bodyguards into custody. Where's Joshua?"

"At the bottom of this cenote, along with the detonator," I reported. "Both are pretty badly broken. Joshua needs a doctor. . . ."

"Quickly!" Joshua moaned from inside the cenote. "I'm in terrible pain!"

"Serves you right!" Zoe yelled down into the hole.

The commando leader apparently understood English. He shouted orders to his men, who immediately snapped into action. Half set about getting into the cenote, while the other half started rounding up the Farkles. The Farkles weren't in trouble; it simply made sense to get them out of there. The Farkles didn't grasp this, though, and they started to panic again.

"YOU CAN'T ARREST US," Edna Farkle explained at the top of her voice. "WE ARE AMERICANS!"

The commando leader himself stayed where he was and kept his gun trained on Murray.

Another ATV arrived. Mike was driving this one, with Catherine Hale riding on the back. Catherine was dressed for a day at the beach in a stylish sundress, although she had two bandoliers of ammunition across her chest and a semiautomatic rifle slung over her shoulder. "Cheerio!" she called out. "Excellent work, children! I see that everything worked out as we'd hoped. . . ." She trailed off, having noticed Alexander, who was gaping at her in surprise. "Oh," she said. "Hello, Alexander. Fancy meeting you here."

"Catherine?" Alexander gasped. "What are you doing here?"

"Just getting a bit of sun," Catherine replied, somewhat weakly.

"With a semiautomatic rifle?" Alexander pressed.

"It's to scare off the iguanas," Catherine said. Then she frowned, not so much at her lame excuse, but because she'd had to make it in the first place. Her features hardened as she appeared to make a decision. "Actually, the truth is, I'm a spy for MI6."

Alexander looked even more startled than before. He began to blabber like Paul Lee. "You? But you . . . er . . . I . . . well . . . um . . . So . . . that gun isn't for the iguanas?"

"No. It was for SPYDER," Catherine said. "I've been working with Erica and her friends to defeat them, seeing as your own agency was compromised."

Cyrus was staring at Catherine himself, looking more angry at her than astonished. "How long have you been a spy?" he demanded.

"As long as I've known you," Catherine replied a bit sheepishly.

"C'mon, Grandpa," Erica said. "You don't think I got this good just by learning from *you*?"

"You told me you were a florist!" Alexander said to Catherine accusingly.

"I had to," Catherine explained. "It was my cover."

"I had a cover too," Alexander said petulantly. "But I didn't keep the truth a secret from you."

"You were probably supposed to, though, weren't you?" Catherine asked.

"Er . . . yes," Alexander agreed, reddening around the ears. "I guess so."

By now, all the Farkles had been rounded up and were being herded back down the road toward the resort. "I PAID FOR A SNORKEL TRIP TO A CENOTE!" Edna Farkle proclaimed. "I HAD BETTER GET A REFUND FOR THIS, OR I WILL WRITE A VERY BAD REVIEW ONLINE. *COMPRENDE?*"

Meanwhile, the commandos tasked with recovering Joshua Hallal had rigged a rope over the edge of the cenote and were preparing to rappel down into it.

Zoe looked at Erica accusingly. "You didn't really sacrifice yourself for us at all, did you?" she asked.

"What are you talking about?" Erica replied.

"Back at the villa," I said. "When Zoe and Mike had been taken hostage. You only *wanted* SPYDER to think they had caught you, right? Because you were planning to switch the detonators all along. Otherwise, why would you have even had the decoy on you?"

Mike now caught on as well. "That was all planned out?" he asked Catherine. "Your shot at SPYDER's yacht with that grenade was just a diversion for Erica? You wouldn't have missed them unless you wanted to."

Catherine didn't say anything. But a coy smile played across her face.

"You weren't looking out for us at all!" Zoe said accusingly to Erica. "You were only using our capture to further your plans!"

"Plans to stop SPYDER from destroying a good portion of earth," Erica reminded her. "Which worked, I'd like to point out."

Cyrus turned on Catherine. "You had a chance to blow up SPYDER's top brass and you didn't?"

Catherine sighed. "Unlike SPYDER, I don't believe in killing people if it can be avoided."

"But now they got away!" Cyrus exclaimed. "The most despicable people on earth! It could take us years to track them down again!"

"Maybe not," Murray said.

Everyone turned to him, surprised.

"You know how to find them?" I asked.

"Of course." Murray opened his hand to reveal something that had been clenched in his fist: the silver key that had been on the chain around Joshua Hallal's neck. He must have snatched it as Joshua had fallen into the cenote. "This is literally the key to destroying SPYDER once and for all."

"How's it work?" Zoe asked.

"I'd be happy to explain that," Murray said. "In exchange for my freedom."

There was a sudden shift in the mood around the clearing. Up until that point, everything had been quite tense, with the Hales discovering that Catherine was a spy, and Zoe accusing Erica of falsely sacrificing herself, and the fact that we were all hot and sweaty and tired from the chaos of the morning. But now there was a palpable sense of excitement. I could see it on everyone's faces: Catherine and Alexander and Cyrus and Mike and Zoe and Erica and even Murray.

I could feel it in myself, too. The leaders of SPYDER might have escaped, but we had dealt them a serious blow. We had thwarted their plans *again*, and this time, they had lost billions of dollars without hope of more investments. Their only option would be to hole up in a safe place—and if we knew where that was, we could finally get the jump on them. For once, we might be a step ahead of SPYDER, rather than a step behind.

Mike was grinning the broadest of all of us, his smile stretching from ear to ear. "Sounds like fun," he said. "Who's up for another adventure?"

To the members of Operation Tiger Shark:

Given the events of the last few days, it is evident that the CIA has been completely compromised by SPYDER. The two agents I trusted to ensure your safe flight down to Mexico—agents I was sure were incorruptible—turned out to have been corrupted by SPYDER. (They also turned out to be expendable. And crocodile food. Serves them right.)

At this point, though, no one in the CIA can be trusted. If we are going to go after SPYDER's leadership, we are going to have to do it ourselves, without any help from the Agency. In fact, the Agency cannot even know we are *thinking* about this mission, let alone pursuing it.

We have no choice but to go rogue . . . again.

Obviously, this is asking a lot of all of you, especially considering that most of you are not yet of legal voting age. But you represent the best—and perhaps the only—chance we have to take down SPYDER once and for all.

It is my duty to make you aware that this mission may be extremely dangerous. And given the rogue status, should it end in failure, the CIA will likely disavow your status as agents (or agents-in-training). I will understand if you do not want to participate in such a perilous endeavor. I won't be happy about it, but I will understand.

Given the nature of this decision, I know it is not to be taken lightly. Still, time is of the essence. SPYDER is on the ropes, but we still need to act fast to take advantage of their situation. The more time we give them, the better their chance to recover.

Therefore, this mission will begin at 1200 hours today. Let me know if you are in or out.

Cyrus

Destroy this message after reading.

ONE FINAL NOTE

The day I finished the first draft of this book, President Donald Trump informed the world that the United States would no longer be part of the Paris Accords, effectively abdicating the role of this country in fighting climate change.

Therefore, I had to rewrite the scene in which Joshua Hallal discusses SPYDER's plans to hasten the melting of Antarctica. Originally, SPYDER's plan was to try to undo all the work the governments of the world were doing to fight climate change. Now, as you have read, he simply claims that climate change isn't happening fast enough.

As rewriting goes, that didn't cause me too much trouble, though. But sadly, Trump's decision may end up causing far more trouble for me, and you, and pretty much every other human being alive.

The truth is, climate change is happening, and humans are responsible. Almost every scientist on earth who knows what they are talking about agrees on this.

What is absolutely disheartening is how this topic has been politicized. It should not be a political statement to say "I believe in science," but somehow, that has happened. So let me be clear: I am not making a political statement here. I am making a statement based on plenty of research and careful analysis and reading the work of people far more qualified to write about the subject than me. In the same way that I can flatly say that there is plenty of evidence that the earth is round and elephants are being hunted to extinction, I can say that climate change is happening, and that human behavior is responsible. Even worse, if we don't do anything, very bad things are going to happen to this planet, and every living thing is going to suffer as a result. Acting like this won't happen, or claiming that it's all a hoax, is sticking your head in the sand.

The good news is you can still make a difference, but the bad news is time is running out to do it. You can do things at home, like encouraging your parents to drive more fuel-efficient cars (which is by far the most effective way to cut down on your own impact on global warming) or trying to save energy around the house. But you can also make a difference on a bigger scale by writing letters or e-mails to your U.S. representatives and senators, telling them that you are worried about a future of unchecked climate change, and asking that they take action. Even though you might only be a kid, they'll still listen to your voice. In fact, they might be *more* likely to listen to you if you're a kid they have to explain their actions to.

If you are still young, you're going to be living on this planet for many, many years to come. I truly hope it's a planet where the ice caps haven't melted and the major coastal cities of earth aren't underwater (and, for that matter, that there are still elephants in the wild). Even though there are plenty of people out there who recognize the problem of climate change and are doing everything in their power to reverse it, the fact remains that we humans have done a crappy job of taking care of our planet. And that trend isn't going to change unless you want it to.

So get involved. Climate change might be a joke in this book, but it's no joke in real life.

acknowledgments

As we were putting the finishing touches on this book, my wife, Suzanne, died very suddenly. This was devastating to me, our children, our extended family, and Suzanne's hundreds of friends. However, even in tragedy, there can be a few rays of light—and one of those was the incredible way in which the publishing community came together to support me and my children at this terrible time. I am deeply indebted to everyone on my team at Simon & Schuster: Liz Kossnar, Justin Chanda, Anne Zafian, Lucy Ruth Cummins, Aubrey Churchward, Audrey Gibbons, Lisa Moraleda, Jenica Nasworthy, Chrissy Noh, Jessica Harold, KeriLee Horan, Christina Pecorale, Victor Iannone, Emily Hutton, Caitlin Nalven, Diego Molano Rodriguez, and Theresa Pang. Additional thanks must be given to my amazing agent, Jennifer Joel.

My fellow authors also rallied to my aid. James Ponti and Sarah Mlynowski were available whenever I needed to talk. Rose Brock and her team of incredible volunteers bent over backward to give my children a fantastic weekend at the North Texas Teen Book Festival. My kids' favorite authors, Ally Carter and Nathan Hale, were unbelievably generous with time, entertaining my children for hours, but I'm also incredibly thankful for Jennifer L. and Matt

Holm, Varian Johnson, Lauren Myracle, Emily Jenkins, Julie Buxbaum, Jennifer E. Smith, Christina Soontornvat, Julia DeVillers, Adele Griffin, Michael Buckley, Jenny Han, Pablo Cartaya, Brendan Kiely, Soman Chainani, Christina Diaz Gonzalez, Jeramey Kraatz, Rebecca Stead, Ronald L. Smith, Lauren Tarshis, Michael Merschel, Morgan Matson, Robin Benway, and Dav Pilkey. They're not just amazing authors—they're amazing people as well.

And then, there are my friends from outside the publishing world. The list of every single person who was there for me would fill this entire book, but I simply must thank my Suzanne, Darragh and Ciara Howard, Ken and Carol Parker, David and Tara Stern, Cheryl and David Bosnak, Rachel Bendavid and Jon Steinberg, Channing Dungey and Scott Power, Sheryl Gibbs, Michelle Ellenbogen, Lennlee Keep, John Janke, Jeff Peachin and Kristin Byrd, Mark and DeLynn Middleman, Chris Kuklinski and Kira Meers, Joel Delman and Mieke Holkeboer, Bill and Carol Rotko, Drew Filus and Andrea Berloff, Cori Wellins, Julie Lynn and Doug Smith, David and Angelique Higgins, Learka Bosnak and Zack Smith, Marc and Vivian Zachary, Chris Heisen and Laura Diamond, Adam Zarembok, Jamie Gordon, Shawn and Ashley Mendel, Tiffany Daniel and Mike Murphy, Marty Scott and Bellinda Alvarez, Gabrielle Stanton and Tris Carpenter, Tracey Underwood and Brian Keyser, Albert

Sukoff, Chip Touhey, Craig Perry—and Courtney Spikes, who worked so hard to introduce Suzanne and me in the first place, knowing we'd hit it off. I'm sure I have missed hundreds of other people I should have named, and I apologize profusely for that.

Finally, this book was probably more inspired by my wife than any other I have written. She was the one who had first suggested that we visit Quintana Roo in Mexico, and we had such a lovely time there that we returned two more times. Suzanne was far more adventurous than she ever fully realized; with her, I explored hidden ruins, swam in cenotes, and boated through nature preserves. We never stayed at Aquarius (because it doesn't exist) but Suzanne did always find fantastic hotels and delicious restaurants. The final research trip for this book was a full-family affair, with my parents, Ronald and Jane Gibbs; Suzanne's parents, Carole and Barry (who also served as our amateur travel agent); and my favorite junior researchers, Dashiell and Violet. Thank you all for all your help.

And Suzanne, thank you for being my wife for fourteen wonderful years. Without your support for my writing career, these books might never have existed. I love you to the moon and back, infinity and beyond, always and forever.

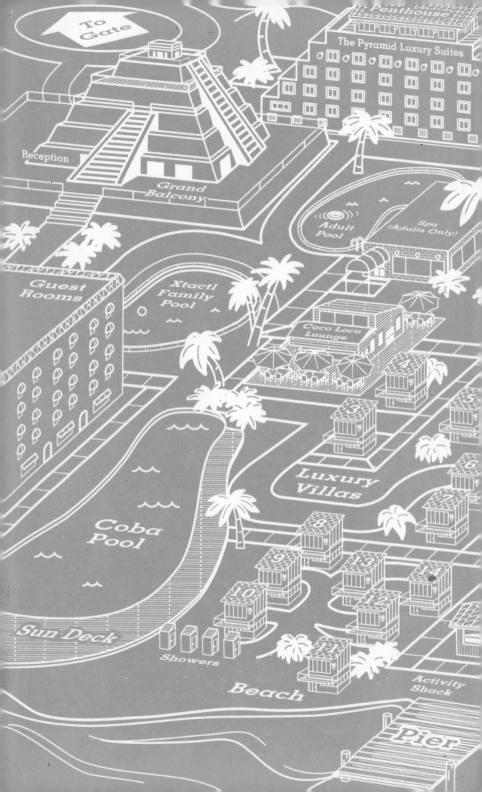